The

Healing

Prophet

By

Susan Davis Sandberg

Cover design by John Sandberg
Cover picture by Chinnapong, Shutterstock.com

To my loving daughter-in-law, Mary, whose effervescent spirit brings joy to those around her

Chapter 1

Lying on his back in bed, Stanley Praetzel sighed happily in the aftermath of a pleasant sexual encounter which the doctors had told him wouldn't happen for months.

"So what did I promise to do?" he whispered.

"To let me go to the office."

"I told everyone we were taking a week off," Stanley protested. "I thought we would go riding this morning."

"We'll go this afternoon," Aleta said. "That is, we'll put you on Minx's back and see if you can handle it. It is pretty soon. I thought I told you Friday would be your first day of activity."

"So what am I suppose to do with my morning?"

"Let Bertha and Jamara do what nurses do with patients recovering from major surgery."

"They are not bathing me!"

Aleta smiled. "Be nice."

"I am always nice. I am also modest. Aleta, these two work for us. Moreover, Bertha is my mother-in-law!"

"They've both seen lots of naked men, which I haven't by the way."

"Don't change the subject," he growled. "Why can't you bathe me?"

"Because I will have my suit on."

"Do it now before you put your suit on."

"Don't be ridiculous. If I do, I'll be late for work."

"Aleta, you're a partner. You can be late."

"The senior partner wouldn't like it."

"I'm the senior partner."

"I know that."

"And?"

"And what?" Aleta challenged. "You demand punctuality."

"You aren't always on time," Stanley pointed out.

"I am frequently legitimately delayed."

"Make this one of those times."

"Stanley, I can't do that. You'll know it's fake."

"But I am asking you to stay home. Bosses can do that."

She kissed him lightly and rolled out of bed.

"Just lay there and enjoy the view," she called as she entered the bathroom.

"What view?" Stanley muttered as she turned on the shower.

He called out to her, "Where are my crutches?"

"Where you left them," she called back.

"You aren't going to wait on me at all, are you?" Stanley asked when she stepped out of the shower.

She toweled herself dry and began to dress.

"Do you need someone to wait on you?" Aleta asked.

"I was looking forward to that," he said encouragingly.

She opened the door and called to Bertha to come into the bedroom.

"Aleta, I want..." he began.

He hastily pulled up the sheet as Bertha stepped into the room.

"He needs nursing," Aleta said. "I have to leave for work shortly."

"Bertha, go away!" Stanley declared. "I can take care of myself."

"Potty him, bathe him, dress and feed him," Aleta ordered as she began dressing.

"I am not a baby!" Stanley protested.

"No, you're not. You're a convalescent. You've had major surgery and I asked too much of you yesterday. That's what you've been telling me all morning, so we're taking a step back." Aleta stated firmly. "Bertha, he is not to go anywhere unassisted including to the bathroom."

Stanley sighed heavily as he laid back down, "Bertha, I'll wait. See that she gets breakfast."

"Yes, Sir," Bertha said.

Before Aleta finished dressing, Jamara appeared. Paul, their resident artist, snuck in behind her.

"Do you want to use the toilet before your bath?" Jamara asked as she offered Stanley his crutches.

"I am not dressed," Stanley said.

Aleta eyed him reproachfully.

"She's not dressing you to go ten steps. And she is accompanying you. Now behave!"

"Objection!" Stanley quipped.

"Noted," Aleta replied, nodding at Jamara. "He's all yours. I think the party last night may have been too much."

"You put me to bed almost before it started," Stanley recalled, annoyed.

"I won't be long," Aleta said.

"You have special clients coming?" Stanley asked.

"I do."

Suddenly Stanley remembered the message Harriet had delivered.

Let Aleta work.

Now it made sense. At the time he had promised to obey without fully understanding what 'work' Aleta needed to be free to do. Harriet had not enlightened him. She often had only the words given to her. Nothing more.

Harriet, a prophet like her granddaughter, also had a special ability. When she was given a message to deliver, she could walk past guards posted to protect either Aleta or Stanley unseen. That ability gave emphasis to her words.

During her surprise visit to him in the hospital, Stanley had told Aleta's grandmother that he believed that Aleta had the power to heal. Harriet had readily accepted that as a real possibility. At the time, he thought that was the work he was to let Aleta do.

Now he realized that perhaps it was her work as a lawyer he was to let her do.

"I promised," he said. "So you can go, but I want you to know I want you with me."

"I will be awhile," Aleta said.

"What did you say?" Stanley asked, puzzled.

"I didn't say anything," Aleta protested.

"You said you'd be awhile."

"Why would I say that?" Aleta charged.

"Because you're a prophet," Stanley said, "and you tell the truth even when you don't yet know what it is."

"Don't do that!" Aleta snapped.

"What?"

"Give me new powers," Aleta charged. "I can't handle the ones I've got."

"That's what you said, Ma'am," Jamara put in.

Aleta burst into tears. "I know it is. Stanley never lies to me."

"Except when I don't tell you I'm going to have my leg chopped off."

"Don't do that either!" Aleta scolded.

"What?"

"Protect me like that."

"I wasn't protecting you. I was protecting me."

"From me?" Aleta gasped.

"Of course, from you. I'm not afraid of anyone else."

"Why would you be afraid of me?" Aleta asked, her expression a mixture of bewilderment and apprehension.

"Because you can talk me into anything."

"I wouldn't interfere with something like that," she declared adamantly.

Stanley raised one eyebrow.

Aleta thought for a moment then blurted out her defense, "The surgery on your ear was something else. You had them fuss with your nose. Besides I finally agreed."

"After Dr. Cook made you."

"He made sense."

"And I didn't?"

"I wasn't listening to you. I was too busy trying to persuade you."

Stanley laughed.

"You are delightful, Aleta. I am not afraid of you anymore."

Aleta huffed, "That was silly."

"I don't know if I would call it silly. You're a formidable woman."

"I am not! I'm not even thirty yet!"

"Formidable doesn't come at a certain age."

"It comes older than I am. That I know."

"Go to work. You've won every round this morning," Stanley grinned impishly. "Go fight injustice while I suffer alone."

"Stanley, you aren't suffering. You feel fine. And this house is full of people. Go spend time watching Paul paint or visit the barn and talk to Hubbs or hold Gerard."

She paused when he frowned.

"You said I was to stay in bed," he reminded her. "Well?"

"So which is it? Do I get to visit or am I confined to bed?"

Aleta frowned as she considered the problem for a few minutes.

"Jamara, he can go anywhere as long as he stays in his wheelchair and he doesn't get in or out of it unattended."

"Yes, Ma'am," Jamara said smiling.

Aleta scowled at Stanley.

"There! Now are you satisfied?" she snapped.

"Yes, Ma'am," he flipped out.

"But, Jamara, the minute he even looks tired, he goes back to bed!"

"Yes, Ma'am," Jamara responded. "Don't worry. We both be used to handling obstreperous patients."

"Good," Aleta said as she breezed out of the room.

"What? No kiss," Stanley muttered.

The door reopened and Aleta returned.

"Almost forgot your kiss. How did I ever expect to get through the day without it?"

She leaned over and kissed him with such love, he felt warm all over.

As she closed the door, Aleta's mind wandered back to the words she had spoken unknowingly. Why was she going to be a while? What was going to happen? A feeling of unease settled over her.

She tried to brush it away.

Don't be silly, she told herself. The danger is all in the past.

After the door closed, while Jamara was busy in the bathroom readying the supplies necessary to change the bandage covering the stump midway between the knee and ankle on his left leg, Stanley pushed himself into a sitting position and looked down at his new half leg.

Paul stood silently, watching and waiting.

Chapter 2

Aleta's tall, muscular uncle waited for Stanley to notice him before stepping out of the shadows.

His movement startled Stanley.

"Didn't you know I was coming?" Paul asked.

"Jamara said bath," Stanley mentioned.

"That's because you didn't want us to tell Aleta," Paul explained. "Jamara is ready to wrap your leg and I've got my swim suit on under my work pants."

"Is that why the sketch pad?"

"No one ever asks me what I'm doing when I'm carrying it," Paul said simply.

Stanley smiled at Paul.

"Your invisibility cloak?"

"If I were you, I'd sleep in pajamas," Paul suggested.

"Aleta always...never mind."

"And she won't let you put them back on."

"I don't reuse clothing."

"And since Jamara was going to bathe you anyway, Aleta figured you didn't need fresh pajamas for two minutes."

"Something like that."

"I noticed the towel."

"Jamara understands, but even so..."

"You want to wash yourself."

"I don't mind if Aleta does it."

"No wonder you were so upset with her leaving."

"You heard?"

"Just the high points," Paul remarked. "You do know why she left, don't you?"

"She had something at the office to attend to."

"She didn't want to change your bandage."

"I would have had Jamara do that."

"I think she was worried somehow she'd be involved."

"How do you know?"

"Bertha told me," Paul said. "Moreover Aleta's going to have trouble when it's removed for good."

"The leg will be healed before that happens."

"You should maybe get fitted for a sock," Paul suggested.

"But I am not getting a prosthesis," Stanley pointed out.

"Just a suggestion."

Twenty minutes later, when they emerged from the shower, Paul said, "I could help you dress completely, but Jamara needs to change that bandage."

"Shorts are okay considering the alternative," Stanley said. "Can you help me shower each day until I get a handrail installed?"

"Sure," Paul agreed readily. "Anything else?"

"How about storing some of your canvases on my bedroom wall?"

"Sure. That would be a good place for them."

"I'd like something to look at when I wake in the morning."

"Aren't you facing the picture window?"

"Not anymore," Stanley said and then was silent.

"I will put them up today," Paul promised.

After Stanley's bandage was changed, Paul helped him dress in his jeans because Stanley was determined to visit the barn that morning to check out the hoist Paul's brother Robert had constructed to help Stanley mount his horse.

"Why the shirt and tie?" Paul asked as he helped Stanley dress.

"I hear voices," Stanley said. "I can change my shirt myself later. I've already made enough of an inroad into your work day."

Paul was silent. Stanley was struggling with not being able to change clothes easily. Paul decided Stanley would appreciate no discussion at this time.

Later, wheeled into the kitchen, Stanley greeted the police chiefs of Willow Glen and Arborville.

Willow Glen Police Chief Tom Milani never appeared unless there was a crime that somehow affected Stanley. Short, chunky, of Italian descent, Tom appreciated Bertha's fresh baked rolls. Lyle West, Arborville's chief, would have been out of his territory except that he'd been named Interim Chief of the Tri-City force. A man of short stature, West had earned the respect of his force as well as his fellow chiefs because nobody could outshoot him or outthink him except perhaps Stanley. He and Milani were sitting at the table with fresh baked rolls and mugs of steaming coffee in front of them.

"We need you," Lyle said. "We wouldn't have come except for the fact that you spent a whole day at your office yesterday."

"I'm on sick leave," Stanley quipped. "Even volunteer deputies get sick leave. If they don't, I quit."

"Let me repeat," Lyle stated firmly. "We need you."

"No, you don't. Your brains are every bit as sharp as mine and they don't have to deal with the adjustments I am having to deal with."

"Shove it!" Lyle said. "You've had three whole days off. We've got a serial killer on our hands."

"Three days! Most people don't even come up for air for seventeen days."

"Seventeen?" Lyle scoffed. "You just had a leg removed. You weren't in an accident and left with multiple injuries."

"Just a leg!" Stanley snapped, and then did an abrupt turnaround. "I'm glad someone thinks my brain is still intact. I don't think Aleta thinks it is."

"Speaking of Aleta," Tom inserted. "She didn't try to contact us, did she?"

Stanley shook his head.

"She slept soundly all night."

"And her visions would wake her wouldn't they?" Tom persisted.

"They always have."

"Must be like that last serial killer case," Tom concluded. "She didn't see those either."

"The bodies were just discovered," Lyle said. "We want you on this from the start."

"He can't go nowhere," Jamara said. "He be convalescing."

"You aren't planning to take him to the crime scene, are you?" Bertha asked.

Tom grabbed his roll and coffee before he answered, "Yes."

"He be going nowhere. He be staying here," Jamara argued.

"When we say he's confined to his wheelchair," Bertha put in. "We mean he's confined."

"We will take it too," Lyle said.

"He not be switching to crutches no matter what," Jamara ordered. "Those be Aleta's orders."

"We will work it out," Lyle said.

"Don't feed me breakfast," Stanley said. "I don't want to lose it in my lap."

"Should we be calling Mrs. Praetzel?" Jamara asked Bertha.

"Don't," Stanley declared. "I will stay in my wheelchair."

"Should one of us be going?" Jamara asked Bertha.

"I will take care of him," Lyle said.

When Stanley was settled in the front seat of Lyle's car, Bertha rushed from the house and handed him several folded bags.

"Lunch?" Stanley asked.

"Deposit bags," she said.

"It's a stomach churning sight," Lyle commented.

"And you told Bertha this and she let me go?" Stanley asked as Lyle turned on his flashing lights and sped down the driveway after Tom.

"Could she have stopped you?"

"No."

"So she took care of you," Lyle said. "That's what servants do."

"How bad is it really?"

"Check to see how many bags she gave you."

Stanley looked.

"Six! I don't have that much...never mind. I get the picture."

"Did she put your badge in the bag?"

"My badge?"

"This is a crime scene. We don't let just anyone walk in you know."

Stanley dug his badge out of the bag and pinned it on. "I am dressed for riding."

"You mean because you're wearing jeans?" Lyle questioned. "Stanley, you've got a shirt and tie on. You're in a wheelchair. Who's going to notice?"

"I don't know how much good I'll be, I couldn't even remember to change pants," Stanley grumbled.

"You remembered pens and a notebook," Lyle pointed out.

"I don't feel together enough for this. My brain has been dulled by the trauma."

"I heard you were brilliant yesterday. A million-dollar fee on a paternity suit."

"Special circumstances."

"Outstanding representation," Lyle countered.

"Aleta scared the bejeebers out of them. I can't believe she shook Jacob Waldenstein. He's one of Chicago's top lawyers."

"Aleta's reputation has grown faster even than your mother's did when she was a young lawyer."

"We had to give Aleta a raise."

"She's a partner."

"I mean raise what she charges. Mother said it was too low. Alice agreed."

"Your secretary had a vote?"

"Everyone had a vote. They did it at lunch. Everyone's rate took a whopping jump but mine. Alice didn't think the county would go for me getting a raise."

"I thought they only paid half."

"They may pay less than that in the future."

"You don't need the money."

"I don't want to be the lowest paid lawyer in the firm."

"It won't help you know. People will still line up to see Aleta."

"I know."

"You want me to make you famous?" Lyle asked as he pulled onto the college campus.

"No. Absolutely not!"

"Too late. Justin has spotted us," Lyle said. "Be nice. We need good press on this one."

"When am I not nice?"

"When you're not nice."

"He's got a TV crew," Stanley exclaimed.

"This is a big story."

"I am missing a leg!" Stanley cried.

"I know."

"I mean. I will be in a wheelchair. Everyone will know I lost my leg."

"It was a secret?"

"Well, hardly, considering all my friends were at Aleta's celebration last night, but I didn't want everyone to know."

"Just tell me who you don't want to know and I will tell Justin, and he can see that they don't see the TV broadcast."

"I haven't adjusted to that fact myself yet."

"Stanley, you've adjusted. I don't know how you did it, but take it from your best friend, you've adjusted."

"I don't feel adjusted."

"We're here," Lyle said. "Pretend then! I don't want to be castigated for heartlessly prying a sick man from his bed to work on a case."

"The truth is the truth." Stanley stated.

"Lie a little."

I don't lie."

"Well, do whatever it was you did when you didn't tell Aleta until after the fact what you were going into the hospital for."

"I didn't want to upset her."

"Well don't upset me," Lyle charged. "I'm giving you the best assignments."

"I am a volunteer!"

"We're going to institute a training program for volunteers. They're going to write parking tickets and handle the paperwork. But you will get assignments like this one-- real plums."

Tom opened the door and pulled out the wheelchair. Justin spotted him and rushed over with his television crew. They filmed moving Stanley into the chair and then Justin, mike in hand, began asking questions.

Lyle took over.

"Mr. Praetzel is here as a special investigator for the Tri-City Combined Police force," Chief Lyle West announced. "As you know, he was successful in helping us track down a serial rapist-murderer that had terrorized a number of counties in Northern Illinois."

"Are the police stumped so soon?" Justin asked. "Is that why you were called in, Mr. Praetzel?"

"Not at all," Stanley answered, taking over. "I was called in early because the smartest move the police can make is to involve all their experts from the beginning. That way less gets missed. Rather than twelve or fourteen victims, we may have only half or a third that number."

"So expect more killings?"

"The chiefs expect more killings. Their experience has told them that. And they aren't fooling around."

"I understand you just underwent major surgery." Justin inserted.

Stanley took a deep breath.

"Yes, I had the lower third of my left leg removed."

"Cancer?"

"Primary bone cancer," Stanley replied.

Chief Milani cut Justin off with an abrupt, "More later."

Stanley was wheeled down the corridor of the Willow Glen College women's dormitory toward the room of the first victim.

Chapter 3

Back in Willow Glen, Aleta saw a line of people when she entered the rear door leading to the ground floor lobby of the law firm of Praetzel, Locke and Praetzel. The line extended from the glass doors leading to the second floor where Alice sat behind a desk which everyone who entered had to pass. She was not a receptionist. She was in charge. It had been a one-man office a year ago. Now the second floor suite of offices housed three partners and four associates, a law clerk, three more secretaries and a research assistant. Stanley Praetzel owned the renovated the tree-lined Main Street of Willow Glen, all of whose shops catered to the wealthy citizenry of Willow Glen, consequently, his firm's suite of offices was in a unique location that appealed to rich and poor alike.

Aleta entered the back door, walked to the tiny elevator and took it to the second floor. She greeted Alice with, "Has Tim done his thing?"

Alice nodded. "We weren't sure, Mrs. Praetzel..."

Aleta acknowledged her assumption as correct.

"There are three women together in line that I want to see," Aleta said. "Also the man with three small children.

Have Tim put him in the library and put cartoons on the
television for the children."

"What about the others?"

"How busy is my mother-in-law?"

"It's her last day."

"Ask her to come see me at her convenience," Aleta
said. "Give me five minutes. Then send in the first in line."

Aleta's attractive gray-haired mother-in-law entered
Aleta's office a few minutes later. A former Superior Court
Judge, Lydia Davis had resigned from the bench to return to
practicing law in her son's fledgling law firm, which had
expanded rapidly after Aleta joined the firm. She had
followed in her husband's footsteps as he had left his firm
earlier to join is son's firm and practice something besides
criminal law. Now, Lydia was returning to the bench with the
promise of a position on the Appellate Court as the carrot
that persuaded her to return to the bench.

"I was planning to do the initial interviews today,"
Lydia Davis said. "It doesn't seem to matter to people that
we announced that we aren't taking clients. They come
anyway."

"I am here for certain clients," Aleta said. "I will let
Alice send the rest to you."

"Does she know which ones?"

Tim stepped in into the room and announced, "I put
the children in the library. The women are waiting. Dr.
Schwartzman sent over another friend. He said Dr.
Schwartzman said he was to see you. He is in an unusual
situation. A dangerous one."

"Stanley's not going to be happy about that," Aleta
commented. "I have two clients ahead of him, but I'll see
him this morning. Take his lunch order. And send in the
ladies.

She turned to her mother-in-law. "Judge Davis, these
three would be best served by you."

"I thought they were special clients—ones you came in for," Lydia queried.

"They are, but things are not what they seem."

Tim ushered in the three women. The tallest of the three, a woman with high cheekbones reminiscent of her Indian ancestry, placed three folders in front of Aleta, and three hundred dollars in bills of various denominations.

"We need an hour of legal advice," Gladys Whitehorse said.

Aleta extended her hand. As Gladys took it, they both felt a warmth that was so pleasant, neither let go.

Aleta noted a puzzled look on the gaunt face. It was followed immediately by an absence of pain in the eyes.

"You are in constant pain, aren't you?" Aleta asked.

"I was until a moment ago," Gladys Whitehorse responded.

Aleta patted their joined hands.

"I believe God answered your prayer."

"How long have I got?"

"I don't know," Aleta said. "Longer than you had when you walked into this office."

"What did you do?" Lydia asked.

"God took away Miss Whitehorse's pain," Aleta said.

"I feel good," Gladys said, puzzled. "I feel well."

"You were sick?" Judge Davis asked.

"Cancer," Gladys responded. "Brain cancer."

"No!" Valerie cried, and then turned to their other companion. "Maria, did you know?"

"I felt it," Maria said. "I don't feel it now."

"Ladies, may I introduce Judge Davis. This is her last day helping us out. She returns to the bench tomorrow. I am putting you in her capable hands."

Daniel Wallace entered her office a few moments later. He was a muscular man just shy of six-feet tall, short blonde hair and one arm in a sling. His right hand gripped the tiny hand of a blue-eyed boy of two. The boy's two older sisters clung to their father's suit coat. He introduced his children proudly. "Becky is four and a half, Jenny is three and three quarters and Scott is almost two."

"Do you like to watch fish swim?' Aleta asked the children. The two girls bobbed their heads and the boy shouted, "No!"

"He always says that to any suggestion," his father said by way of explanation.

"He can stay here and one of my secretaries will watch him while the rest of us go look at the fish swimming."

"No," Scott shouted.

"If you want to come with me, you will have to hold my hand," Aleta said.

The boy grabbed her hand and she led the small family into Stanley's office.

Standing in the center of the room, the awed children stared at the huge tanks. Becky moved nearer, her eyes on the little fan-tailed gold fish darting in and out among the Koi.

"Do they have names?" Becky asked.

"Yes," Aleta replied. "My husband named each one after a friend."

"Who's this?" Becky said.

"Martha Cook," Aleta said.

Becky pointed again.

"Judge Lydia Davis, his mother." Aleta responded.

"Which one are you?" Becky asked.

"The tiny goldfish that can't sit still."

The girls giggled.

Aleta regarded their father and raised a brow. He responded to her unspoken query.

"Yes, I could leave them here for a few minutes so we could talk."

Tim came in as soon as Aleta buzzed Alice.

"That was quick," Aleta said.

"Your husband's on television," Tim blurted out. "On the news. Hurry!"

"Watch the children," Aleta said, saying their names as she pointed to each. "Becky, Jenny and Scott."

"Go! Go!" Tim urged her.

Daniel Wallace followed Aleta to the library. Once Aleta appeared, her father-in-law switched to another news channel hoping that by so doing Aleta would see the entire segment.

She saw Stanley being helped from the Arborville police chief's car to a waiting wheelchair which was manned by Chief Tom Milani personally.

Aleta stared at the screen in utter disbelief.

"What is he doing out of bed?"

The entire room chuckled.

Justin Conway, Tri-City Register's star reporter, who wore as a second hat the role of local TV newsman, approached the trio and interviewed Stanley briefly.

As they were wheeling Stanley into the dormitory, Aleta murmured, "He can't investigate a murder! He's convalescing. Doesn't Lyle know that?"

"The reporter knows," Maya quipped. "Those cops are in deep shit!"

She was right. Justin Conway came on the screen and openly questioned Chief West's decision to have Stanley involved in a crime scene so soon after major surgery.

Aleta rushed out of the library.

"Alice, get me through to Justin Conway. He's on the air. Tell him I want to speak to him."

Daniel Wallace, who had followed her, not knowing what else to do, tailed her into her office. She waved him into a seat.

The group in the library stayed glued to the set as Justin promised them a live interview with Aleta Praetzel who had called with regard to the show.

"Mrs. Praetzel," he said, his phone on speaker. The TV camera crew in the studio hastily inserted a photo of

Aleta Praetzel in the corner of the screen as they reviewed the live feed.

"Did you know your husband was drafted for this duty?"

"Justin, you know full well that neither Chief West nor Chief Milani would endanger my husband in any way. You will not go down that road."

"It's a question that needs asking?"

"No, it doesn't. It's irrelevant. Stanley's head wasn't cut off. It was his leg. You need a refresher course in anatomy if you believe brain cells reside in either foot, especially the left foot.

"But his was major surgery. Pain killers would interfere with his thinking."

"They would if he were on any."

"Then the pain would color his thinking."

"It would if he had much."

"Then simply residual weakness," Justin argued.

"You interviewed him," Aleta said. "Didn't he seem as sharp as ever. You know him. Tell the truth."

Justin smiled into the camera. "You've got me there. He did respond as a man in full command of his mental faculties."

"Your camera captured him emerging from the car. Did he appear in pain?"

"No, he didn't."

"The doctors said he could go anywhere he pleased in a wheelchair. Wasn't a wheelchair provided?"

"Yes, it was."

"So he is adhering to his doctors' orders and helping the police. There's nothing wrong with that."

Justin nodded smiling.

"He did make a quicker than normal recovery, didn't he?"

"The doctors have said so."

"He had surgery only four days ago. Don't you think that Chief West was presumptive to ask him to do this?"

"No," Aleta stated. "Absolutely not! Stanley worked a full day at the office yesterday and we had a party last night and Chief West was there as was Chief Milani. They were acting on knowledge, not guesswork."

"Tell me, Mrs. Praetzel, did you heal your husband?"

"Absolutely not!" Aleta cried. "I am a prophet. I am not a healer."

"Three days after major surgery and he is back at work. I leave it to my listeners. Do you think our local prophet has other powers?"

Aleta slammed down the phone.

Daniel Wallace flinched. Aleta saw it.

She laughed.

"Don't worry. I don't throw things," Aleta assured him. "So your wife throws things? How did she break your arm?"

"With a cast iron frying pan."

"Was she swinging at you or one of the children?"

"I'm not sure. When she flies into a rage, she hits whoever's closest."

"You're a pretty muscular man."

"And my wife is a thin woman, but she wields a mean bat or, in this case, skillet."

"And you take it so she won't hit the children?"

"All I know is that if she doesn't hit me, she will hit them. She started out just using her fists and I got black and blue but that's all. Lately, though, she's gotten worse and she's begun using objects."

"Like the frying pan?"

"And a bat. Once a knife."

"Did you report these attacks to the police?"

"I used to, but they laughed at me. I thought that after she broke my finger with the bat that I would be believed, but I wasn't. When she used a knife I had to go to the hospital for stitches. I reported that. I had to. The police did nothing. As I said, they laughed at me."

"What city?"

"Oakwood."

"How long ago?"

"Before the new chief came on."

"Did you report this incident?"

"No. I didn't want to be laughed at again. I came here instead."

"We're going to report it together," Aleta said. "You do know I don't handle divorce cases."

"Yes, I know. I am not sure I want a divorce," Daniel Wallace said. "Stella Woodbridge said you were a victim's lawyer. I don't know what that is exactly but, she said if anyone could help me you could."

"How do you know Stella?" Aleta said, remembering with fondness the octogenarian, who was a key witness in a case.

"She was a close friend of my grandmother whose house I now live in," Daniel said, and then continued, "I need help. There are places for battered wives to go. I spent last night in the car with the kids. I watched my wife leave for work this morning and I snuck back into the house so we could change clothes and then we came here."

"Don't you have a friend's house you could go to?"

"Phyllis would look there. Someone would get hurt."

"Such a shelter would only be temporary," Aleta said. "Why are you here?"

"I want my wife to get help." Daniel said. "It would have to be a hospital in order for her insurance to pay and for her to keep her job. I don't want to ruin her."

"What alternatives have you considered?"

"Running away."

"And?"

"Divorce, but she might get custody."

"What would happen if you went back to work?" Aleta asked.

"You mean switch roles back?"

"Yes."

"I would be willing if the therapist said that would help her. I like being with my children, but I liked my job too."

"Teacher?" Aleta guessed.

"Teacher and coach," Daniel said.

"We're going to take this one step at a time" Aleta said pressing her intercom, "Alice, please tell Chief Peets I wish to see him about a crime in his town."

She paused for a moment and then said, "It's urgent."

"It's not urgent," Daniel corrected.

"Yes, it is," Aleta responded, the blood draining from her face.

"Why is it urgent?"

"I saw your death," Aleta replied.

"Are you psychic?"

"No. I am a prophet. I sometimes see murders before they happen."

"How about these two girls who died at the college last night? Did you see those murders?"

"No."

"Why not?"

"I don't know."

"That's not good enough. I'm sure you think you saw something or you sensed something, but that doesn't mean it's going to happen."

"Yes, it does," Aleta said firmly.

"Okay, tell me how I'm going to die."

"When you open your front door and step inside your house, you're going to be shot in the chest," Aleta predicted.

"Who's going to shoot me?"

"I don't know."

"My wife doesn't own a gun." Daniel said. "Besides she's at work."

"Prove me wrong?" Aleta challenged.

"What?" Daniel gasped. "Go home and get shot?"

"I would never advise that!" Aleta exclaimed. "All I want is for you to give me permission to ask Chief Peets to send one of his men to your house to search for a gun."

"What will that prove?"

"If someone is there with a gun, won't that give my warning some credibility."

"I guess."

"Your children need you."

"I will feel foolish if they find nothing."

"As I said before, I am sending the police. Not you."

"I guess I have nothing to lose."

Chapter 4

Meanwhile, at the college dormitory where a young coed had been brutally murdered, Stanley had used two of the barf bags Bertha had given him before he was able to quell the tendency of his stomach to literally throw itself up with the partly digested contents of the meal he'd eaten the night before.

He scowled at Lyle.

"If you'd tell me in advance," he snapped. "I wouldn't stuff myself at my parties. In fact, I wouldn't eat at all."

Lyle snapped back. "If you'd stop hogging Aleta's attention, maybe she would have prophesied and..."

Stanley's glowering visage cut him off.

"Sorry. I forgot."

"Forgot what?" Tom asked.

"Never mind. I was out of line. Aleta is open to receive visions no matter what she's doing."

"Surely there are times?" Tom posed.

Lyle shook his head.

"And you know this?" Tom asked.

"Yes, I do."

The banter relaxed Stanley enough to begin taking notes. Hawk was already working the room. Natsumi was on the second case. The coroner arrived thirty minutes after Stanley.

"Another messy one," he commented. "Everyone clear out."

Stanley was wheeled to the second victim's room. His stomach lurched, but he kept it from turning inside out in its effort to dispel what his other senses were loading into his brain.

The girl lay naked on the bed, hands and feet tied to the corners of the bed, her mouth taped. She had obviously been raped first. The multiple knife cuts were deep. Blood was everywhere.

Stanley noted everything. What he didn't know was that both West and Milani had assigned their best men to position themselves in the doorway at the alternate crime scene and take notes as well. Neither Lyle nor Tom thought Stanley would miss anything, but Peter French and Matt Carradine were eager for the challenge.

The cell phone taped to each girl's ear became the hallmark by which the cases were linked. Focus would center on those first.

To Stanley's mind they were incidental. They were the fuse that lit the bomb of rage that resulted in an explosion of hate that showered the room with blood.

How could the perp escape without being covered in blood? Of course, he might have been. The deaths occurred in the wee hours of the morning when the dorm halls were empty.

He noted that the first girl's room was neat. Even her dirty clothes in the net basket were folded to fit exactly. Only the shorts on top were simply thrown in.

The closet doors were open. All the clothes were hanging neatly in a prescribed order. The only clothes on the floor were the slacks and the long-sleeved shirt she'd been wearing. Underneath Stanley could see her panties and the strap of her bra. All were bloodstained.

Stanley wondered if she'd just gotten in from a late date and been surprised when she entered the room. Otherwise, her pajamas would be on the floor as well. He surveyed the room carefully from his chair, looking for her shoes. Had she removed them, put them away and then been surprised. He asked Hawk who told him they were under the bed.

"Kicked or placed?" Stanley asked.

"Placed neatly."

The second room was a chaotic jumble of clothes, magazines, scrunched potato chip bags, empty soda cans and books turned upside down. In the mess there was a second cell phone besides the one plastered against the victim's ear.

Even in chaos, Stanley reasoned, there is a pattern.

What is out of place, he asked himself.

There was no bra with the clothes nearest the bed. It was draped with the others on the lamp on the dresser. The panties, however, were underneath the slacks and long-sleeved sweat shirt on the floor nearest the bed. The girl's nightgown was there too in the jumble of soiled clothes, tossed carelessly on the side of the pile. All her shoes were scattered on the closet floor.

Stanley surveyed the group—red, blue, tan, black, white, pink, and orange.

"You see any green shoes anywhere?" Stanley asked Natsumi.

"Should there be?" Natsumi asked.

"Yes," Stanley replied. "What size did she wear?"

"Eight," Natsumi answered.

"You both got photos of everything?" Stanley inquired.

"We did," Natsumi replied.

"Take more in that room," Stanley asked. "Please."

"Anything in particular?" Natsumi asked.

"Something's out of place."

"Everything is out of place," Natsumi responded, smiling. "But I will take more pictures."

The coroner came and shooed everyone away. Natsumi took pictures and the coroner grumbled about that being something she should have done earlier. Natsumi apologized and continued shooting.

"Have you got anything?" Lyle asked Stanley.

"The perp was small," Stanley said.

"That's all?" Tom pressed.

"No sign of a struggle."

"How did the killer get the upper hand?" Tom asked.

"A stun gun," Stanley responded.

"What do I tell the news media?" Lyle asked.

"As little as possible," Stanley said.

"Do we have leads?" Lyle asked.

"Yes." Stanley said. "And we'll have more after the coroner's report. I believe you're in for a surprise."

"Are you going to tell us," Lyle asked.

"No."

"Then you are going to the autopsy with us."

"I need my rest."

"The morgue has tables," Lyle said.

"You're kidding?"

"You're holding out on us." Tom said. "Deputies can't do that."

"Check with Matt," Lyle said told Tom. "I'll see if Peter has any idea what Stanley came up with."

"I'm not sleeping on a table at the morgue," Stanley declared. "I'm a private citizen. You need to take me home when I ask."

"You're a deputy on duty right now," Lyle said. "You go home when your shift is over."

"You're really pushing me, Lyle," Stanley charged, irked.

"Chief!" Lyle shot back.

"I hope the morgue tables have padding, Chief," Stanley returned, his tone apologetic. "I do need to lay down."

"I have a blanket in my car you can use as a pillow."

"I will need that for my leg."

"We'll fix you up," Tom assured him.

And fix him up they did—in a hospital bed on the second floor of the Tri-City Hospital.

"I can't get in bed dressed," he protested.

"We don't expect you to," Lyle said. "We got a hospital gown for you. Show him Tom."

"Extra long," Tom grinned, holding it up.

"I am not a patient!" Stanley declared vociferously.

"I promised Wayne I'd get you here," Lyle said. "Now strip!"

"You promised Dr. Cook?" Stanley queried, surprised.

"Yes," came the terse reply.

"When?" Stanley pressed.

"After he saw you on television."

Stanley pulled off his tie, then his shirt. He folded both neatly and put them on a chair.

"He wasn't happy, was he?" Stanley ventured.

"That's putting it mildly."

"He can't put me back in the hospital."

"I'm putting you here so you can write your report and rest your leg."

"No autopsy?"

"That's scheduled for at one o'clock. That'll give you time to write your report and have your MRI."

"What MRI?"

"The one Dr. Cook has ordered."

"On my nickel?"

"He and Michael want to see what's happening with your leg."

"Nothing's happening with my leg. It's fine."

Dr. Cook walked in. "Aren't you undressed yet?"

"I'm still arguing," Stanley shot back.

"I thought you said he was on duty," Dr. Cook questioned.

"He is!" Lyle stated.

His tone held a warning.

Stanley pulled off his undershirt and held out his arms for the gown. Tom tied it behind his neck and Stanley wriggled out of his jeans.

He folded his undershirt and then his jeans.

"Everything!" Cook ordered. "You aren't changing hospital rules."

"Tom's idea of long isn't mine," Stanley quipped.

A stern look from Chief West forced Stanley to remove his last bit of clothing.

"The MRI comes first," Dr. Cook said. "I know you guys. You'll spirit him away if I don't grab him."

An orderly came in with a gurney.

Lyle smiled at Stanley as they wheeled him out. "Your leg is getting a rest. That's what you wanted."

"An MRI doesn't hurt, does it?" Tom asked.

"No. Stanley's just pissed."

"And why are we pissing him off? The poor guy just lost a leg, for God's sake!" Tom exclaimed.

"That's the reason. While we'll accommodate his handicap, we'll treat him as we would if he weren't missing that leg."

"I think you're treating him a bit harder." Tom noted.

"I know I am," Lyle said. "He knows it too, but it's okay. He can quit being a volunteer deputy anytime he wants. We both know that. He likes being a part-time cop."

"Really?" Tom returned, surprised. "I read a lot of resentment."

"And a lot of eagerness. He wants to be pushed."

"No one wants to see what we saw this morning," Tom insisted.

"We need him," Lyle said. "He's already figured out half the puzzle. Let's see if either of our guys did."

Meanwhile in Oakwood, Chief Alan Peets' two uniformed officers found Phyllis Wallace at home. They searched for the gun and found it under a couch cushion where she had hastily shoved it when they had announced their presence.

She was arrested for possession of an illegal firearm and called her lawyer, Fred Dunn, a noted Chicago divorce attorney.

Chief Peets meanwhile took Daniel Wallace's statement at the law offices of Praetzel, Locke and Praetzel and added the assault charge before Dunn arrived to consult with his client.

"You can't go home," Aleta told Daniel Wallace.

"I'm beginning to see that," Daniel said. "But where do I go?"

"You need a safe house." Aleta mused aloud. "And you can't leave the children so you can't work."

"I don't have any money of my own."

"And you can't really be seen while she's loose on bail."

"You think she will get bail?"

"I'm sure of it," Aleta said. "Alice will order lunch for you and the children. I have arrangements to make."

"The children need their toys," Daniel said.

"That's one of the arrangements," Aleta responded. "I'm going to send Karyn in to get a list of essentials for you and the children. Karyn recently moved out of her home with two small children so she'll be able to help you not forget anything truly important. Tim and Karyn will pack for you while your wife is being arraigned. Two of Oakwood's police officers will accompany them and watch. We don't want you accused of stealing."

"Where are the kids and I going?"

"I am arranging for a foundation to purchase a home as a haven for battered men and their children."

"Such arrangements would take months."

"I have an in with the head of such a foundation. I expect to have you settled by the end of the day."

"That would truly be a miracle!"

"No. That would be my ingenuity. The prophecy was a miracle," Aleta said pressing the intercom.

"Alice, get me Bertha and then Mrs. Cook and then Mrs. Morales," Aleta ordered. "Is Chief Peets still here?"

"Yes, he is."

"Would you have him step into my office, please." Aleta said. "Also, I need Tim and Karyn right away."

"Why all this haste?" Daniel Wallace asked.

"What's the first thing you would do if you were your wife and you found out your husband had discovered you were planning a divorce."

"Change the locks on the house. Phyllis is very possessive."

"Don't have Tim and Karyn fetch anything your wife thinks is hers even if you like it and she doesn't."

"She'll destroy it."

"Probably," Aleta agreed.

"I hate to..."

Aleta cut in sharply. "You are trying to save your children."

Daniel nodded reluctantly.

Chief Peets, Karyn and Tim entered as Aleta's phone light flashed. She picked up the phone and asked Bertha to hold and spelled out the first part of her plan.

When the three left her office, she asked Bertha about Stanley.

"He's in the hospital. Dr. Cook wanted to do another MRI," Bertha reported. "He'll be there for a couple hours Chief West said."

"Why is Dr. Cook doing an MRI?"

Mr. Praetzel said his leg needed a rest and Chief West got worried. Mr. Praetzel is not one for complaining," Bertha explained. "Chief West did say that Mr. Praetzel said he felt fine."

"Do you know his room number?"

"205," Bertha said.

"I have an emergency here. I'll call him as soon as I can."

"Chief West said nobody was worried."

"I'm worried."

"Yes, Ma'am."

Stanley was back in his room when Aleta called.

"You had an MRI," she accused.

"It wasn't my idea."

"Didn't you complain about your leg?"

"My leg feels fine. I was trying to get out of watching an autopsy and..."

Aleta burst in.

"Lyle was going to drag you to an autopsy? In your condition?"

"Viewing an autopsy is not something I would have wanted to do when I was well either."

"Oh, I guess not," Aleta said settling down. "So you used your leg as an excuse?"

"Yes," Stanley said. "Now tell me what took you so long? You didn't do anything this morning that will get me shot, did you?"

"Maybe just a little bit," Aleta confessed. "But I had Peets confiscate her gun."

"Someone came at you with a gun?"

"I had a vision. She was going to shoot our new client. He's one of the reasons I came in this morning."

"You mean we have two people gunning for us?" Stanley sputtered. "Did you have two visions?"

"No. The other client was a trio of old ladies." Aleta said. "I healed one and let your mother handle their legal problems."

"She's only got a day," Stanley pointed out.

"They only paid for an hour," Aleta said. "I think she can manage that."

"Whom did you heal?"

"She doesn't know she's been healed."

"How could she not know?" Stanley questioned.

"I told her God took away her pain," Aleta said.

"Did He?"

"Yes. She said she felt well."

"And?" Stanley pressed.

"She asked me how much longer she had."

"And?" Stanley asked.

"I told her I didn't know" Aleta responded. "And I don't."

"You misled her," Stanley said.

"Go to your autopsy. It'll give you something to think about besides what I'm doing."

Aleta, however, was mistaken.

Just after he hung up, he received a visit from his two doctors.

"Jamara told us it was time to remove the whole bandage," Dr. Taekman said.

Stanley objected. "You can't!"

"Why not?"

"Bertha says Aleta won't be able to handle it."

"She's been handling everything so far," Dr. Taekman pointed out.

"That's because I have a big bandage covering half my leg."

"She's a big girl," Dr. Taekman said.

"She has limits," Stanley countered. "Why can't I keep it on for the normal ten days?"

"Because it's time for it to come off," Dr. Taekman insisted.

"Can't I refuse?" Stanley said, his eyes seeking support from Dr. Cook.

"We must do what's right for the leg," Dr. Cook said. "Wear long pants until she can handle it."

"I'm not sure I'm ready," Stanley enjoined.

Dr. Taekman smiled. "You're as ready as you'll ever be."

Dr. Cook buzzed for the nurse.

Stanley objected. "You mean you aren't doing it?"

"What? And find out we're wrong and it's a bloody mess," Michael commented soberly.

"We got you an orthopedic oncologist," Dr. Cook said as an aside.

"I wasn't planning to get one."

"We thought you might not," Dr. Cook said. "We had him read the MRI with us. He said the upper leg looks clean. So does your other leg."

"You did them both?"

"You were just lying there," Wayne Cook said. "It seemed prudent."

"It doesn't jump from leg to leg."

"We don't know how you got it the first time."

"You did the whole right leg," Stanley pointed out petulantly.

"Of course," Dr. Cook said. He turned to his companion. "Here it comes."

"That'll cost more than half a left leg."

Michael chuckled. "No one will ever accuse you of not knowing where every dollar goes."

"How much more?" Stanley asked.

"I thought we'd go for double," Wayne Cook said.

"Too much," Stanley snapped.

"MRI fees aren't negotiable," Dr. Taekman put in.

"Everything is negotiable," Stanley shot back. "How expensive is this new orthopedic oncologist I don't want, don't need, and am not going to use."

"We're going to use him to read your MRI's," Wayne Cook said. "He's going to hold your hand while the dressing is removed.

"I don't need my hand held!" Stanley protested loudly.

"Be nice." Dr. Cook said as Dr. Taekman brought Dr. Curtis Jurgen into the room.

Dr. Jurgen extended his hand. "I understand you don't want an oncologist."

"Dr. Cook and Dr. Taekman have jumped the gun. I haven't decided what course of treatment I want next, if any."

"We could make an appointment and discuss your options."

"I already know my options," Stanley said tersely.

"Perhaps a review of statistics would help," Dr. Jurgen offered.

"I've reviewed them. I am as current on the treatment of bone cancer as you are."

"Then you know the efficacy of radiation therapy in cases of primary bone cancer."

"Yes."

"Chemotherapy will attack any cancer cells that might be developing elsewhere. You're a young man and cancer at your age needs to be attacked vigorously."

"That's what I did."

"You probably didn't need to lose the leg. With a well-structured regime of chemotherapy and radiation we could probably have excised the tumor, inserted a prosthesis and saved the leg."

"I weighed that option," Stanley said coldly. "Dr. Jurgen, thank you for your time but I am not going to be using your services in the near future. Michael, he's the wrong man for me. Please show the doctor out."

Dr. Cook motioned to the nurse to get started. He sat down beside Stanley as Dr. Taekman led Dr. Jurgen out of the room.

"Knowledgeable men who can read cancer in the bone are hard to find, Stanley," Dr. Cook said.

"He second-guessed me."

"That was a mistake."

"He went further, Wayne, and you know it."

"He's tops in his field."

"Then get me someone at the bottom."

"You don't mean that."

"Let me find someone."

"You haven't found a single doctor on your own."

"I found you."

"Oh, Stanley, what a short memory you have. Wasn't it a little over a month ago that, despite my caring for you for almost a year which included house calls, you still didn't think of me as your doctor."

"Find me someone like you. I need to work into trusting a doctor."

"That's not how it's done," Dr. Cook said.

"Dr. Taekman delivered Lauren's baby."

Dr. Cook's jaw dropped. "What has that to do with anything?"

"You're all the doctor I need," Stanley said.

"I'm not an expert in radiation therapy."

"I'm not going that route yet."

"Nor chemotherapy."

"I have something else in mind. I just need someone to haul me in here and do an MRI without my requesting one. You're what I need."

"You're risking the rest of your leg."

"I am a man who is, above all, cautious," Stanley said. "In business I study before I make a decision. To outsiders I may appear to be taking huge risks, but I'm not. My body is not something I take casually. You respect me. You let me fuss about the money because you know it doesn't matter. Michael doesn't quite get it yet, but he loves Aleta. He'll put up with me for her sake. But, you. You like me too."

"The nurse is finished, Stanley. Do you want to look at your leg?"

"No."

"You may go, nurse," Dr. Cook said.

Then Dr. Cook moved to the end of the bed and studied the stump.

"We did a good job," he said. "And it is completely healed which is remarkable."

He drew the sheet over the leg.

"Take your time," Dr. Cook said kindly. "Get used to the feel of it. Don't rush."

"Can you excuse me from the autopsy?"

"You mean write you a note?" Cook smirked.

"If you think Lyle would...never mind. I want to see if my theory is right."

"Being active appears to agree with you."

"I'm contentious."

"Hey, now's the time you can get away with it. Enjoy it!"

Stanley smiled. "Thanks, Doc."

Just before one o'clock Stanley discovered that he couldn't dress without looking at his leg. With the dressing on, the end of his leg didn't quite compute. Now there was his bare knee with nothing but a bare stump below it.

As he pulled on his shorts he felt the cloth brush his knee. That felt normal, but the sight of an empty space where his ankle and foot had been was surreal.

Aleta's not going to like this one bit, he thought.

Lyle arrived in time to help him with his jeans.

"They took off the bandage," Lyle said calmly. "Looks good."

His comment spurred Stanley to glance down again.

"Yeh," he said. "They did a good job."

"Come on," Lyle said. "Let's go cheer you up."

"We're going to an autopsy," Stanley cracked.

"Two autopsies. It will take all afternoon unless your theory makes sense after the first one."

Stanley handed Lyle the laptop. "Both reports are in there. Aleta's at the office making people angry."

"Peets told me," Lyle said. "But one of them is in jail.

"Lyle, she healed someone."

"At the office?"

"Where else?"

"Here, at the hospital, where we could maybe cover it up," Lyle said wistfully.

"She said the woman doesn't know."

"Tell her to stop it. We're too busy with a serial killer on the loose to deal with crowd control."

"Lyle, try to remember just exactly who Aleta answers to."

"Can't you make her stay home?"

"Let me drink my coffee," Stanley said, reaching for the cup on his tray.

"Isn't it cold?"

"I need the caffeine."

"Let me get you a hot cup from the vending machine."

"That stuff tastes like tar."

"Suit yourself," Lyle shrugged.

Stanley drank the coffee so fast he barely tasted it.

"Now I'm ready," he said.

Five minutes later he was wheeled into the hospital morgue. He found that Lyle had guessed that his wheelchair was too low for him to have a clear view of the proceedings.

"We got you a gurney to sit on," Lyle told him.

"The wheelchair will work fine" Stanley protested. "I can hear everything. I don't need to see. Honest."

"We need your full participation in this," Lyle said, rolling over the gurney.

Tom and he hoisted Stanley up onto it and then sat on either side of him as the coroner began his examination.

"Did French's report give you a clue to what Stanley's holding back?" Tom asked.

Lyle shook his head.

"It was thorough, but there was nothing surprising in it."

"Same with Matt's."

"You had two regular guys second-guess me?"

"They want to be investigators," Lyle said. "You're their teacher."

"Then let me teach them," Stanley said.

"Go ahead," Lyle said. "We could all learn."

"I thought maybe we could go somewhere else," Stanley suggested. "Even my hospital room is better than this."

"Talk so I can't hear you," the coroner said. 'Better yet, don't talk at all."

"We'll be quiet," West said.

A few moments later, Stanley nudged Lyle.

"Poison," he whispered hoarsely. "I'm burning up. Can't talk. Can't see."

Lyle glanced over.

"Good God! You're beet red," Lyle cried.

Tom turned at Lyle's shout and the two chiefs simultaneously leaped from the gurney, and together they eased Stanley down.

The coroner, who looked up annoyed at the interruption, quickly realized that one of the spectators was in crisis.

Stanley choked out, "Get Cook and Aleta."

The coroner rushed over.

"No cutting," Stanley uttered through dry lips.

Behind him he heard Lyle talking to Dr. Cook on his cell.

"Aleta," Stanley tried to call out, but her name stuck in his throat.

His thirst was incredibly intense and he couldn't seem to catch his breath. The doctor looked into his eyes and the glare from the overhead lights hurt. He squeezed them shut.

An oxygen mask was put over his face. Moments later a strong hand took hold of his. He couldn't bring himself to open his eyes. Dr. Cook's voice assured him that he wasn't going to die.

Then he felt himself moving. The hand continued to grip his through the journey around corners, up several floors in the elevator, down a long hall and into a quiet room where orders were given rapidly.

The hand left his and Stanley felt the sting of a needle in his arm.

"I am giving you another poison to battle the one that appears to have taken over your body," Dr. Cook said. "It's sometimes called an antidote."

Stanley latched on to the last word. There was an antidote.

"You're going to be with us a while," Dr. Cook said. "Chief West insists you change rooms; however, that will happen later. We need you in intensive care for twenty-four hours.

Stanley tried to nod but he didn't think his head moved. The oxygen mask told him not to speak.

He was stripped and gowned. Heart monitors were placed on his chest. An automatic blood pressure cuff circled his arm. Two IV's were started. A clip was attached to a finger. He felt a band of material wrapped around his right ankle. Another band was wrapped around each wrist. A catheter was inserted in his penis. The oxygen mask remained in place.

His throat was no longer burning and he wasn't as thirsty. He felt cooler. The shot was working.

He opened his eyes. Dr. Cook was standing over him.

"Why the restraints?" he croaked.

"Atropine is nasty. It can cause hallucinations, disorientation and even aggressive behavior in a few hours or a few days after ingestion. The restraints are meant to keep you from hurting yourself."

"Aleta?" Stanley whispered hoarsely.

"Lyle said no visitors."

"Just Aleta," Stanley emphasized, his voice cracking as he spoke.

"Sorry no," Dr. Cook said. "She obeys you. She'll remove the restraints."

"I could explain" he stammered.

Dr. Cook shook his head.

Stanley's eyes widened when he realized what was about to happen.

"No," he choked.

Dr. Cook proceeded to tell him why.

"Both the poison and the antidote cause respiratory collapse," he related solemnly. "There is still the possibility of convulsions from the one and bronchial constriction from the other. I don't want to wait for either to happen."

"Getting better," Stanley proclaimed.

"Yes, you are. And if it were anyone else, I would wait until you displayed some symptoms; however, your body isn't acting normally. This is a slow acting poison and if your body reacts at an accelerated rate, I may not be able to act fast enough."

"No Aleta," Stanley gasped.

"Right," Dr. Cook said, signaling the nurse who wheeled over a cart.

Stanley was surprised at how quickly Dr. Cook worked.

The overriding sensation was that his air was being cut off. Were he not tied down, he wasn't sure he wouldn't have tried to block the move.

"There," Dr. Cook exclaimed. "It's in."

Even then, Stanley's inclination was to remove it. His hands went up and both were stopped by the restraints.

Why had he agreed to this, he wondered. He had no idea what he'd agreed to. Maybe death would be better. Suppose he never got well enough to have it removed. The thought terrified him.

He didn't have time for another thought. Dizziness spun his mind around. As his body convulsed, he lost consciousness.

Chapter 5

When Aleta arrived home that night, she was overjoyed when she saw Lyle West's car in the driveway. She was puzzled at the presence of several other cars, but not perturbed. They were all friends.

When she opened the door Tank and Scooby greeted her enthusiastically.

She looked around for Stanley.

"He's not here, Aleta," Bertha said.

The blood drained from Aleta's face and her father rushed to her side, but she brushed off his offer of help. She noticed that Lettie and Jocelyn weren't there although both their fathers were. Something was terribly wrong.

"Does everybody know but me?" she charged.

"Let's take a walk," Lyle said quietly. "I have things to share only with you."

The last sentence turned her around. She followed Lyle out the door. The group watched them through the large picture window in the living room. They walked halfway, then stopped.

Aleta said, "We're alone. Tell me everything."

"He's alive," Lyle said.

"I sensed that," Aleta said.

"He was poisoned."

"Poisoned?"

Lyle began with the autopsy. The beginning was always a good place to start. He ended with the convulsion ending in a coma.

"I must see him," Aleta determined.

"Stanley's afraid he'll order you to do something that in his right mind he wouldn't," Lyle said. "So Dr. Cook promised him you wouldn't come. Nor for that matter would anyone else."

"Stanley doesn't know I hold his life as more precious than my wedding vow," Aleta said. "I will not undo the arrangement he agreed to."

"So you won't try to see him."

"Stanley knows I obey a higher power," Aleta said. "I have a message for him, so are you going to drive me or not?"

"The men on the door have their orders," Lyle said.

"Then let them stop me."

"You aren't your grandmother."

"I know," Aleta said. "I won't make a scene."

"I won't escort you in," Lyle warned.

"If I'm turned away, that's okay," Aleta said. "I feel I need to go."

Lyle escorted her to his car and without a word to anyone, the two left the grounds.

Inside the house, Bertha was the first to speak.

"She insisted on talking to Dr. Cook," Bertha guessed and they all agreed.

At the hospital, Aleta left the elevator and walked straight toward the room where the two police guards were standing guard outside the door.

Lyle stopped at the nurse's station and asked where Dr. Cook was.

He watched Aleta approach the two guards. They appeared not to see her. She passed them and entered the room.

He followed her. Jamara rose from her chair when he entered. Her eyes didn't dart between him and Aleta and Lyle realized that Jamara didn't see Aleta either. Lyle saw that one of the beds in the six-bed intensive care unit was occupied by Stanley's doctor.

"If we talk," Lyle whispered. "Will we wake Dr. Cook?"

Jamara shook her head, so Lyle sat down and asked for an update. Meanwhile, Aleta drew the curtain around the bed.

Lyle sat back and watched the monitors with Jamara.

"At least he's still alive," Lyle murmured.

"That he is," Jamara said.

"How long are you on?"

"Midnight."

"If you're a praying woman, now's the time for it."

To his surprise, Jamara bowed her head and Lyle could tell she was doing just that.

He sat silently, watching and waiting. He hadn't meant she should pray that very second.

Aleta approached the bed and pulled back the sheet. She stared speechless at the exposed stump.

"You were right," she said softly. "It's another reality. Somehow it wasn't real when it was hidden. I know the space was there, but now I'm seeing the end. Oh, Stanley don't leave me because I am weak."

She put her hand on his leg and ran it down to the knee and didn't stop until her fingers were holding the stump.

She saw a reflexive movement and she bent over and kissed his knee. She placed her other hand alongside the first, remembering how he said he loved her touch.

"Please, God," she prayed. "Give him back to me."

She wanted so to let him know she was there and that she loved him, but she couldn't think of what else to do.

She let her hands caress him watching for any response. She kissed his closed eyes as she laid her hand on his forehead, whispering in his ear that she loved him and he was still a beautiful man.

Suddenly, she started and jumped away.

"Don't argue with me! I am using the word beautiful correctly."

She moved her hand down his body toward his leg.

"It's your head that needs fixing. How dare you try to keep me out?"

She paused part way there.

"I will put it where I choose. And yes I see the catheter. I am not dumb either."

One hand paused on his penis while the other travelled to just beyond his knee.

"You used to like me to hold it," she said. "Yes, you are fully exposed. I am your wife. I get to do this. You know how much I love to look at your body."

Her hands stayed where they were--both of them.

"I know you're hooked up to monitors and you can't speak. I rather enjoy the fact that your heart rate is increasing. It was a bit too slow.

"You can open your eyes. No one disobeyed your orders. God sent me. I did a Grams' number on the guards. Even Jamara didn't see me. She's your nurse this evening. Dr. Cook is napping which is why I drew the curtain.

"Open your eyes and I'll tell you what God's message is."

Stanley opened his eyes.

"Yea though I walk through the valley of the shadow of death, I will fear no evil, for thou art with me."

Aleta ran her hand up his leg.

"It's still a beautiful leg."

He frowned.

"No, God didn't say that part. I did...And why wouldn't He use a scripture you know? Isn't that where you were?"

Aleta pulled the sheet up. "I have to go. I'm not a hallucination. Tell me what you want me to do and I'll do it only I can't touch any of these contraptions. You have a way to go yet and one or more of them will save your life. And I want it saved. So aside from that what do you want?"

Aleta paused. "Really? Of course I'll do it...I don't care what others think...Well, yes, I do care, but I'll do it anyway."

She drew back the curtain.

The noise startled Jamara who looked up as Aleta went through the door.

"Your praying helped," Lyle said. "I think our patient is awake."

Jamara rushed to Stanley's bedside.

"You're awake," she said. "Let me tell Dr. Cook."

Lyle came to Stanley's bedside and took his hand. "I need to take your wife home. No one else knows she was here."

Stanley heard Jamara talking to Dr. Cook a few beds away and realized that neither of them heard Lyle.

"She knows the rules," Lyle said. "She did a Harriet number."

Stanley squeezed his hand.

"You're welcome," Lyle murmured, "Welcome back."

"You're awake!" Dr. Cook exclaimed. "We got that tube in just in time. You seized right afterward."

"I need to go," Lyle said. "I'll be back later."

He signaled Dr. Cook to follow him. When they were out of earshot, he told Dr. Cook that Aleta had been there.

"She didn't touch anything?" Dr. Cook questioned.

"I couldn't see because she pulled the curtain," Lyle reported, "But none of the monitors went berserk."

"Didn't Jamara notice the curtain?"

"She was praying," Lyle said. "She didn't see Aleta come or go. Neither did my guards."

"How come you did?"

"Maybe because I accompanied her."

"So she followed you in."

"Reverse that. I followed her in," Lyle said. "Everyone saw me. Jamara and I talked before I told her to pray."

"You told her?"

"Why not? It seemed as good a suggestion as any at the time. His heartbeat took a jump and I'm guessing Aleta touched him."

"Stanley will think I broke my promise," Cook moaned.

"Aleta told him you didn't," Lyle said. "She told him the contraptions needed to stay in place for a few more days."

"She said that?"

"It seems she takes orders from someone other than Stanley."

"So he's not out of the woods yet?"

"I would guess not," Lyle responded.

"That's good to know."

"I believe she turned him around," Lyle said.

"I would agree. He was sinking fast."

"And you fell asleep?"

"Yes, I did," Dr. Cook confessed. "I don't know what came over me. I never nap during the day."

"I will be back," Lyle said.

"I thought you had a dog show this weekend."

"You do remember trivia, don't you?"

"Some," Dr. Cook admitted.

"I am not going. Lauren was terribly disappointed, but, she did agree that I couldn't leave."

"Will she go alone?"

"No."

Ten minutes later, as Chief Lyle West began to drive out of the hospital parking lot, Aleta burst into tears. He stopped the car instantly and put his arm around her. She cried on his shoulder for a long time.

He handed her a handkerchief when she slowed down. She tried to dry his uniform with it, but he told her it was for her use.

"I made a mess of your uniform," she sniffled.

"I have others."

"I am sorry" she murmured. "It was so hard to see him like that."

"I know."

"I am okay now. You can take me home. I have to pack."

"Where are you going?"

"Lauren and I are going to the dog show."

"Does she know this?" Lyle asked.

"Not yet."

"We weren't planning to go. I have to work."

"Of course you do, but Lauren doesn't. And Stanley wants a video of me at the show. Actually, I think he wants to see everyone, but he only asked for me."

"He wants you," Lyle said, "but if you're watching anyone, he will want to be doing it with you."

"Harriet and Claude will be there. Claude will operate the camera for me."

"You've got this all worked out, haven't you?"

"Am I missing something?"

"Who's going to drive you?"

"We can't drive ourselves?"

"No."

"Oh."

When they arrived at Aleta's house, several RV's were parked down the long driveway.

"That's your car," Aleta noted.

Lyle growled, "What does Lauren think she's doing. She can't drive alone to the dog show?"

"Grams is here!" Aleta cried. "Lauren and I are going to the show. It's been arranged."

And it had indeed been arranged.

Stanley's father had agreed to drive. His mother was seated in the passenger seat. Seated at the small table behind them, Lauren and Aleta nibbled on sandwiches Bertha had prepared. Each had a carton of milk and a slice of apple pie.

Prior to their leaving, Harriet took Lydia aside and told her that Aleta had seen Stanley.

Lydia eyed her skeptically.

"You haven't even talked to her," she accused.

"I know her."

"Lyle said Dr. Cook was adamant about there being no visitors," Stanley's mother contended.

"She would never leave if she hadn't," Harriet declared. "If you want first hand information, ride with her and get it."

Once they were underway, Lydia approached the subject directly. "Harriet says you saw Stanley."

"Yes, I did," Aleta responded.

Lauren West's surprise burst forth in protest, "Lyle would never..."

"He didn't, "Aleta said. "He has told you about Grams walking past his guards, hasn't he?"

"Yes, but...you mean?"

"Yes."

"I don't understand," Stanley's mother said.

Aleta took another bite of sandwich and let Lauren explain.

"When Harriet has a message, she can pass by the guards Lyle puts in front of the door, and they don't see her come or go."

"I had a message for Stanley," Aleta remarked.

"How was he?" Lydia asked, boring straight to the core of her concern.

"Terrible," Aleta said. "Dr. Cook was right. Stanley wouldn't want anyone to see him like that."

"Oh, my God!" Lydia breathed aghast. "Please tell me he's not dying."

"But he is," Aleta said calmly. "I told him he needed to suffer through several more days trussed up as he was..."

"What do you mean trussed up?" Lydia prodded.

"He was in restraints. He had a tube down his throat, two IV's and various monitoring systems were in place. He couldn't move or speak."

"Restraints?" Lydia questioned, shocked by what she'd just heard and unable to move past the first word on the list."

"He had given up," Aleta said. "This was too heavy a burden on top of his recent loss. He had let go of life. He was in a deep coma."

"Why didn't you stay?"

"My job was done and Stanley had a request."

"I thought he couldn't speak," his mother charged.

"He couldn't, but somehow I knew what he wanted."

"Tell us, Aleta," his father said kindly.

Lydia fell silent. She realized she'd been conducting an inquisition. She softened her tone.

"Please let us help."

"You are," Aleta said. "Without you I never would have been able to go to the dog show. Stanley wants a video of me showing dogs."

"Do you have film?" Hubert asked.

"You know Stanley. We have lots of film," Aleta said. "And I even remembered the camera."

"I will follow you around and videotape you." Hubert offered.

"That would be great!" Aleta exclaimed.

"Won't Stanley feel as if we all abandoned him?" Lydia worried.

"I can't think about that," Aleta said. "All I know is that Lyle is going to tell him I went to the dog show as he asked and his parents drove me. Then he'll know I truly understood him. And a video will be like a visit."

"You think he'll be hospitalized that long?"

Lauren spoke up. "Lyle said Stanley ingested a lot of poison. If it doesn't kill you within the first twenty-four hours, it messes with your brain."

"So he'll be there a while," Hubert summarized. "I suggest we plunge into doing what he requested."

"I can't help worrying," Lydia wife moaned.

"Yes, you can," Hubert said," And you will. I'm going to take you up on your wedding vow. I am calling in the obey part."

"I am not doing that," Lydia protested.

"You promised," Aleta said calmly. "And you are a woman of your word. And Stanley will absolutely love hearing this story."

"You said he was dying," Lydia challenged.

"Yes, I did."

"So how can you be so calm?"

"I have got to believe Stanley will make it. If I am wrong, then I will cry. But right now I am rejoicing because he has awakened from his coma."

"Doesn't that mean he's no longer dying?" Lydia probed hopefully.

"No, it doesn't. And in your heart you know that that's a false hope," Aleta said. "He is dying. Our taking this trip tells him, we all think he's going to live. He needs to believe that."

"Lydia, stop pressing," Hubert said. "Aleta can't promise you Stanley will live."

"But she's a prophet!" Lydia wailed, her worry consuming her.

"He forbid me to come. God took care of that. I did not go to say goodbye. I went to tell him he was in the valley of the shadow of death but that God was with him."

"So you told him he wasn't done," Lydia said thoughtfully.

"His two best friends are with him," Aleta said. "And we are preparing a gift for him."

Hubert spoke up again. "Now will you stop worrying, Lydia?"

"If you say so," Lydia acquiesced.

"I guess I count that as compliance," Hubert commented ruefully.

"You'd better," Lydia quipped, "Because it is."

Several hours later, as darkness was approaching, the two RV's pulled into their assigned spaces in the lot at the fairgrounds assigned to RV parking.

Tom Wilson, saw the two big RV's arrive and he went over to Harriet's rig and asked about Aleta and Stanley.

"Aleta's here," Harriet said. "She's with Lauren. Stanley is in the hospital. There's a serial rapist-murderer and..."

"I saw Stanley on television," Tom said. "Did he really lose a leg?"

"Yes," Harriet said. "After that interview he was poisoned. He's critical."

"And Aleta's here?"

"At Stanley's request," Harried responded.

Aleta approached with Hubert following with a camcorder.

"Lyle called to give me a heads up," Aleta said. "He and Stanley had made a couple of wagers. Morgan has to beat Holly. That's one wager. Tank has to place higher in group than Morgan. Five days on that one. Two on the first."

Tom laughed. "Those two can't help it can they?"

"Lyle needs to win to keep Stanley on as a deputy. Lyle's counting his down time because he was on the case when he was poisoned. He's only got twelve days. It's not enough."

"So how much room have you in your schedule Aleta?"

I'm showing Morgan in the Breed only, and I am taking Tank as far as I can."

"So you are free to take Maggie?"

"Always," Aleta said. "Is George Sciretta here?"

"I will call him. He will drive down tonight. Bulldogs are in at nine. You know he always comes to watch you handle Maggie."

"Labs are at eight," Aleta said.

A second handler came running up.

"Hey! No more plans without me getting in a lick," Chuck Rigden called as he got nearer. "You are such a sneak, Tom Wilson!"

"The Chinese Shar-Pei," Tom said quickly.

Aleta laughed. "Yes."

"Tom!" Chuck roared. "Cut it out. I need her on Rolex."

"Same time as Wolfhounds," Tom said.

"I brought Tank," Aleta elaborated.

"Can't Harriet or Lauren show him?" Chuck asked hopefully.

"Grams will be on Stoney and Lauren's arm isn't healed," Aleta explained. "Now tell me, why aren't you showing the better Saint in Breed? Why are you putting your stamp on a lesser animal?"

"I have an obligation to an older client," Chuck hedged.

"You have only two more shows with Rolex. Why not go all out at these two shows?"

"I could lose my older client."

"Maybe. But you're sending the wrong message when you arrange for me to beat you," Aleta pointed out, then abruptly added, "Yes, I'll take in the Bullmastiff and the Collie."

"How did you know?" Chuck asked.

Tom chuckled. "We aren't the only ones who studies the judging schedule."

"What about Auggie?" Chuck asked, referring to Aleta's Pug.

"Grams is on him through the end of the circuit," Aleta said, and then looked at the camera. "Wish you were here, Stanley."

Hubert turned off the camera.

"You are holding up remarkably well, my dear," he said as he walked her back to the RV that she was sharing with Lauren.

"I am as worried as Mom. I wanted to stay at his bedside so much."

"Why didn't you?"

"It's going to sound silly, but I didn't want to get Lyle in trouble."

"And?"

"And I wouldn't be able to keep from crying and that would drain him."

"Oh, I think you are under better control than that."

Aleta burst into tears.

"Oh, Dad. He's so terribly, terribly sick. I'm so afraid he's going to die."

Her father-in-law gathered her into his arms.

"When you were talking to Lydia, didn't you listen to your own words?" Hubert asked softly.

He felt her head shake.

"Ah, well. That sounds normal," Hubert murmured and then added, "Lyle must be feeling rotten about now."

"Lyle?" Aleta hiccupped, pulling back.

"He put him in harm's way."

"No, he didn't!" Aleta declared, her anger dispensing her tears. "He and Tom would have laid down their lives to protect him. Lyle knew Stanley's mind would love the challenge. He was restoring him...Dad, have you got your cell on you?"

Hubert handed him the small phone and walked her to the RV.

"It doesn't have Lyle's number," she complained.

Hubert opened the door to the RV and called, "Lauren, what's Lyle's number?"

"Never mind," Aleta said. "I'll use my phone. If he sees it's me, he'll answer right away."

As they stepped inside the RV, Hubert asked, "What is it?"

"You gave me an idea, Dad."

"Me?"

"What idea?" Lydia asked.

"Damned if I know," Hubert muttered, thoroughly bewildered.

"Lyle, it's me. I'm calling about Stanley," Aleta said. "You have got to engage his mind. Can you work out a signal he can use to respond?"

"Am I on speaker?" Lyle asked.

"Lauren, Hubert and Lydia are listening."

"Stanley communicates with me by squeezing my hand," Lyle said.

"The murders," Aleta hurried on. "Ask him questions."

"He needs rest."

"He needs not to be stressed."

"Exactly."

"Do you have any idea how stressful not being able to speak is?" Aleta shot back. "Stanley's mind has been working since this happened. He desperately needs to communicate his thoughts."

"He's not up-to-date on the most recent forensic or medical reports."

"Bring him up-to-date!" Aleta ordered. "You're still paying him."

"Aleta, he's barely hanging on."

"Don't you think I know that?" Aleta snapped. "Give him three responses: yes, no, and possibly."

"Possibly?"

"Isn't there frequently more than one possibility inherent in a piece of evidence? Lyle, you're a lawyer. Think like one!"

"I am a cop."

"Stanley is a lawyer. Now's the time when you need to think like him."

"Dr. Cook might not agree," Lyle put forth.

"He put me in charge of Stanley's recovery. Remind him I brought Stanley out of his coma."

"How did you know I told him?"

"Because you know he needs to know everything in order to save Stanley's life," Aleta shared. "Tell Wayne to trust me on this. I've been there."

"Are you at the show?"

"Hubert got some great footage of Tom and Chuck plying me to show half their strings. If Lauren wasn't still nursing that shoulder, I would have offered her up as a sacrificial lamb."

Lyle laughed. "I can see that shoulder being miraculously healed sometimes this weekend."

Aleta put her hand on Lauren's shoulder.

"Oh, that feels good," Lauren murmured.

"What feels good?" Lyle demanded.

"Lyle, we have chaperones!" Lauren laughed. "Honestly!"

"Aleta's massaging her shoulder," Hubert said merrily.

Lydia piped up, "Hubert and I are sleeping in Harriet's RV. Too many dogs in this one. Tank takes up the whole hallway."

"Lyle, you switched topics on me," Aleta said. "I almost let you get away with it."

"Stanley will want news about you," Lyle returned.

"Stanley does not need news. Stanley needs to be useful. He needs to communicate. Don't let him go silent to his grave."

"Why do you think he's dying?" Lyle asked, upset with Aleta's pressing him.

"Because he is," Aleta said. "Lyle stop blaming his condition on yourself. Stanley could have said no. He didn't. He wanted to be useful. Don't you know that's what drives him?"

"I shouldn't have taken him to a crime scene in his condition," Lyle asserted.

"You didn't poison him!" Aleta exclaimed. "Get on the same page I'm on."

"I am not killing my best friend!" Lyle swore. "That I am not doing."

"Will you ask him one question?" Aleta pleaded.

"No!"

Aleta handed the phone to Lauren.

"Tell your husband that it's okay." Aleta urged quietly. "It was too much to ask. He is suffering so. Tell him Stanley holds him blameless in this as do I."

Aleta then went outside. Hubert and Lydia followed her.

"You gave up," Stanley's mother scolded.

"Maybe if I tried," Hubert offered.

"Lyle has too much on his plate," Aleta responded. "He is terrified that Stanley is going to die. Give him time to consider my request."

"Perhaps if we..." Lydia began.

"Pressured him?" Aleta finished. "You don't think I didn't hit him in the gut with both barrels?"

Hubert turned to his wife. "Lydia, you have to admit she did that."

Slowly Lydia nodded.

"Let's get our stuff and invade Harriet and Claude's privacy," Hubert suggested to his wife.

Lydia's mind leaped onto Hubert's comment.

"This isn't their honeymoon."

"According to Claude, it hasn't ended yet," Hubert chuckled. "But remember. We were invited."

Chapter 6

Lyle West went back to Stanley's bedside. Stanley's eyes were closed. Lyle thought about what Aleta had proposed. He turned away.

When Stanley is on the road to recovery, Lyle decided, then I'll pick his brain. Not now.

Aleta was right about Stanley hovering on the brink of death. Dr. Cook hadn't left the room. He had called other doctors in and gone over the test results with each one. None had examined Stanley except Dr. Taekman.

Michael spoke with Lyle briefly. "I'm surprised Stanley agreed to the tube and the restraints; however, we would have lost him had the tube not been put in when it was."

"He looks bad," Lyle said.

"Grave is the term I use for someone in his condition." Dr. Taekman said. "It's one step beyond critical."

"He's dying?"

"He's as close as he can be and not be dead," Dr. Taekman said. "Every minute counts. The longer he hangs on the better the chance he will make it. The first twenty-four hours are the most critical."

"What are his chances?" Lyle had asked. He needed hope.

"Not good."

It was after that conversation that Stanley had had a convulsion and lapsed into a coma. Dr. Taekman had gone home to talk with Martha. He had promised Wayne he would spell him at midnight.

Now Lyle stood in the aisle way, not certain what to do. He recalled Dr. Taekman's words. Even though Stanley had roused from his coma and Dr. Cook was pleased with that, Lyle was told Stanley wasn't better. He was only awake. The poison had invaded his whole system.

When Dr. Cook approached the bed, Lyle followed.

Dr. Cook took Stanley's hand and said, "I want you to squeeze once for yes and twice for no. Try it once."

Dr. Cook nodded as Stanley complied.

"Three times for 'maybe,'" Lyle burst in. "That will tell you Stanley wants more information."

Lyle paused because Dr. Cook was studying him. Abashed at having interrupted the doctor, Lyle looked down.

Dr. Cook nodded.

"That makes sense."

He turned his attention back to Stanley. "I want to monitor your brain waves...no?"

Stanley squeezed twice again.

Dr. Cook paused. "I heard you the first time. It won't hurt."

Stanley squeezed once.

"I wish I could guess why," Dr. Cook said.

"He doesn't want to be monitored more than he is already," Lyle offered.

"He affirmed what you said, Lyle," Dr. Cook said. "Now he is squeezing my hand three times. What does he want to know?"

"Probably he wants to know why," Lyle guessed.

Stanley squeezed Dr. Cook's hand once.

"I am hoping I can predict the onset of a seizure and mitigate its severity."

One squeeze told Dr. Cook to go ahead.

"Why did you change your mind?" Dr. Cook asked.

"Because you listened to him," Lyle guessed. "You let him be in control."

"Where'd you learn that?" Dr. Cook asked, indicating that Stanley was agreeing.

Lyle shrugged. If he told them it was Aleta, both would press him for more information and he wasn't eager to share the fact that he and Aleta had argued.

Suddenly, Stanley began to seize.

"Nurse!" Dr. Cook shouted. "Diazepam."

Jamara hurried over with the shot. Without the restrains it would have taken several people to hold Stanley down so the shot could be given. As it was, Lyle only had to pin down one arm.

The thrashing lessened and eventually ceased altogether. Stanley's eyes, however, closed and stayed closed.

At midnight Dr. Taekman entered the guarded intensive care room, as did Eunice Rivers.

Jamara brought Eunice up to date and left after a few minutes.

Dr. Cook didn't follow suit.

"I am not leaving," he declared.

"Catch forty winks then," Dr. Taekman suggested. "I will wake you if there's a major shift in Stanley's condition."

Lyle was sitting beside Stanley's bed, holding his hand.

"You take a break too," Michael said.

"I am fine," Lyle said. "I want Stanley to know he's not alone."

"You're exhausted. You can't keep this up." Dr. Taekman declared. "You take a break or I will boot you out."

Lyle eyed him with a hint of amusement in his gaze.
"And whose men do you think are guarding this
room?"

Stanley squeezed Lyle's hand lightly.

"He squeezed my hand," Lyle announced.

Dr. Cook who had just made it to the bed at the end of
the room, spun around and hurried to Stanley's bedside.

"A reflex?" Dr. Taekman queried.

"We're communicating via hand pressure," Dr. Cook
said.

"Ask him a question," Lyle prompted.

"Are you feeling better?" Dr. Cook asked.

"Three squeezes," Lyle reported.

"Wasn't that a yes or no question?" Dr. Cook asked.

"You're talking to a lawyer," West responded
remembering what Alta had said. "Too general. Be
specific."

A single squeeze told Lyle he was correct.

"You had a seizure," Dr. Cook said. "We gave you a
shot of valium to relax your muscles and soften the muscle
contraction."

"He squeezed my hand twice," Lyle reported.

"What's he saying no to. That's what I did," Dr.
Cook said.

"Three squeezes," Lyle said. "Stanley, was there a
problem with the valium?"

Stanley squeezed once.

Dr. Cook took Stanley's hand.

"No more valium?" he asked.

One squeeze meant yes.

Dr. Taekman took Stanley's hand. "You want us to
give you valium should you have another seizure?"

Two squeezes.

"No," Lyle said.

Stanley's finger pointed to his head.

"Do you want the brain monitors removed?" Lyle
asked.

Dr. Taekman reported a single squeeze.

"Don't you want us to continue to monitor your brain activity?" Dr. Taekman asked.

Two squeezes verified Stanley's instructions. Dr. Taekman recorded the request and the time. The machine at the nurse's station sounded an alarm.

Eunice hurried to shut it off.

"Done!" Dr. Cook said. "Do you want us to do nothing when you have a seizure?"

"Three squeezes," Dr. Taekman reported. "What does that mean?"

"He didn't like the question," Dr. Cook said. "Give his hand back to Lyle while we talk."

The two doctors moved away and Stanley signed an "a" and Lyle guessed Aleta.

"You want to know what she told me, don't you?"

A squeeze told Lyle he did.

"I fought with her," Lyle stated.

Stanley squeezed his friend's hand once. Then he let go of Lyle's hand. Immediately, Stanley's eyes rolled and his body shook.

"Doctors!" Lyle cried.

Both rushed to Stanley's bedside. The convulsion wracked his body while both doctors watched helplessly.

When the nurse offered Dr. Cook the shot, he shook his head.

"He's not in his right mind," Eunice insisted, holding out the syringe.

Lyle pushed her hand away.

"Stanley is not psychotic."

"At least not yet," Dr. Taekman ruminated. "What do we do if that happens?"

The convulsion eventually ran its course and Stanley lay still and unresponsive. The heart monitor told everyone he was still alive.

Lyle's cell phone vibrated. He took the call.

"I have another double rape murder," Lyle told the doctors. "I will be back as soon as I can. Someone hold Stanley's hand. Tell him I need him."

Having said that, he left.

Eunice stepped up, "I can do that. I can read the monitors here as well as back there."

She sat down in the chair that Lyle had vacated. She took Stanley's hand and spoke to him softly.

"We're still here, Stanley, except for Lyle who had to leave. He said to tell you he needed you. He said he would be back."

When Stanley seized, Aleta woke with a start. She dressed hurriedly and left the RV. She knocked on the door to her grandmother's RV and asked for the keys to the car she had brought.

"Where are you going?" her grandmother asked.

"Stanley needs me now."

Hubert, a light sleeper, joined Harriet at the door.

"I'll drive her," he stated. "I don't want her driving alone."

"Lauren came running up dressed in her robe and slippers. "What's going on?"

Hubert ducked inside and began to dress. Lydia woke up and asked him what was happening. He told her.

Harriet told Lauren at the same time.

"Lyle will help him," Lauren responded. "I know he will."

"Lyle is gone," Aleta said.

"He wouldn't leave Stanley," Lauren declared.

"Something's terribly wrong. Stanley needs me."

"I will call Lyle," Lauren offered. "He's right there."

Aleta's response was definite.

"I am the one that's needed. Lyle is busy. Martha is directing him."

"That means he's saving someone's life," Harriet said. "Aleta needs to go."

Hubert appeared.

"I'm ready. Lydia will help where needed."

"I will show your dogs until you return," Harriet offered.

"Me too," Lauren said. "My shoulder feels great."

Hubert unlocked the car door and slipped into the driver's seat. Aleta climbed in and waved as they pulled away.

As they left the fairgrounds, Aleta addressed her concerns aloud.

"I have never done anything like this before."

"It's alright," Hubert said. "I know how close you and Stanley are."

"You think Stanley is calling for me?"

"That wouldn't surprise me."

"That would explain why the feelings are so vague."

"You mean God is clearer?"

"Yes."

"If it's Stanley, it's just as important to go."

"If it's not God, I may not be able to enter Stanley's room."

"Stanley can rescind that order."

"If he's able to communicate," Aleta worried aloud.

"Suppose we take this one step at a time," Hubert said. "First we get there."

"You're right," Aleta said. "We're on our way. We've taken the first step. God didn't stop us. We both have keen minds. We'll figure out how to get to Stanley somehow."

"If you sleep, your mind will be sharper," Hubert suggested. He didn't add that she needed rest for the baby's sake.'

Aleta crawled into the back seat and laid down.

Hubert smiled. When she took as a suggestion, she embraced it completely. He turned on his favorite music station and increased his speed by fifteen miles an hour. Traffic was sparse. The mid-Illinois roads were flat and straight, the towns few, and the almost full moon in a cloudless sky lit the area far beyond the high beams of the car's headlights.

Like Stanley, his father needed little sleep. The two hours Hubert had gotten were enough to keep him alert for the entire journey.

He skirted Chicago on the west and turned east once well past the suburbs that clung to the city like barnacles on a ship. It had taken three hours to drive to the show in the RV's. He made the trip back in just under two hours.

He woke Aleta after he parked.

She seemed to wake as quickly as she had fallen asleep.

"It's quarter to three," her father-in-law said. "We made good time."

"We need to hurry," Aleta said, rushing toward the Emergency Entrance. Hubert ran after her and puffed lightly as he landed in the elevator just as the doors closed.

"We could be stopped," he cautioned.

"Take my hand," she ordered. "If I can pass unseen, then so can you. Say nothing."

Hubert nodded as the elevator door opened.

The two at the nurse's station didn't even glance up. Aleta headed straight for the two guards, paused momentarily waiting for them to move apart and then opened the door.

A nurse was rushing toward the medicine cabinet by her desk. Hubert recognized Eunice Rivers.

Aleta breezed right past her.

Hubert gasped when he saw his son in the throes of a convulsion that was causing him to flail his arms, arch his back and twist as much as the restraints would allow.

Hubert heard Eunice call the doctors by name. There were two white-coated forms on the beds in the far corner. She opened the cabinet and took out a vial of diazepam and a syringe.

As Aleta drew the curtain around the bed, she handed Hubert the chart.

"Read," she whispered.

Ignoring the writhing of the man on the bed, Hubert read the chart.

"No drugs for seizures," he hissed.

Aleta put one hand on Stanley's forehead and slipped the other under the sheet.

"I'm here," she whispered. "I came. I heard you."

Eunice grabbed the curtain intending to push it open.

Hubert stepped around it. Startled, Eunice's hand fell away.

"What are you doing with that needle," he asked.

"I am going to inject him with valium," Eunice stated flatly. "This seizure is worse than the last one."

"The chart says no shot is to be given during a seizure."

"I know what it says," Eunice declared and then elaborated. "It was Mr. Praetzel who gave that order. I was there."

"I want his order obeyed."

"Do you want him to die?"

"No."

"Then stand aside," Eunice ordered.

"No," Hubert vowed. "You will not disobey his order."

"He is not a doctor!" Eunice cried.

"Neither are you," Hubert said.

"I will wake the doctor," Eunice decided.

She hurried over to the beds and shook each one in turn. Neither stirred.

Hubert followed her.

"Don't worry. Aleta is with her husband," he informed her.

"You aren't supposed to be here," Eunice declared.

"Check the monitors," Hubert suggested. "If you think a doctor is needed," I will help you wake one."

Eunice took the tray back to the desk and set it down. She began to watch the monitors. Hubert continued to stand guard.

He could hear Aleta speaking to Stanley. Her voice was soft, but her words weren't marred by tears.

"Of course, it's me," she said. "Do other women touch you there?"

There was a pause and Hubert smiled.

"Well, I know I told them to bathe you and I included all your parts, but does it feel like I'm bathing you?"

Hubert couldn't bring himself to move out of earshot.

"Well, you should know the difference. And the catheter is no excuse...Of course, I don't know how it feels. I'm not built like you."

Hubert glanced toward the other beds to see if either doctor was stirring.

"This episode is over, Stanley," Aleta said. "The nurse almost gave you Valium. Lyle isn't here. Both doctors are sound asleep. Your father stopped her...Yes I brought him, or rather he brought me...Yes, he saw you in the middle of a seizure. I had him read your orders. He defended your right to choose. That's what I may become—a victim's advocate...Well, of course I know that's what being a defense lawyer is some of the time, but that's not what I mean, and you know it, and it's time for you to open your eyes and see that it's really me. You haven't gone crazy yet."

Hubert wanted so to be on the other side of the curtain.

He listened as Aleta spoke again. "Yes, I will cover you up, but can I show your father your leg? It really looks good. I know it wasn't cosmetic surgery, but it looks good. You can even wear shorts...Don't get in a huff...Aren't you ever planning to go swimming with your sons? Weren't you planning to exercise your leg swimming laps. Were you planning on doing that in your sweats? They'll fall off, you know."

Hubert smiled. Was Stanley awake? Her patter sounded as if he were answering her. Hubert could almost fill in the gaps.

"That's only one eye," Aleta said. "If you don't open the other one, I will leave you half-covered...There that's better. Did Lyle teach you some way to communicate? Don't wave your hand at me. I'm not moving either hand...Oh, alright, if you insist...There...Now can I show your father your leg? It's not a private part...Honestly, Stanley, it's a leg. Well, half a leg, but still a leg...There, I covered it...Now can he come in?"

Hubert heard his name called and he ducked around the curtain.

"Your mother's back at the dog show. She plans to help," his father told Stanley.

Aleta laughed. "She has no idea what that means, does she?"

Stanley held out his other hand and Hubert moved around the bed and took it.

"Do the restraints bother you?" Hubert asked.

Stanley squeezed his hand once.

"Do you want me to remove them?

Stanley's two squeezes were strong.

"Are you expecting more seizures?"

Stanley responded with a single squeeze.

"Are you afraid of being poisoned again?" Hubert asked.

The response was three squeezes.

"What does three mean?" Hubert asked Aleta.

"Possibly," Aleta responded.

"Does the medication have side effects?" Hubert asked.

One squeeze affirmed that.

"It supposedly keeps the seizures under control," his father posed.

One squeeze told Hubert his son had considered that.

Aleta stood abruptly. "Hubert, we need to go."

"So soon?" Hubert asked, regret coating his query.

"Stanley, I am sorry. I have to get your father away from here now," Aleta asserted.

Stanley realized his wife had received a vision. He squeezed both their hands once.

Aleta leaned over and kissed him.

"I know that is the toughest battle you've ever fought, but I promise you I will do anything you ask if you make it through this. So think up something you really want from me."

Hubert said nothing. He knew his voice would betray him. As he left, he plucked out a business card and set it on the tray with the shot.

"A reminder," he said. "Stanley knows what he's doing."

Eunice nodded and then began to cry. It was so soft Hubert almost didn't notice. He stopped.

"I won't tell Dr. Cook. Just give Stanley the respect he deserves."

"I was afraid he would die before I could ask him."

"Ask him what?"

"If he ever hires women associates."

Hubert tapped the card. "When you're done being reminded, send Kay to see me."

When Chief Lyle West arrived at the scene of the slayings in the freshman dormitory, Peter French and Matt Carradine were already there taking notes. Silently, he and Chief Milani studied the scene while Hawk worked the room. Natsumi was in the bathroom. Both rooms were primary crime scenes. The girl on the bed had been tortured, raped and murdered. The girl in the bathroom has been stabbed in the heart but was otherwise untouched.

"I had suggested that the girls double up," Chief Milani told Lyle. "I thought they would be safer. It's a lone assailant. I figured he could only surprise one. The other would call for help."

"Don't beat yourself up, Tom," Lyle responded. "It was a good plan. What we need to figure out is how he got in."

"Is Stanley able to talk yet?"

"He's barely alive," Lyle said. "Aleta said I should involve him, but then she's a hundred miles away. She doesn't realize how weak he is."

"What are his chances?" Tom asked, not realizing that Justin was close enough to hear what was being said.

"Well, he's dropped into another coma," Lyle reported. "I don't have much hope."

Justin shoved a microphone between the two chiefs and asked, "Any comment?"

Tom exploded. "Who let you in here?"

"Nobody," Justin replied. "So, I gather the one girl was killed because she was a witness."

Chief West walked Justin out. "We aren't ready to make a statement yet, but you will be the first reporter we talk to."

Justin Conway signaled his cameraman to catch him being escorted out by Chief West. Once on the steps he spoke directly into the camera.

Two young women were slain last night by the coed killer. One was apparently the target. The other was merely a witness. The police are stymied by the apparent ease with which the assailant gained access to the room and the speed with which he took down both women without either sounding an alarm."

"Missing from the investigative team is Willow Glen's children's lawyer, Stanley Praetzel, who was responsible for identifying the Tri-City area serial rapist-murderer as the same killer that has been active for over a year in various outlying counties. Stanley Praetzel had been called upon when the first two slain coeds were found less than twenty-four hours ago. He was barely four days post-op having lost his left leg to bone cancer; however, he was obviously deemed a threat as he was served poisoned coffee while at the hospital waiting for the coroner to begin the autopsies."

"Justin stopped while the footage of Stanley was rerun. Then he continued.

"Stanley Praetzel now lies in a coma. He is not expected to live. And with him will die whatever insights he may have been able to offer with regard to the coed killer's identity."

Justin's broadcast was picked up by all the networks.

Hubert heard the newscast as he was driving south through Chicago. Aleta had insisted that he go east and then south after which she'd curled up in the back seat and fallen asleep.

Hubert realized that no one knew yet that Stanley had awakened from his coma. The source must have been Chief Lyle West. He wondered if Lydia had heard the broadcast.

It had been a strange night. Lydia never slept well when she was worried. He decided not to take a chance. He dialed her number.

She answered immediately.

"Is he dead?" she asked.

"He's awake," Hubert said. "Aleta brought him out of the coma."

"But the news..."

"I got to talk to him, Lydia. I got to hold his hand," Hubert said. "He's not dying. When I get there I will fill you in."

"You're on your way back?" Lydia asked, her tone laced with disapproval.

"Aleta said my life was in danger," he said. "I can't figure out who would be after me, so I think that I was killed along with Aleta. She can't predict her own death you know."

"Couldn't you have told West or Milani, so you could have stayed with Stanley?"

"Aleta chose," Hubert said. "Stanley understood. I gather that when she gets these visions, she's shown a way out and she takes it."

"But..."

"Stanley's clinging to Aleta's love. It's his lifeline. He needs to feel she is safely hidden."

"So he's getter better."

"He's holding his own."

"I want to know that he's going to live!" Lydia declared. "What did Dr. Cook say are his chances?"

"We didn't speak to him."

"Wasn't he there?"

"Both he and Dr. Taekman were sleeping a few beds away."

"Who was watching Stanley?"

"The nurse," Hubert replied. "I have so much to tell you, Lydia. I'll be there in a little less than two hours."

"Wake me."

Chapter 7

Martha Cook's phone call pulled Chief Lyle West from the crime scene. He managed to get past the reporters crowded around the entrance to the dormitory with a brief comment.

Justin ran back to his car and tuned in on the police band.

West was giving an address.

"Clear the house. I'm getting the dog," Chief West told his dispatcher.

Justin climbed into the news van.

"There's another story breaking in Arborville."

"The station wants you to stay on this," the cameraman said. "The coroner just arrived."

"Here's the address," Justin said.

"Looks familiar."

"It should. You shot pictures of the house when Stuart Fouts was running around attacking older women. One of his victims lived there."

"We need you to be here and give us the patter to go with the coroner's exit."

"Put the camera on me now," Justin said. "I will give you your introduction."

The cameraman focused on him.

"We're standing a short distance away from the building the coroner has just entered. The Head of the Joint Chiefs has just left. We will wait for the coroner before following Chief West to the site of another major crime. The doors are opening. Here come the bodies of two young women who just this morning were looking forward to four years of college life."

He made a cut sign and the cameraman stopped filming.

Then Justin jumped into his car and took off. One of the TV crewman looked at the cameraman.

"You gonna tell the station manager?"

"We got our lead. He told them where he was going. We can ask after we get this segment if we should follow."

"Suppose they say no."

"Then we hang here. I'm not risking my job."

Justin slid his car to a stop several houses away from the one where two squad cars were parked.

There was a crowd despite it being the wee hours of the morning. Many were in robes and slippers but one family group caught his eye.

Justin walked over to the tall father of three small children.

"May I hold the boy for you?" Justin asked. "Your daughters seem frightened. Maybe they need to be held a bit too."

"You're Justin Conway, aren't you?" Daniel Wallace said. "I read your stuff all the time. You're a terrific reporter."

Justin's smile was broad as he reached for the little boy.

"Come on little man. Let your daddy comfort your sisters."

"Name's Daniel Wallace," the muscular man said, scooping up both daughters. The little girls clung to his neck.

"This is Tonia Morales' house. Are you relatives?" Justin asked.

"It's a shelter now. That man over there is the supervisor of the shelter."

"Why don't you tell me about it?"

"Because if you use my name, my wife will know where I am. She was planning to kill me."

"How do you know?"

"The police found her at my house with a gun. Aleta Praetzel sent them. I still can't believe it."

"Wasn't she arrested?"

"She's out on bail."

"How come everyone is out here. Is she in the house?"

"Oh, no. She can't come near me. Mrs. Praetzel got a restraining order."

"So why are we all standing around?" Justin said.

He noticed that Daniel stiffened. Casually, he continued, "Oh, wait. I know. We're waiting for the dog."

"Big dog," Becky said.

"A bomb sniffing dog?" Justin guessed. "But why would you need him? Didn't someone find the bomb?"

"Chief West got a call," Daniel said, "And his men came and took all of us out of the house. We weren't allowed to take anything."

"Mrs. Fouts must have planted one of Doyle's bombs in the house," Justin murmured. "She sure had it in for Tonia Morales."

"I read about Mrs. Praetzel having voice-activated bombs planted everywhere, but all those were found."

"Doyle made other kinds too," Justin said. "Stuart Fouts had a stack at his house. And they are cleverly disguised."

"Like how?" Daniel asked.

"He put one of the voice-activated one in the mobile above Aleta's baby's crib."

"So that's why we had to leave everything," Daniel concluded.

"I didn't know we had a house for abused men in Arborville," Justin commented.

"Aleta arranged it with someone named Martha."

"Martha Cook?"

"No, the last name was longer."

"Martha Cook Taekman?"

"That's it. I thought it was a funny name: Cook-Take-Man."

"Martha Cook married Dr. Michael Taekman about six months ago."

"But she's ninety!"

Justin smiled. "Every bit of that. He courted her for six years. I guess she finally believed he was serious."

The TV truck drove up. Justin handed the young boy back to his father and ran toward the truck as West's car drove up. The cameraman was out and filming as Chief West held his car door for a slender young girl with a giant black dog. The camera followed the girl, the dog and Chief West going into the house. The bomb squad pulled up shortly afterward.

Justin ordered the cameraman to stay up close.

"Where's West?" Sergeant Ronnell Silva asked one of the uniformed officers. Justin and his cameraman moved closer.

"Inside with the girl and the dog," the officer said.

"There's a girl and a dog in there?" Silva barked.

"They're looking for the bombs," the officer said.

"Is he crazy?"

"The dog's good," the officer said. "It's Hawk's dog."

"Tell him I'm here," Silva said.

"Yes Sir," the officer responded, opening his radio. "Silva's here with his team."

The officer turned to Sergeant Silva.

"Chief West says you can come in. They've found one bomb. The dog is searching the rest of the house."

"Ask him if he's bringing it out."

The officer repeated the query and then said, "It's under a burner in the stove top. He said he's not touching it. That's your job."

"Tell him we aren't going in until he and the girl and the dog come out. We don't intend to be blown up by amateurs."

Silva made his pronouncement loud enough for the TV cameraman to catch every word. The cameraman wasn't the only one who caught the whole tirade. West heard it via his man's radio.

The young officer smiled when he received Chief West's reply. Justin moved closer so as not to miss a word. His tape recorder was also on. They would edit the TV footage, but his editor would print his story in its entirety.

"Chief West says he will be out as soon as he is sure the house is safe for you to come in," the officer said.

Justin stepped forward and shoved a mike in Sergeant Silva's face.

"How did West know that there were bombs in the house?"

"He got a report from one of the prophets he said."

"Which prophet called Chief West?"

"Who knows? One of the crazies."

"He found a bomb," Justin said. "If it had gone off, people would be dead."

Daniel tapped Justin on the shoulder. "I'll give you an interview."

Justin had the cameraman swing around and had Daniel introduce his children.

"I understand you are the first family to use this new safe house for men," Justin began.

Daniel nodded.

"I had nowhere to go and no money. I gave up my job to take care of the kids. My wife likes working."

Slowly, Justin brought out the arrest of Daniel's wife and why he needed a safe place to stay temporarily. It was a nice interview and would make it onto the air waves only because the children were cute and obviously afraid. It added a touch of humanity to the bomb scene. Real lives had been saved. The prophets were still at work. As they had said repeatedly, they received the prophesies. They didn't generate them. This story gave balance to the evening's events. Two girls were murdered. A family of four didn't die.

All this Justin managed to stick in his summation before Chief West, Paige Monroe and her huge black Newfoundland emerged from the house. Chief West was carrying a suitcase as was Paige.

"There's a bomb in here," West said as he handed his suitcase to Sergeant Silva.

"Topper says it's C-4. It looks like the trigger is attached to the latch."

Silva handed the case off to one of his officers who stashed it in their van.

"The other C-4 bomb is attached to the right rear burner of the stove," West went on. "Topper says there are no more C-4 bombs. I suspect there are no more bombs, but, you can search if you like."

"And I suppose you know the who, why and how too." Silva quipped sarcastically.

"Yes," Chief West said. "Now, if you'll do your job, I'll get back to mine."

Chief West walked over to the man with the three children and said, "I have temporary housing for you and your children. Come with me."

"All our things are in the house." Daniel said.

"Not all," West said. "Paige packed a suitcase. She says it will get you through the night. She says Topper says all the animals on the beds are safe. She packed a few."

Daniel was nodding. "Thank you so much."

"You'll be staying with an old friend. She's parked down the street," West said, taking the hand of the younger girl. The camera caught the family leaving with the police chief carrying a suitcase in one hand.

That was the last anyone saw of them. That same night all the clothes and toys taken from their home earlier were removed from the safe house and disappeared as well.

Chapter 8

Three hours after he left, Chief West re-entered Stanley's room. The two doctors were sound asleep. The nurse was at her desk staring at the monitor.

"No one is holding his hand," Lyle snapped.

"He's awake," Eunice said. "Aleta was here. So was his father."

Lyle left and checked with his guards who reported that there had been no visitors.

"Hubert Praetzel left his card to remind me," Eunice said when Lyle reappeared.

"About what?"

"It's personal."

Lyle decided not to pursue the matter. He hurried over to Stanley's bedside and took his hand.

A squeeze told him Stanley was awake.

"Aleta was here?" he asked.

Stanley responded with a firm squeeze.

"And your father?"

Stanley opened his eyes. Lyle smiled at him. "You look better. She woke you up from the coma, didn't she?"

The single squeeze was emphatic.

"I wish I knew how, so I could do it."

A double squeeze caught Lyle unprepared. A laugh burst out.

"Don't worry I won't do whatever it was she did. It is nice to know how close your brain is to that particular bit of your anatomy."

Lyle removed his coat and sat down.

"I wish you could have been with me. French and Carradine were there each trying frantically to notice everything."

Stanley squeezed Lyle's hand four times.

"Four?" Lyle said. "What does that mean?'"

Stanley let go and held up three fingers.

"Are we playing charades?" Lyle asked.

Stanley made a circle with his thumb and forefinger.

"Okay. Three words."

Stanley held up one finger.

"First word."

Stanley pointed to himself.

"You."

He shook his hand and pointed to Lyle and then himself.

"You and me."

Stanley made a circle, then held up three fingers.

"Me. The first word is me!" Lyle explained. "So it's me, blank, blank. No, it's I, blank, blank."

Stanley made a circle. Then he put up two fingers.

"Second word."

Stanley held up three fingers.

"Three letters." Lyle said. "A verb?"

Stanley tapped his hand once.

"I can?" Lyle asked.

Stanley lifted his hand slightly and made a gesture in the air.

"Write," Lyle guessed. "You can write?"

Stanley snapped his fingers then he patted his bed under his hand and pretended to write.

Lyle rushed over to the next bed and removed the chart and set it under Stanley's hand.

"Why didn't Aleta tell me?" Lyle asked.

"She didn't know," Stanley wrote. The handwriting was crooked but legible. It extended only part way across the page and then started again. It was obvious Stanley couldn't see the paper.

"Summarize the crime," he wrote. "Then we'll go over it slowly."

Lyle did that. His overview was fast and complete.

"Start at the door," Stanley wrote.

"No sign that force was used."

"They let in the perp?"

"It appears so," Lyle responded. "Hawk said there were burn marks on the thighs."

"That's how she got in," Stanley wrote.

"She?"

"Our perp is a woman."

"A woman?" Lyle repeated.

"The women were scared," Stanley wrote. "They would never have let a man in the room."

"They would have let a boyfriend or a brother in," Lyle said, then nixed his own idea.

"She came offering stun guns." Stanley wrote. "She insisted on showing the girls how they worked."

"So they let her in," Lyle said. "Now how do we figure out who it is and then prove it?"

"She likes to wear their clothes during the attack and then discard them in plain sight," Stanley wrote. "That's why some of the clothes had way too much blood on them."

"And the missing shoes?" Lyle asked. "The green ones?"

"Haven't worked that out yet?" Stanley wrote. "Were any shoes missing today?"

"We can't tell," Lyle said.

"If Hawk looks at the neckband of the bloodiest clothes, he may find DNA that doesn't belong to the victim."

"By itself, that won't be enough."

"It will if he finds DNA on all three of the victims' clothes that is the same, "Stanley wrote.

"We need a motive," Lyle said. "I'm going to bring you Peter and Matt's reports and the photos and see if you can glean anything more from them."

"Coroner's report," Stanley wrote.

"I may as well bring my desk and set up shop in here."

"What's this about a desk?" Dr. Cook interrupted, drawing aside the partially-closed curtain.

"Stanley can write!" Lyle exclaimed.

"Why does he need to?"

"I had to play charades to find that out!" Lyle snapped.

"Bet that was fun," Dr. Cook grinned.

"You could have told me!"

"Why?" Dr. Cook asked picking up Stanley's chart.

"Because I had questions."

Dr. Cook took Stanley's hand. "You had another seizure. Are you sure you don't want us to give you a shot to lessen the convulsions?"

One squeeze.

"So is Lyle making you work even now?""

One squeeze.

"He's never going to let you off the hook, is he?"

"How come you slept through his last seizure?" Lyle charged, nettled.

"Don't get in a tiff over my comments," Dr. Cook hastened to say. "Stanley obviously benefits from your presence."

"He's still glowing because Aleta was here."

"Aleta?"

"She brought his father. They breezed right past my guards. Very disconcerting."

"I thought she was at a dog show."

"Hubert drove her back for some reason, probably because you were asleep."

"Dr. Taekman was supposed to take this shift," Dr. Cook remarked thoughtfully. "His sleeping makes no sense."

Suddenly, Chief West rushed over to the bed where the portly doctor lay. He saw two mugs on the night stand.

"Whose cups are these?"

"The nearly full one is mine. Didn't much like the chicory in coffee. Michael thought it was great."

"Where'd the coffee come from?"

"I asked for coffee from the kitchen. They sent it up." Dr. Cook replied, beginning to realize what Lyle was suggesting.

He took Michael's pulse and then took out his stethoscope and listened to his heart. He tested the unconscious man's reflexes and palpated his arm and leg muscles. He immediately called out instructions to Eunice who rushed to do his bidding.

"Michael isn't going to be happy about this," Dr. Cook told Lyle, "but he's my grandmother's husband. I am taking no chances. I have no idea how much chloral hydrate was in the coffee.

As Lyle watched, Dr. Cook proceeded to pump Dr. Taekman's stomach.

"Isn't it too late?" Lyle asked.

"Michael ate a huge meal. I'm hoping not all the choral hydrate was absorbed. I only took a sip and I was out for hours. There was enough in there to kill a man. This was no ordinary Mickey Finn."

When he finished, Dr. Cook inserted a breathing tube and fastened an oxygen mask in place.

"Lyle, you have to let Grams in here," Dr. Cook said. "I am not moving Michael."

"Of course," Lyle said. "Call her."

From the bed on the opposite side of the room, Stanley tapped his tablet. Lyle read the note.

"Send all short people on staff home. Male and female."

"Male?"

"Disguised," Stanley wrote. "Keep the old fat ones who are short."

"If you think I'm giving that order, you're crazy." Lyle declared.

Stanley held up his tablet on which he'd drawn a smiley face.

"Stop enjoying yourself!" Lyle groused. "This could cost me my job."

"Welcome to Praetzel, Locke and Praetzel," Stanley wrote.

"This is your doing," Lyle growled. "I am not sure how it is, but, I will figure it out."

Stanley scrawled, "Good men are hard to find."

"Don't quote me to me," Lyle grumbled. "It would serve you right if Martha replaces me with you."

"Want me to lie for you?" Stanley wrote.

"Lie? I haven't done anything wrong," Lyle asserted.

"Now you're on the right page!" Stanley wrote.

By the time Martha arrived, the hospital was locked down. She saw Oakwood police paired with men from Willow Glen. An Arborville officer was waiting for her. He escorted her through the maze of guards to the eight-bed intensive care unit which her husband now shared with Stanley Praetzel.

Her grandson met her and hugged her gently and then apologized as he walked her in.

"Why are you apologizing?" Martha asked, her thin high-pitched voice carrying to the farthest corners of the long room.

"I didn't notice Michael's condition until Lyle pointed it out."

"Stanley snapped his fingers and Martha went over to him. He held out his clipboard.

"Wayne was drugged too," she read aloud.

She held up the clipboard and asked, "Is this true?"
Dr. Cook nodded.

"None of us got any sign he was stricken," Martha
said. "God knew you would do what was necessary to save
his life."

"You called Harriet?" Dr. Cook asked.

"Right after you called me," his grandmother said.
"And Aleta and Jocelyn."

"Aleta was here last night," Dr. Cook told her.
"Stanley's convulsions were more violent than before.
Eunice couldn't wake us."

"I guess Aleta succeeded in what she came to do,"
Martha concluded. "Don't fret, Wayne. This person after
Stanley is evil. And clever. I've hired Ed..."

She stopped when Stanley snapped his fingers. She
went over to see what he had written.

"Have Ed see me. I can cut the field in half."

"Can't Lyle?" Martha asked.

"I am not under the same constraints," Stanley wrote.
"Is it daylight yet?"

"No," Martha said.

"Get him here now."

Martha looked at her grandson. Dr. Cook took her
aside. "Stanley is still having seizures and he knows that
psychotic behavior could follow. He is lucid now. He may
not be in a few hours or a few days."

"What kind of psychotic behavior?"

"Mania, delirium, hallucinations, aggressive
behavior—any one or all—or if we're lucky, none. That's
why he's in restraints."

"Will Michael be okay if I leave for a few minutes?"

"Grams, his doctor's with him," Wayne reminded her.

"Oh yes," Martha smiles and patted his cheek. "I
sometimes forget I raised a doctor."

Thirty minutes later Martha was back with Ed
Ornstein, the short, tubby private investigator who had
accompanied Aleta from California. He had and married a
woman whose friends lived in the Tri-City area. He happily
moved his one-man business.

"Hi Stanley," Ed said. "Talk about a string of rotten
luck! How's the leg?"

"Martha, you and me," Stanley wrote.

"Dr. Cook chuckled. "That just excludes me."

"And Lyle," Stanley wrote.

"Oh, go ahead. Have your meeting. I will go hold
Michael's hand and talk to him."

Martha looked up, distressed.

"I will tell him you're here," Wayne told his
grandmother. "Take care of business."

"It's a woman," Stanley wrote. "A small woman.
She wants us to believe she's a man."

"Well, she fooled me," Ed quipped. "The knife's
what done it. It ain't a woman's weapon."

"Poison is," Stanley wrote. "But it was the clothes
that told me. She wanted to not have any blood on her
clothes so she disrobed in the bathroom and wore her
victims' clothes only not their underwear."

"How do you know that?" Martha asked.

"The underwear was under the clothes, not on top."

Martha nodded.

"She took a pair of green shoes from the second
victim, a size eight." Stanley wrote.

"So you figure she wears a size 8?" Ed asked.

"The green shoes are a red herring," Martha put in.

"I am the only one who noticed," Stanley wrote.

"If no one noticed that was okay because she was
only worried about a person like you," Martha explained.
"They were meant to sidetrack you."

"I've been studying these cases," Ed said.

Martha nodded.

Ed took a deep breath and continued. "Nobody was in the wrong place at the wrong time. The girl stabbed in the bathroom was a target too, only our killer don't want us to see that."

"Explain," Stanley wrote.

"Both girls was stunned by a Taser in the thigh. No way that weren't done the same time or one of them would've been outta there. That means two guns. She knew there was two in the room. On top of that she knew which two. She threw you another red herring and you swallowed it."

Stanley began to write. "I am putting one-hundred thousand dollars at your disposal. Bribe whomever you need to. The rest is yours. Martha is paying you for your services. This is on top of that."

Martha laughed when she read the note. It was a high-pitched cackle and Michael stirred in his bed.

"I am glad you agree that I hired him," she quipped.

"Give to Bertha," Stanley wrote on the top of the page.

Neither of his two listeners questioned the fact that Stanley's housekeeper had the combination to his home safe.

"I been thinking," Ed said. "We maybe got this gal's motive all..."

Stanley scribbled furiously.

"Rage!"

"Yeh, I go along with that, but why Cook and Taekman?"

"They are taking care of me," Stanley wrote.

"Red herring!" Ed snapped. "Your case ain't hard. Another doc could take over easy. I figure she was aiming for these two on purpose."

"She's into hurting people," Stanley wrote.

"Yeh, that's how I see it too." Ed said. "There be lots of ways to hurt folks. Look I gotta go and get started. Stanley, you ain't got nothing to do for a couple days. You can work on why she hates rich people."

"If that were true," Stanley wrote. "She would have sent a cup of coffee in for Lyle."

"Don't you know?" Ed asked. "It's sitting on the nurse's desk."

A few minutes after Ed left, Stanley had another seizure. As his body was convulsing, Martha laid her hand on his arm.

Eunice, who was watching the monitor, called Dr. Cook's attention to Stanley's condition.

Wayne hurried over and then stopped. His grandmother was stroking Stanley's forehead and whispering the same phrases over and over.

"Aleta loves you. She told me to tell you that."

Chapter 9

At the fairgrounds near Springfield, Aleta and Lauren were awakened by Tank and Morgan whining to go out.

"I guess some sweet smelling bitches have been put in their pens," Aleta said as she left the bedroom, shutting the door behind her.

Tank whined to leave with her. It had been decided that Lauren would sleep on the couch since Morgan was used to roaming the inside of her R.V. Tank was relegated to the bedroom with Aleta.

"I didn't think you'd make it back," Lauren commented.

"Had to leave. Some people were after me, I think. They killed Hubert. That is, they would have," Aleta stuttered. "Stanley understood. I am not used to explaining my actions. Stanley always understands. So does Lyle."

"I wasn't criticizing,' Lauren said. "I was just surprised. That's all."

Aleta smiled. "No more so than me. One good thing. Hubert got to see Stanley. Lydia would have broken down for sure."

"She's a strong lady."

"So, how's your shoulder?" Aleta asked.

"It feels great!"

"Are you up to taking Tank in?"

"I'd love to!" Lauren returned, confused. "Why aren't you showing him?"

"Because Chuck is about to beg."

A soft knock on the door brought Lauren to the window. "It's Chuck. How did you..."

"No magic. I saw him leave his RV from the bedroom window," Aleta explained. "Open the door and give him the good news."

"Lauren opened the door and said, "Aleta's letting me show Tank. Isn't that great!"

Aleta laughed. "I didn't mean that news. What Chuck wants to hear is that I'm willing to show Rolex."

"Will you?" Chuck asked. "I took your words to heart. Honest. But I know Rolex's family will never let me take him on tour. I need to keep the Saint I have."

"I will be there for Rolex," Aleta said. "Stanley will get a kick out of Lauren showing Tank."

"Will Stanley show again?"

Aleta shook her head sadly.

"He's decided to be one-legged for a while."

"I thought doctors fitted...oh, heck. It's none of my business. He's a level-headed guy. He will know when he's ready."

Movement behind Chuck made Aleta peer around his hefty frame.

"Hubert!" Aleta exclaimed. "I didn't see you there."

"Stanley will want everything," Hubert said.

"Did you get any sleep at all?" Aleta asked.

"Enough. Martha called Harriet again," Hubert said. "Ed is on the case. Stanley was a big help."

"That reminds me," Lauren said. "Lyle called after you left the hospital. He said to tell you that Daniel Wallace and his children are safe. Paige and Topper found two of Doyle's bombs in Tonia Morales' house. As a thank you,

Lyle is having one of his men drive Paige down here for the show. Hawk will fetch her tomorrow afternoon."

"Is she entered?" Aleta asked.

"Beatrice entered her in all the shows close to home as part of her wedding gift. She knew Paige would never ask," Lauren explained. "Lyle told me I better beat you today because Stanley is using up all the hours he owes."

"Why are you letting me show Morgan then?"

"Lyle knows today's judge likes chocolates."

"Stanley doesn't know all this," Aleta complained.

"Sure he does. Lyle told him," Lauren told her. "Stanley is betting on you."

A firm knock startled the two women. Lauren opened the door to see the smiling face of Lieutenant Peter French.

"Whoa!" Aleta exclaimed. "What brings you here?"

"Either of you claim this chocolate dog. He seems to think this is his RV."

Aleta peeked out.

"Scooby! How did you get here?"

"Chief West thought it only fair to give you a choice," French said. "I am to stay the weekend. I would appreciate it if the two of you would act like Siamese twins."

"Help me set up the pens," Lauren said. "And then we can talk."

After the dogs were penned and given water, French set up the chairs, sat down and began talking.

"Chief West had me drive Paige and Topper to the show. He had someone else picked out. But when the two doctors went down, he decided I was more experienced at guarding people at a show."

"He sent just you?"

"He couldn't spare anyone else. He told me to use Claude and ask Hubert Praetzel to help. He's locked down the hospital and the search is on for the serial killer. Milani has his men guarding the dorm. Hawk and Natsumi are working around the clock. Paige and Topper will be coming home with me. We will be following your RV."

"You skipped right over the part about what kind of danger we're in," Aleta said.

"When Chief West's coffee was poisoned..."

"Lyle's coffee?" Lauren gasped.

"Three mugs were delivered--one for each doctor and one for him. To go on, that's when he started worrying about you two. You are not to drink anything but what you brought. I brought a case of ice tea and a case of water. Bertha sent down yogurt and sandwiches for both of you to snack on. And this part I don't understand, but Lyle said neither of you was to use anyone else's bait. What does that mean?"

"We bait the dogs in the ring, usually with liver cooked in garlic." Aleta said. "We carry the bait in our mouths."

"Ugh!" French said.

"That's why I don't eat the bait. I use cheese and chicken when I can." Aleta remarked.

"I only brought liver," Lauren commented.

"I will make do," Aleta said. "Let's get dressed and figure out who's going to show Morgan."

"You aren't?" Lauren asked.

"Lyle sent down Scooby."

"He doesn't want you to win," Lauren observed knowingly.

"I would hate to lose with Morgan. He's the best Lab in the country right now."

"Except for Holly," Lauren said defensively.

"Morgan's better," Aleta said.

"Prove it!" Lauren challenged.

"Double the bet," Aleta dared her.

"Why not quadruple the bet. Make it really worthwhile?" Lauren challenged.

"We're as bad as our husbands," Aleta snickered. "How many days?"

"Eight," Lauren responded.

"You're on!" Aleta declared.

When Aleta and Lauren approached the ring they were dressed in colors that would best show off the dogs when they stood behind them. Aleta wore a pale blue suit with a short jacket with short sleeves under which she wore a long-sleeved filmy pastel multi-colored blouse with full sleeves. Around her neck was the sapphire pendant Stanley had given her as an anniversary gift. Lauren was attired in a forest green print dress with a flowing skirt. She wore a twisted chain of gold as her only piece of jewelry.

Not to be outdone, Harriet wore a flowing pale turquoise skirt which with her slender hips made her appear younger than her seventy-one years. The blouse was a lighter shade of the same color and provided a beautiful backdrop for Scooby's rich chocolate brown coat.

Judge Derrick Copeda was surprised at the quality of the champions at a show where the Lab entry didn't make two points. There were more than the usual number of chocolates in the classes, but he couldn't deny the young black bitch in the 12-to-18 class. Minx, Morgan's daughter, took Winner's Bitch. Beatrice, outfitted in bright yellow, which was Ed's favorite color and which her former boyfriend hated, fit into the group of ladies in the Breed ring. Tom Wilson was in his usual blue coat and pale beige slacks.

His attire would provide a contrasting backdrop when he stacked his black Lab.

There was nothing casual about dog showing. Stanley, an impeccable dresser, fit in well. Both professional handlers, Tom Wilson and Chuck Rigden had enjoyed watching Aleta accumulate show dogs and were equally surprised to find that Stanley was a born handler. He was a quick study and Tom had found teaching him pleasurable. Tom had sold him Tank whose owners thought he was too big. Chuck had sold him Auggie whose owner was impatient with the little dog's seeming inability to take Best in Show. He was maturing too slowly in their eyes.

On the circuit, Harriet had been commandeered by the two pros to help with a dog or two. Her skill was equal to theirs and better than that of their assistants and her appearance in multiple rings led some judges to believe she was a pro. She regularly showed two dogs from vastly different groups. Handlers usually began in similar groups. Rarely did they show a toy and a sporting dog, but she was regularly in both Groups. It wasn't long before, after multiple Group Ones, Auggie took a Best in Show. The next weekend he took another. The Chessie meanwhile consistently placed in the Sporting Group. He won Best in Show at the Chesapeake National and at the local Specialty two days later. He gathered an all-breed Best in Show following the two Specialties. Harriet, knowing that Stoney would get a good look as a double Specialty winner, elected to have Chuck show Auggie in the Best in Show competition on the final day of that circuit and she took her beloved Stoney to that Best in Show win.

Harriet had told Claude that she was satisfied and they could skip the rest of the circuit and go hunting. When plans were made to take Aleta to the show so she wouldn't mope all weekend, Claude had readily agreed that they should go to the show.

"I don't hate going," he said. "I like being with you."

"But we both love to hunt," she replied. "And we'll miss some of the season when Keeper's pups need more care and there's Paul's art show next weekend."

"We keep forgetting we're retired now. We can go up north on Tuesday and hunt Wednesday and Thursday and be back in time for Paul's show."

Harriet had kissed him with such passion that he remembered why he'd married her.

Now, as Claude watched his wife enter the ring, he kept his camera on her. Standing beside him Hubert was concentrating on Aleta. Both men, however, followed Lauren as she moved Holly around the ring.

Without their realizing it, both men caught the two men standing beside Arborville's Lieutenant Peter French.

Hubert's camera caught Peter's expression of surprise and moved on. Claude's camera caught French just as he began to fall. The two men held French up and moved him quietly away from the ring. Claude, whose focus was on Lauren didn't know what had been caught by his lens.

Harriet, who had ended her run and was facing Scooby, saw French being taken away. As she watched Lauren pull up behind her, Harriet got a vision. To her surprise it wasn't of Peter French, but of Lauren.

As they waited in line while the judge went over Morgan, Harriet spoke to Lauren.

"The action I'm going to suggest after the judge chooses the Best of Breed winner is going to be bizarre."

Lauren looked at Harriet quizzically.

"I received a prophetic vision. It concerned you."

"Me?"

"Remember how many times Aleta has saved your husband's life."

Lauren nodded.

"After you get your ribbon, you must take Holly and run as fast as you can to Aleta's RV. Put your ribbon on the counter. Put Holly in Tank's crate and crawl in with her. Lock the door."

"French is here," Lauren pointed out.

Harriet appeared to ignore her comment. She rushed on. "Don't answer anyone who calls your name. No one! I will come for you when it's safe."

Banner was being moved by Tom Watson. Lauren pointed to clue Harriet into the fact that she was up next.

"Aleta's life depends on no one knowing where you are. No one!" Harriet whispered earnestly as she moved Scooby to the place where the judge was individually examining the dogs. She looked back at Lauren who mouthed a single word.

"French?"

Harriet shook her head. Scooby pranced in place in response. Harriet checked his legs as the judge moved toward the dog.

"He's young," he said and Harriet knew she had lost.

"You gave his sister Winners," Harriet commented.

"Really," Judge Copeda said.

"You have a good eye," Harriet said. "I like that in a judge."

"You realize you aren't supposed to talk to a judge this way."

"You've already told me you like my dog, but he's too young to get the Breed. Isn't it over for me?" Harriet quipped good-naturedly.

"You've been around," the judge observed.

He was still smiling when he approached Lauren. He paused for a long time to study the chocolate bitch. She was superb, every bit as outstanding as the black males especially the first one.

He remembered seeing a photo in Canine Chronicles of a chocolate bitch that had taken Best in Show that year. As he studied Holly he realized this was the bitch.

He moved her to the front of the line and saw her handler turn to the handler behind her and say something. He assumed she was asking the handler on the male to give her room. What Lauren asked Aleta to do was go all out. To the judge's surprise the handler on the black male did just that. To his utter amazement, the chocolate bitch had both reach and power, but more than that, she had drive. She refused to be overtaken.

Holly took the Breed, Morgan took Best Opposite and Minx took Best of Winners.

Harriet whispered to Aleta to go to the building, and then congratulated Beatrice.

Finally, coming to Lauren, Harriet ordered tersely, "Run! Now!"

She pointed at the ring ropes on the side nearest the building as she spoke. Lauren heard not only the urgency but the authority in Harriet's rough voice. She rushed toward the ring rope away from the entrance to the ring, ducked under the rope and began to run.

She was behind the building before anyone around the ring moved to follow. She ran along the side of the long aluminum building inside of which were four rings reserved for small dogs. As she reached the end she ran toward the stand of trees that marked the edge of the gravel road leading to the section where the RV's were parked.

Why did I leave French, she puzzled. Then she remembered Harriet's head shake. Something had happened to French. She had to tell Lyle. She resolved to call as soon as she reached the RV.

She ran around the outside of the big RV's causing the dogs in the nearby pens to bark.

They'll give me away, she thought. She slowed to a walk and cut across the road to where Aleta's RV was parked, its door facing away from the fairgrounds. She passed the Arborville police car and considered fetching the keys from the RV and driving away.

She opened the RV door and set the ribbon on the counter. She opened the door to the extra large crate that took up half the aisle way. She looked around for her cell phone, but even as she did so, she knew instinctively that she was out of time.

Holly stood in front of her crate and Lauren forgot about calling Lyle. Panic had begun to take over. She took Holly's leash and guided her into Tank's crate. She undid the show leash and Holly turned to leave the strange crate. Lauren blocked her exit.

Then realizing that she'd mess up her outfit if she climbed into the crate, she unzipped the skirt and stepped out of it. She folded it and laid it on top of the crate. The blouse followed. Then pushing Holly back, she crawled into the crate.

She positioned the latch in the open position by curling her fingers around the outside. She switched her hold to the fingers of her hand on the inside, then she pulled the door closed and released her hold. The bars sprang into place. She and Holly were locked in, only Holly was in the back and she was in the front wearing a white satin slip.

Holly's not a small dog, she thought. What were you thinking, Harriet? How did I even manage to get in? How am I ever going to get out? Harriet, didn't it occur to you I might be claustrophobic? Or that Holly wouldn't like being squeezed in a crate with me?

Slowly as these thoughts were racing through her mind, Lauren eased herself backwards. Holly, grumbling, finally moved forward toward the door.

Lauren was still trying to figure out how to get herself out of a crawl when she felt the RV shake.

My slip, she thought. It's too white.

Quickly she pulled it over her head and shoved it up near the door under Holly. She looked down. The bra would have to go too. It stood out in the dark interior of the crate. She slipped it off, rolled it into a ball and tucked it in the corner. She heard the click as the outside door handle was turned. Heavy steps on the metal stairs brought Holly to her feet barking. Lauren sat back on her haunches as Holly's tail rose. Lauren bowed her head because the tail hit her in her face. Unbeknownst to Lauren, her auburn hair in the dim light of the crate looked like an extension of the chocolate-coated Labrador.

The two men searched the RV, opening every cupboard, leaving only the door to Holly's crate untouched.

"She's not here," said one, shouting over the racket Holly was making.

"She's hiding," came the response. The voice was lower, but it carried through Holly's constant barking. "Here's her ribbon. We were too quick not to see her leave."

"She changed clothes," noted the second man.

Inside the crate, Lauren began to quiver. Her fear had chilled her to the bone. She couldn't stop. The crate shook. Holly's barking became frenzied.

"I tell you she's gone!" yelled the higher-pitched voice.

Lauren's cell phone rang.

Lauren held her breath. She heard the men rush toward the sound.

"What did you think?" the high-pitched voice snarled. "That I didn't look in the glove compartment?"

"Okay, so that wasn't necessary," the other grumped.

"This thing isn't big enough for secret panels," the high-pitched voice claimed. "She's not here and I can't stand the damned dog one more second."

"Did you look in his crate?"

"He takes up the whole thing."

Lauren knew the man's eyes were peering through the bars on the door of the crate. Her shaking stopped as her fear froze her in place. Why was it they couldn't see her? Then she remembered how, when she was checking the whereabouts of her dogs and she peered into the crates in the semi-darkness, she couldn't see the back section at all.

Aleta and she had drawn all the shades in the RV as they dressed and had left them closed. It would keep the RV cooler when the sun rose higher in the sky.

She heard the door open. She felt the RV shake as just one and then the other left the RV. She sat very still listening for what seemed like a long time. Her legs were getting stiff. She had to change position. Slowly she tried to ease one leg along the side of the crate but Holly grumped as Lauren crowded her. Lauren quickly realized she had no room to maneuver at all.

How did I ever manage to squeeze back here, she wondered.

She curled, laying her head on her arms. She was extremely uncomfortable.

The threat had been real, she realized. She wondered if she could have gotten away if she had just kept going.

Suddenly, the RV shook. Holly barked as the door opened.

A familiar voice called out.

"Aleta, Lauren, are you here?"

It was Beatrice. Holly quieted at once.

Lauren was about to respond when her cell phone rang. Beatrice moved to the front of the RV. Lauren suddenly didn't want to be seen practically naked. She decided to wait for Harriet.

Beatrice answered the phone.

"Hi Lyle...No, they're not here...Lauren took the Breed with Holly, Aleta took Best Opposite with Morgan, and Minx took Best of Winners which gave her two points. She won over a chocolate which surprised me. Aleta told me afterward that Stanley owes you eight days. She said she and Lauren changed the bet...I'll tell Lauren you called when I see her...Goodbye."

Lauren thought about the position she was in. Her legs were beginning to cramp.

Why am I waiting? I can have Beatrice move Holly to her crate, she reasoned. I can put on my bra before I get out. It would take some explaining, but Beatrice was one of the Tontine group. They all trusted Harriet implicitly.

"You be a good girl, Holly," Beatrice said. "You're in the big crate so you'll be well rested for Group. We all want you to shine. Such a smashing pair you were! And how you ran! I think even Aleta was surprised that you could stay ahead of Morgan."

Lauren liked the kindness in the tone. She hadn't known that Beatrice cared about her. She was a bit abashed at her reticence to ask Beatrice for help.

"Well?" said a strident female voice.

Lauren almost jumped.

"Oh, they aren't here. Lauren must have come back to change and then left. She won't be showing until three. As for Aleta she wasn't expecting to be here at all, so she's not showing any dogs but her own. She probably went off with Lauren. She be back for Tank at eleven."

"I think I'll just wait here," said the deep voice of the man who had searched the RV earlier. "Just in case she comes back before then."

"I'll look around," the other man said.

Holly stood watching and then settled with her head on Lauren's arm.

Lauren dozed. When she woke, she wished she could stretch. The phone rang. She instinctively knew it was Lyle.

He knows something's wrong, she realized.

Oh, don't come down here, she urged silently.

Fifteen minutes later the phone rang again. Then it didn't ring anymore.

Lyle called Claude who was carrying his cell.

"What's going on? I can't raise French and Lauren isn't answering her cell."

"We don't know how many there are," Claude said. "Harriet's in charge. She's in the ring."

"Where's Lauren?"

"Harriet stashed her some place."

"Where's French?"

"Harriet knows. He's not in any danger though."

"Is Aleta okay?"

"Harriet says she will be as long as she doesn't leave the building. Trouble is the toilets in the women's restroom are backed up."

"Take Aleta into the men's," Lyle ordered. "Fish that badge out of your pocket and use it."

"I'm filming."

"Hand the camera to someone else," Lyle said.

"Lydia, come here," Claude called. "Pin this on me, then take the camera."

"Okay, Chief, anything else?" Claude asked.

"Tell Harriet to call me."

Ten minutes later, Harriet called.

"I am in the men's room," she said. "Can you hear me?"

He heard Aleta laugh in the background. "She's confined me to this building forever with only the men's john working."

"Hush, child," Harriet scolded.

"Harriet, what's going on?"

"Beatrice said there were three strangers outside Aleta's RV looking for Aleta and Lauren," Harriet reported. "Beatrice said the two men were together. The woman wasn't with them. She and one of the men split to search the grounds. The other man stayed."

"Where's Lauren?"

"Safe."

"Where's French?"

"Alive."

"Alive where?"

"Haven't had time to look."

"Well, take time!"

"My job is to keep Lauren and Aleta safe. And that's what I am doing."

"You're showing dogs!" Lyle exclaimed.

"And Claude is filming me and the crowd. Bet Stanley will recognize the woman who poisoned him."

Chief Lyle West took a deep breath. She was doing everything he would have done. His voice lost its edge.

"Tell Claude to keep filming," he said evenly.

"Hubert's on Aleta. We should have everyone who's here on film by the end of the show," Harriet said. "Someone will bring it to the hospital around seven."

"Are you telling me I am to stay here," Lyle said tersely.

"You are too tired to drive. I can feel Lauren's worry that you might come and get hurt," Harriet said. "Besides Aleta doesn't want you here either. She wants you taking care of Stanley."

"I should be there," Lyle insisted.

"Most chiefs stay behind their desks doing chief things. They don't go running all over the place making targets of themselves which you seem to do a lot!" Harriet asserted.

Her rough voice made her words seem like an order. Lyle bristled. "I will send someone for the film."

"Can you send him down this morning?" Harriet asked. "We could use another cop car to scare off the bad guys."

"You are so manipulative, Harriet," Lyle griped.

"That's what Claude says."

Lyle called Ed on his cell and told him about the videotaping.

"Yeh," Ed said. "There was three of us going at it."

"Where are you?"

"In my car driving north. I had to see Beatrice show. Minx won again. She's sure a pretty little lady."

"You were at the hospital earlier," Lyle puzzled.

"Yeh, I had to speed a bit, but I made it."

"Did you film much of the crowd."

"Some. By accident," Ed said. "I was focusing on Beatrice and Minx."

"French disappeared when the Labs were showing," Lyle said. "See if you got any shots of that."

"Take me an hour before I can begin looking at the film," Ed said. "You going down?"

"Yes. Can you maybe get some of the photos over to Stanley?" Lyle asked.

"Don't you know?" Ed asked.

"Know what?"

"He can't see."

"Of course he can see!" Lyle exclaimed.

"It's blurry," Ed said.

"He can't see photos?" Lyle questioned, dismayed.

"Nope."

"So getting the tape to him won't do much good, will it?"

"Nope," but I'll pick up the other tapes tomorrow morning. I got other ways to check on who's there."

"You're going down to the show tomorrow too?"

"It's important to Beatrice," Ed said. "She wants me to see her win."

"And if she loses?"

"Then we have sex."

"That seems backwards," Lyle remarked.

"Hey, don't queer it for me. I got a good thing going."

Chapter 10

Lyle charged into Stanley's hospital room.

"You didn't tell me your sight is blurry."

"So?" Stanley wrote.

"I've got to leave," Lyle blurted out. "Our wives are in trouble. How can I leave if you can't see?"

"What's happening?" Stanley wrote.

"Harriet has them stashed in different places. She won't tell me where Lauren is. I can only deduce I would be more upset than I am now."

"Aleta?" Stanley wrote.

"She confined her to the building where the toys and bulldogs are being shown. The women's john is flooded."

"Aleta's pregnant. She can't be without facilities." Stanley wrote.

"I took care of it."

"From here?" Stanley wrote.

"Are you going to be okay?"

"I'm planning on it."

Lyle motioned Dr. Cook over.

"Wayne, I've got to go to the dog show. Can you take care of Stanley?"

"That's what I've been doing," Dr. Cook said, smiling.

"You didn't know he couldn't see," Lyle charged.

"He can see. His vision's a bit blurry. That's because his pupils are dilated," Dr. Cook responded evenly.

"You didn't tell me," Lyle declared, irked.

"I am not sure that was the most egregious of Stanley's complaints," Dr. Cook snapped. "You do know what egregious means, don't you?"

Stanley held up his pad. "Be good!"

The two men laughed.

"Who won?" Stanley wrote.

"Holly. You owe me eight days."

"Eight?" Stanley wrote.

"Our wives quadrupled the bet."

"That doesn't count," Stanley wrote.

"Do you want to tell our red-headed wives that we aren't going to honor their bet?"

Stanley waved the suggestion away.

"I thought not. Now, you be good while I'm gone."

"Be good?" Stanley wrote.

"No comas, no going crazy, no dying," Lyle ordered. "Just lie there and vegetate."

Stanley wrote furiously.

When Lyle read what he'd written, he laughed.

Wayne picked up the pad and read the comment aloud.

"When you go to bed, make sure you're next to the right red-head."

Chapter 11

Crouched inside the crate in the RV, Lauren moaned softly. She tried to move but found her muscles refused to respond. It was as if they were locked in the painful position she had first chosen. She began to cry.

Suddenly, she was shaken by the nearness of the voice that spoke.

"There you are," she heard the deep-voiced man shout. "Where have you been?"

"Everywhere," the man with the high-pitched voice replied. "She's nowhere. Neither is that friend of hers."

"They took that big gray dog of hers to the ring," came the response.

"We'll go there now. Remember she won't be in green."

Aleta was never in green, Lauren thought. All this and Aleta would be caught anyway.

"I tell you, they're gone," the high-pitched voice insisted. "Taking out that cop spooked them."

"We're taking one more good look around, then we're coming back here."

"Here? Why?" the high-pitched voice squealed.

"They could be watching this RV and return as soon as I leave."

Inside the RV, Lauren groaned.

Time for me to get out of this crate, she decided.

She moved one hand forward slightly, but her legs wouldn't unfold. They stayed locked in place.

Holly stirred as her pillow began to move.

"Why are you complaining," Lauren chided. "You have half the crate."

Holly rose suddenly and bristled. Lauren heard a growl emerging. It was followed by a loud bark.

Holly's barking drowned out the sound of the door opening, but Lauren could tell by the slight tremble in the floor that someone was in the RV, someone Holly didn't like. Holly's barking grew louder.

Lauren heard the water running and worried lest whoever it was would run the tank dry.

After the water stopped, Lauren thought she heard the refrigerator door being slammed shut.

Holly's incessant barking was stirring Morgan outside. He and Scooby soon joined in.

"Shut the hell up," the woman yelled. "I will leave when I am done."

The water was running again. Suddenly, water was thrown into the crate.

"I said shut up," the woman shouted.

Holly shook off the water, but before she started barking again, Lauren reached up and began to scratch Holly's back just above her tail. Holly quieted her protest to a deep-throated growl.

When the RV door closed, Lauren stayed quiet and unmoving for a few minutes. Holly turned and licked her face.

"Good girl, Holly," Lauren whispered, petting her wet forehead. "She really got you, didn't she?"

She dozed again. A heavy footfall on the stair woke her.

"Not again," she murmured, surprised that Holly didn't bark.

Lauren heard a deep-voiced man inquire, "Is she there? I want to arrange to breed my dog to hers."

"You have a chocolate Lab?" Beatrice asked.

"No, a Wolfhound."

"You'll catch her at the Wolfhound ring."

Beatrice approached the crate, Lauren was about to shout when Holly barked. Beatrice turned around.

"You haven't seen her, have you?" the deep-voiced man asked.

Lauren could tell the door was open. Beatrice told him she hadn't.

Holly went into a barking frenzy.

"I will come back later, Holly," Beatrice said.

And then turning to the gentleman, she said, "Let's go outside."

Lauren heard the door close. Holly didn't stop barking which told Lauren the man was still close by.

These people were very persistent. How did they miss Aleta?

She dozed. Again Holly woke her.

"Quick, inside," she heard Harriet say.

Her rough voice was unmistakable.

"The latch is broken," Harriet said. "Claude, guard the door."

"Where is she?" Aleta asked.

Lauren tried to find her voice but couldn't.

"From what I was able to gather, the man after you thought Lauren was you," Harriet explained, opening the crate door.

Holly bounded out. Aleta hugged her.

Harriet continued her explanation. "I didn't know that earlier. I had to go on what I was given."

"She's all wet," Aleta cut in.

Harriet peered into the crate. "Can you get out or are your legs too stiff?"

"Stiff," Lauren mumbled.

"Your slip's a mess, but your outfit is fine," Harriet said. "Who threw water at you?"

"A woman," Lauren said as Harriet offered her a hand.

"I'm not dressed." Lauren murmured.

"You're planning to pose nude for my son Paul," Harriet quipped. "Give me your hand."

"Aleta, take off your suit so you can give Lauren a massage," Harriet ordered, as she helped Lauren creep toward the bedroom.

"You've had a rough time of it, Lauren. I'm sorry I couldn't get here sooner. It wasn't safe."

"I know," Lauren said, collapsing on the bed. "I'm stiff all over."

Aleta crawled onto the bed and put her hands on Lauren's back and began to massage it.

Lauren sighed heavily.

"My legs are really stiff."

"I'll start with them then," Aleta said.

An hour passed and Lauren dozed. When she woke, Aleta turned her over and worked the front of her thighs and told her about her morning.

"I took the breed with the Chinese Shar-Pei. He is such a neat dog. Tom is doing so much better with him now that he speaks Chinese."

"Tom speaks Chinese?" Lauren asked.

"I taught him the phrase I use. It makes Mrs. Lee titter."

"What's he saying?"

"What I say. If you were a man, you're so handsome I'd marry you."

"Poor Tom."

"Hey, he's winning." Aleta said. "I took the Breed with the Saint. His owners were delighted. The children told me they didn't say his name once while I was in the ring. They were so proud of themselves."

"You taking him into Group?"

"Chuck asked me to and I said yes." Aleta said. "You realize I may not have many shows in my future."

"Stanley will get an artificial leg soon, won't he?"

"He says no."

"Why not?"

"We never got to discuss that before he was poisoned. Somehow it didn't seem right to talk about it too soon after the surgery, especially as he was worried that having only one leg would make him less of a man."

"That's why you were crying when you did my calves."

Aleta changed the subject.

"I lucked out you know. Harriet made me stay in the building they put some of the working and the herding dogs inside because they could fit five rings in that building, so I got to show the Bullmastiff and the Collie both. Harriet called your husband. She told him not to come down."

Lyle doesn't like being bossed."

"So we've all noticed," Aleta chuckled. "Okay sit up and face the other way and let me do that injured shoulder. If you're up to it, you can show Tank in Group."

"Don't you want to win?"

"May I remind you, you beat me today," Aleta said as she put her hands on Lauren's shoulder.

"Oh, that feels so good," Lauren sighed. "And I'd love to take Tank in, but what about your grandmother."

"She's going in with Auggie and Stoney." Aleta said. "I'm going in with Maggie and Mugs. So you can take in Holly and Tank. Doesn't that sound fair to you?"

Aleta took her hands away. "I'm going to the john. Stretch and move around. See if you need more."

Lauren stretched her arms above her head. "The shoulder feels great."

She flopped backwards on the bed and arched her back. "You worked a miracle, Aleta. I thought it would take days."

The toilet flushed masking the sound of the outside door opening.

Lauren closed her eyes and lay on her back and stretched. She spoke softly sensing a person standing in the doorway to the bedroom.

"Aleta, have you ever thought what it would be like to be with a woman, sexually? Have you ever wondered?"

"I'm sure she has," said the male voice from the doorway. "As evidently have you."

Lauren's eyes shot open. "Lyle! You weren't supposed to hear that. That was girl talk."

Lyle closed the door and locked it.

"Lauren, you're a woman, not a girl. That wasn't talk. That was an invitation."

Lauren blushed. In the dim light, Lyle could barely discern the flush.

"Do you want me to leave?" he asked.

"No, of course not! Oh, Lyle, I'm so glad you're here. I was so alone, so afraid...I don't know what I was thinking."

She turned and buried her head in her pillow and cried.

Lyle gathered her up, pillow and all and drew her to him.

"Thoughts aren't sins," he said. "If they were, we'd all be in jail and there'd be no jailers."

"But I might have..." Lauren uttered between sobs.

"And you might not have." Lyle said. "Tell me about your day—all of it."

And Lauren did, right up to when Lyle appeared in the doorway.

"I was so tempted," she confessed.

"Temptation is like that. It tempts people."

Lauren hiccupped a short laugh. "I shouldn't even have such thoughts."

Lyle had one final question. He posed it gently.

"Lauren, was Aleta naked?"

Lauren drew in her breath sharply. "No, of course not! She'd taken off her suit so she wouldn't get it mussed."

Lyle felt himself relax. He hugged his wife and kissed her lovingly. "Thank you for the truth."

Lauren kissed him.

"That's for loving me," she said.

Lyle held her close.

"You have no idea how glad I am you obeyed Harriet and saved your life and Aleta's," Lyle said. "It isn't easy to obey one of the prophets. I know. They never think of ordinary alternatives."

Lauren laughed.

"I agree with you wholeheartedly. Promise me you'll do whatever they ask."

"I have reputation," Lyle said, remembering his last refusal.

"I just lost mine," Lauren said softly. "Come join me in the muddy puddle of lost reputations."

"I like being a clean frog on a lily pad."

"You're an easy target for every kid with a BB gun."

"Are you saying I am foolish?"

"Yes. Risking one's life to save one's reputation is a foolish waste of a priceless gift. Stanley is fighting just to live. Take a lesson from your friend."

"Aleta told you about the restraints."

"Yes."

"You're right. He is stronger than me," Lyle admitted. "And here I've been trying to get him to accept my leadership."

"That's necessary and right," Lauren said. "Aleta says he enjoys working for you."

"For me? Not with me?"

"It's probably a vacation," Lauren commented.

"A vacation!" Lyle snapped. "I've heard police work called many things, but vacation is not one of them."

"He's head of a law firm and in charge of a growing business empire. When he works for you, he doesn't have to think."

"My men are not mindless robots!" Lyle huffed.

"But you direct them."

"Lead them," Lyle corrected.

Lauren laughed.

"If I agree, can I get dressed?"

"Why do you want to get dressed?"

"I am taking Tank into the Hound Group and there are five days on the line."

"Who is Aleta taking in?"

"Mugs, the Bullmastiff." Lauren replied smiling. "And Chuck is on Rolex."

"Did Rufus take the Breed?"

"I have been cooped up in here, lying naked talking to my fully dressed husband for who knows how long. How would I know?"

"Tonight we take up where we are right now."

"Aleta and Tank sleep in this bed."

"Not tonight they don't."

"It's her RV."

"Ed said Beatrice would welcome company."

"And you want me to arrange it."

"You're better at that than I am," Lyle said smiling, knowing she was still worried. "Start by telling her the refrigerator is off limits. I think that woman who was fussing around while you were in the crate did something to the food."

Chapter 12

The Hound Group results were what Aleta and Lauren predicted with Tom Wilson taking first with Madge's red Dachshund, Rufus. Tank took second.

Aleta took a second in the Working Group behind Chuck. She showed the Bullmastiff well and the dog was an excellent representative of his breed, but Rolex was a cut above.

Auggie took first in the Toy Group. Harriet had become a familiar figure in the show ring as she toured with her small string of two dogs. She had been in the final competition frequently, once with her Chessie, multiple times with the Pug. She had taken Best in Show twice with Auggie which moved him up in the national rankings.

Chuck Rigden watched the Toy Group with particular interest. He wished he were handling Auggie again. He silently cursed the former owner for her lack of patience. This was a dog who could be a repetitive Best in Show winner. Auggie had only been a bit slower to mature than most Pugs; however, Aleta had put muscle on him by letting him be a dog. He was energetic and happy and strong. Chuck wanted him in his string again. He wanted to special

him again. He wanted to take him all the way to the top--
repeatedly. His disappointment at losing the Saint would be
assuaged if he could handle the Pug again.

As the afternoon group judging continued, Tom
Wilson talked to Aleta about letting him show Tank at
Westminster. She had asked about Rufus, and he had told
her if both won, Madge would show Rufus. Breeder-
handlers did well in that competition. She agreed to putting
him Tank on Tom's bench.

Immediately afterward, Chuck Rigden cornered Aleta
and talked with her about campaigning Auggie. When he told
her Auggie's former owner was bad-mouthing him because
Harriet had put two Best in Shows on him--something he had
failed to do--Aleta agreed to let him campaign Auggie until
Christmas and at Westminster.

Harriet walked up to the pair after her photo session,
the blue rosette still in her hand.

"Claude's bringing Auggie, Aleta," Harriet said. "I
assume you're taking him in."

"Chuck is. I'm taking in Rolex." Aleta said. "I will
explain later."

"Is Chuck going to campaign Auggie?"

"Until Christmas," Aleta responded, surprised that her
grandmother had guessed.

"Can he start tomorrow?" Harriet asked. "Stoney
thinks Tuesday comes after Saturday."

"I don't understand that one at all." Aleta remarked.

"We told him we were going hunting Tuesday and the
idea turned him on."

"Usually he has to see you clean your guns," Aleta
noted.

"Well that's what we were doing when we told him."

"And you figured he could figure when two days after
tomorrow was?"
"He's a smart dog"

"I'll say," Aleta exclaimed. "He got you to change
your plans to his."

After the Best in Show competition, Aleta sought out her grandmother. Hubert was caught unprepared by her sudden departure. He was changing film in his camcorder. He hurried to catch up and then, because the afternoon had been a warm one and he had been actively filming for hours, he slowed down.

Stanley will like what I have, he realized. I can quit for the day. Aleta needs quiet time.

She had been surprisingly accepting of his presence the entire day. The Best in Show competition was a fitting climax and he had filmed the aftermath as well. He stepped into Harriet's RV to unload the film and came upon Aleta and her grandmother talking.

"Come, sit down," Harriet offered.

"Sit down," Aleta said. "It's not woman talk."

"It's prophet talk," Harriet said.

Curious, Hubert sat down.

"Go on," Harriet said.

"It wasn't a prophetic vision, but just a sort of premonition. Can we get premonitions that aren't true?"

"I doubt it," Harriet said.

"I don't want it to be true."

"Did it have to do with Stanley?"

"No," Aleta responded. "Michael."

"Your baby?" Harriet questioned.

"He's not going to..." Aleta stammered.

"To what?" Harriet pressed.

"I don't know," Aleta cried. "I was talking to him, telling him I wanted to go to Westminister and asking him to hang in there until March and I got this chill. Oh, Grams, am I going to lose my baby?"

"Hubert, you were with Aleta in Stanley's hospital room. Tell me what happened."

"He was having a seizure. It was a bad one. The nurse was going to give Stanley a shot. I talked her out of it.

I was so busy taking care of that situation I didn't pay much
attention to what Aleta was doing."

"Did she have her hand on Stanley?"

"Yes, on his forehead," Hubert said, "But he kept
convulsing even with her hand there. Eventually, the seizure
stopped and he was himself again."

"Just like that?" Harriet inquired sharply.

"Well, er...yes."

"No period of disorientation?"

"Now that you mention it, none."

"Aleta, I believe you have been given a gift. Like the
gift of prophecy, it drains you."

"You were the one who prophesied today, not me."

"I know"

"And you have lots of energy."

"I know," Harriet said, "but I don't fight."

"Neither do I!" Aleta declared.

Her grandmother's raised eyebrow made her back
down.

"Well, maybe sometimes."

"I think your newest gift is sapping your strength,"
Harriet started when a commotion outside interrupted them.

The three rushed out of the RV. Lyle and French were
cuffing two men who were lying on the ground while Garrett
was holding a gun on them. Hubert filmed them being read
their rights.

Harriet took her granddaughter aside. "Aleta, Lyle
has had it. Get your stuff out of your RV and over to
Beatrice's. Lauren needs to take care of him in private."

"Tank?"

"He can spend the night in that giant crate you had
made for him." Harriet said. "Lauren will take care of him.
Scooby's with me. Sleep in tomorrow. Take care of
Michael."

"What are you telling me?"

"You are able to keep going because you are using
the sustenance that should be nurturing your baby."

"I made promises," Aleta argued. "And I don't feel tired. Besides I don't think I can sleep in."

"Suppose I just tell Beatrice not to wake you?" Harriet said. "Okay?"

Aleta nodded.

Chapter 13

Back in the guarded intensive care unit in Tri-City Hospital, Stanley Praetzel lay unmoving, his spirit draining away as time passed with no word. French was down. Lauren was in hiding. Aleta was confined to the building with only her grandparents and his parents--all unarmed--to protect her.

It wasn't that he expected a shoot out, but so many things can happen in a crowd. And Aleta frequently drew a crowd.

Worry about Aleta plagued every waking moment. Sleep-- that great devourer of time--would not visit him.

Eventually, he realized that it was he who had ordered Aleta away. How could he have forgotten that? She'd come anyway--twice.

Why had he done that, he mused. What was he thinking? What had he been worried about?

Oh, yes, he'd been worried about her seeing his leg without its bandage. Well, she'd seen it. He hadn't wanted her to see him in a convulsion. Well, she'd seen that as well. He hadn't wanted her to see him spread eagle on a bed with tubes everywhere. And, she'd seen all of that as well.

Nothing had truly shocked her if he didn't count his being so ill. That had affected her deeply. He could tell her worry was profound. And he couldn't assure her.

Dr. Cook had been grave after the blood test came back. Stanley knew then that he was dying and still he had banned the only person with the power to save him.

The only command he had been given was, "Let Aleta work." And he hadn't done that.

Still, she had come. He now concluded that she was the reason he was still alive.

"Not that I could have stopped her, God," he murmured quietly. "You didn't leave me voice or hand to push her away."

Her touch, however, hadn't instantly healed him. With Jesus a sick woman had only to touch the hem of his garment and she was cured.

He was drained. Not completely, but enough so he could feel it. Did Aleta feel drained? She must have. She always felt drained after her visions. She had received one about his father and he had understood why she had to hurry away. His father was with her. If he was killed, the upshot was she was also.

Why did Harriet hide Lauren and not Aleta?

Because she was told, he determined. The prophets always came up with outlandish requests when they worked to save a life. He hadn't thought about that before. Were their plans outlandish to prevent too much impact on contiguous events occurring simultaneously.

The women were given such a tiny peek into the future. They never saw the perpetrators just the deaths of the victims.

With more details they could do more, but that would be a problem. They were problem solvers—all three. God had kept them reined in.

Did God render him helpless, he wondered. Immediately he dismissed the thought. God didn't poison

him. He had been told the effects of the poison and decided
to protect himself from harming himself before the poison
was completely shed from his body. He had allowed the
restraints. And even though he had protested the insertion of
the breathing tube, he had allowed it.

His thoughts were interrupted by a violent seizure.
He didn't know how long it lasted, but when he began to
wake, he felt nauseous and dizzy. Even though his vision
was blurred and unfocused, he watched as a needle was
inserted into his other arm and a new IV bag hung on a
stanchion. He felt the nurse removing his gown and saw the
shadowy form of Dr. Cook writing on his chart.

He wanted to say that was a bad one. He wanted
some assurance it was the last. He was upset and confused.
He didn't seem to be getting any better.

When the nurse changed Stanley's gown, she took his
pen and tablet and set them on the night stand. Neither were
returned to him.

He felt isolated.

Dr. Cook came to the side of his bed and took his
hand. He tried to squeeze it, but couldn't. What was
happening to him? Fear crept into his thinking.

I am dying, he thought, and I am afraid. Why haven't
I ever been afraid before?

The answer came unbidden. You have never truly
faced death before.

"I am sure you're frightened," Dr. Cook said calmly.
"Your last seizure was worse than any you've had before.
Your body is still shedding large amounts of Atropine. I
don't expect the seizures to stop. I am afraid you're too
weak to squeeze my hand, but can you blink to tell me you
understand?"

Stanley blinked once.

"Do you want me to reinstate the use of valium to
mitigate the seizures?"

Stanley blinked twice.

"You understood that you said no."

Stanley blinked once.

"Let me ask you once more. Despite my advice to the contrary, you do not want me to give you any shots of valium?"

Stanley blinked once.

"I will honor your decision," Dr. Cook said. "Don't worry. I am not losing you."

Stanley heard the bleeps of his heart monitor slow down.

Dr. Cook patted his head, "Try to sleep if you can. Your body is exhausted."

Stanley closed his eyes and listened to the steady bleeps from the heart monitor telling him he was still alive. It relaxed him. Still sleep didn't come.

Hours marched in funereal pace though out the afternoon. They were punctuated by two seizures and Dr. Cook saying after the second, "I won't force medication on you, but I insist on recording the pattern of your brain waves."

Stanley blinked once. It was time to let the doctor do his work as well.

After the patches were set and the new monitor was in place Dr. Cook announced, "Grams heard from Harriet. Are you up for good news?"

Stanley blinked once.

Martha smiled as she pulled up a chair and sat down. She took Stanley's hand and said, "Harriet made me write it all down. It's mostly abbreviations. She said you would understand."

Stanley tried to squeeze her hand and she looked up. "I felt that, Stanley."

His spirit soared and his heart beat faster.

"Calm down," Martha said in her high-pitched voice that was anything but soothing. "I am not going anywhere."

Stanley didn't know how to slow his heart beat.

Martha called to her grandson, "Wayne, come tell me if I am hurting him."

Stanley squeezed her hand twice.

"He says no," she reported as Dr. Cook looked at the printed strip.

"I would say you're helping," Wayne smiled.

He kissed her on the cheek. "You would never hurt anyone."

"Don't get sentimental. You're doctoring right now," Martha quipped. Her grandson kissed her again.

"This is my hospital unit. I can do what I like here."

"Are you done declaring your independence so I can give this poor man news of his wife?" Martha quipped and then, without waiting for his answer, began to read from her notes.

"Aleta took BOB with Maggie. I have in parentheses bulldog. Do you understand because the whole list is like that?"

Stanley squeezed her hand and she listed four more Best of Breeds by name and breed. Stanley wondered what happened to Tank. He didn't realize until Tank's name wasn't on the list that he wanted him to be one of the morning's winners.

"Now comes news of your dogs," Martha went on.

Stanley's heart skipped a beat.

"Harriet showed Auggie. Another BOB. She showed Tank too. Another BOB. And Stoney. BOB."

Stanley didn't know what happened, but he figured Aleta had her reason for not showing his dog.

"Harriet said to tell you Tank was shown outside the building. Two groups of working dogs were shown inside. This is all gibberish to me. Do you understand?"

Stanley squeezed her hand. He remembered that Aleta had been confined to the building by Harriet.

Martha harrumphed, "If you dog show people talked regular talk...yes, I know I seemed to have absorbed a lot when I was there, but I need a catalog in my hand to help me remember. I am ninety, you know. Much as I'm trying to cling to my reasoning and memory, learning new things doesn't come easily anymore."

Stanley squeezed her hand once.

"Okay," Martha said, "As long as you don't think I am stupid."

Stanley squeezed twice.

"Thank you," Martha said. "Rufus and Bella both got BOB with Tom. You know that sounds a bit racy, don't you?"

Stanley squeezed her hand.

"It must be terrible for your mind to be locked up. It takes courage for you to allow it. And I have a long note here about Paige winning BOB and putting another two points on Topper. I assume that's her Newfoundland."

Stanley squeezed her hand.

"Now for the afternoon stuff," Martha said. "Aleta showed Maggie and took a Group Two. She showed Mugs in the Working Group and got a Group Two there too. Lauren took Tank into the Hound Group and got a Group Two. Harriet says that Lauren and Aleta had pitted Tank against Mugs for five days. Five days of what? It doesn't matter because since they tied you still owe Lyle eight days. Do you bet on the dogs in the show? And if you do, how can you bet days? That makes no sense."

Stanley squeezed her hand once.

"Don't tell me it does and then not tell me how."

"Grams," Wayne Cook broke in. "Are you arguing with my patient?"

"Yes. How can people bet days?"

"The bet involves volunteer deputy days. Stanley owes Lyle when he loses. Lyle erases the days owed if Stanley wins."

"Still doesn't strike me as sensible."

"Give him the rest of the news," Wayne urged.

"Harriet took a Group One with Auggie and Stoney both. She had quite a day. Tom took a Group One with

Rufus and Chuck took a Group One with Rolex. Do you know who all these dogs and people are?"

Stanley squeezed her hand once.

"That's good because here's where it gets complicated. Harriet took Stoney into the Best in Show competition. She said for me to start there. Tom took in Rufus. Chuck took in Auggie because the judge favors male handlers and small dogs, so Aleta took in Rolex. He's the Saint Bernard. He's definitely not a small dog. Was Chuck programming Aleta to lose?"

Stanley squeezed twice.

"No? That's what Harriet said. He wanted Auggie to win."

One squeeze.

"You'll have to explain that one to me sometime. Anyway, it seems Aleta thanked the judge for taking time with her dog as he'd already decided against him. That set the judge's teeth on edge so he told Harriet that Chessies are wasted on women and they had a verbal exchange that wasn't nice."

Stanley smiled inwardly. Harriet was the perfect person to own Chessies. She was a headstrong, loyal, brilliant person. She matched her dogs in temperament.

"It seems that the choice was between Rufus and Auggie and the judge started back toward the table when something stopped him. Harriet told me that she thinks her words and Aleta's had finally penetrated and he had stopped to give a last look to honor the quality of the dogs the women had. And he got stuck there trying to decide which to put over which. Harriet said she promised Stoney they would go hunting one day earlier than planned and his tail began to wag faster. Then Aleta whispered the names of the children in Rolex's family and the big Saint got excited and he won."

Stanley squeezed Martha's hand.

"Yes, Aleta won. Harriet said there was no way the judge was going to give her the win. That's what she said, but I think she was a little disappointed."

Stanley squeezed her hand.

After the show, Lyle caught two of the men that were after Lauren and Aleta. They are in jail. A woman had come into the RV where Lauren was hiding inside the crate with Holly and the woman kept opening and closing the refrigerator door. Lyle figures she poisoned some of the food in there. He's sure she's gone."

Stanley squeezed once.

"Harriet said that Aleta healed Lauren's shoulder that morning, then after being jammed in the crate for almost three hours, Lauren could hardly move. Aleta massaged her for a long time and she restored her. Harriet says to tell you this because she thinks that Aleta's healing powers are draining her."

Stanley squeezed Martha's hand as strongly as he could.

"Here's the kicker," Martha said bluntly. "It's affecting the baby."

Stanley was too stunned to respond. That made no sense. A woman's body was set up to nurture the baby it was carrying over itself.

"She told Aleta to sleep in. She said she's going to insist Dr. Chesney check the baby's heart rate before letting Aleta back into the show ring. Now, your question is how does Harriet know this?"

Stanley managed a squeeze. He needed to know.

"She didn't. Aleta had a premonition that she wasn't going to carry the baby to term."

Stanley's heart sank.

Martha patted his hand. "It was a warning. It's meant to help. Like telling a child to look both ways before crossing the street."

Stanley managed a squeeze.

Martha left him alone with his thoughts.

Chapter 14

During the night Stanley had two more seizures. He decided after the first that if Dr. Cook asked him again, he would reverse his decision and let Dr. Cook dictate his treatment.

Dr. Cook, however didn't intend to ask that question again. Jamara, however, who came on at eight, urged Dr. Cook to reconsider.

"Mr. Praetzel was very definite earlier," Dr. Cook responded.

"He is afraid to put more poison in his body," Jamara said. "He's got the Atropine, the physostigmine salicylate and the cancer going at it in every cell in his body. He doesn't think he can handle any more poisons."

"Stanley, is Jamara right?"

Stanley blinked once.

"Have you changed your mind about the Valium?"

Another single blink.

"I don't understand."

"He is trusting you to be his doctor," Jamara offered. "Is that true?"

A single blink.

Dr. Cook then asked the question about the Valium twice couched so as to receive a positive and then a negative response.

"I am noting the change on your chart," Dr. Cook said.

Stanley blinked once.

The second seizure that night was controlled with the Valium. This time the side effects were minimal. The ringing in his ears was much lighter. The Valium made him sleepy and he slept until morning.

Sunday morning, the second day of the show, Aleta didn't wake up at seven. Or eight. She was still sleeping when Beatrice met Harriet at the Lab ring. Tom was there with Banner.

"So Aleta's not on Morgan either?" Tom asked.

"What do you mean either?" Beatrice asked.

"Lauren couldn't wake Lyle this morning either," Harriet explained.

"Who's going to show Morgan?" Beatrice asked.

"Lauren."

"And Holly?"

"I am," Harriet said.

"Who's showing Scooby?" Beatrice asked.

"Paige," Harriet revealed.

"Wolfhounds are at the same time as Chessies," Tom said, approaching Harriet as she was updating Beatrice. "Do you want me to take Tank in?"

"I was planning not to show Stoney," Harriet said. "I promised him no more shows."

"He's a show dog," Tom said. "If you don't bring him out during a show, he'll think he did something wrong yesterday."

"I never thought of that. If we had left as planned, he would have been okay, but we didn't."

"Lauren says she has an eleven o'clock appointment. So there's just me," Tom joshed.

"You aren't last choice," Harriet retorted. "But you're a pro."

"Consider me doing this as Stanley's friend," Tom said. "I would like to do something."

At eleven o'clock when Tom Wilson was taking Tank into the ring, Lauren entered the bedroom in the RV and gazed at her sleeping husband. Slowly she began to undress, carefully hanging up her clothes.

"Wake up, Lyle," she said. "Go shower. You have an eleven o'clock appointment."

Without looking around Lyle rolled out of bed and made his way to the tiny shower room. Lauren heard the water run. She knew he wasn't fully awake.

He re-entered the bedroom a puzzled look on his face. "Did I lose a lot of weight overnight?"

"Those are Stanley's. We're in their RV."

"No wonder I'm using a strange razor." Lyle said, noticing his wife for the first time. "What are you doing?"

"Opening the book to the page you were reading."

"What are you talking about?"

"Last night before you fell asleep you said we needed to pick up where we left off at eleven o'clock."

"It's eleven o'clock?"

Lauren gazed at her husband lovingly. "You've been working too hard. I won the Breed with Morgan so you could have some fun this afternoon, but now I'm not sure you're up for anything but sleep."

Lyle fell back onto the bed. He let the electric razor slip from his hand.

"Wake me in two days."

Lauren looked back at her sleeping husband as she left the RV.

"How's Lyle?" Harriet asked.

"Exhausted," Lauren replied. "He started to get up then fell asleep again."

"Wasn't he hungry?"

"I will wake him later."

"Don't wake him," Harriet said. "He and Aleta are done in. Let's let their bodies wake them."

"I can go along with that," Lauren agreed.

That afternoon, Tank, who had spent the day being shuffled around as Aleta slept, was reunited with Aleta. His enthusiasm soared and Tank poured his energy into pleasing her. That energy coupled with his natural soundness set him apart from the rest of the dogs in the Hound Group. He took a Group One.

Tom approached her afterward and said, "You should take Tank into Best in Show. I will take in Maggie."

"But..."

"Tank would only droop if you handed him back to me. Let's give Stanley's dog a real shot."

"I told Mr. Sciretta that Maggie would always come first," Aleta declared.

Tom left Aleta and went over to George Sciretta. Aleta noticed there was no arguing. Mr. Sciretta approached Aleta.

"Tom says Tank would probably not look good if you handed him off."

"That's true," Aleta said, "but there's no guarantee of a win."

"Tom says Maggie has a really good chance."

"I feel that way too," Aleta said.

"But I don't want to win by taking out Maggie's biggest competition."

"You won't be winning unfairly," Aleta said.

"Your husband is pretty sick, isn't he?"

"Yes, he is."

"And Tank is his dog, right?"

"Yes," Aleta said hesitantly, not sure of what Mr. Sciretta was saying."

"Then, just this once, I am releasing you from your promise. It's a get-well wish to Stanley from me."

"You don't need to do this," Aleta said. "I am not asking it. And I'm not expecting it. Maggie has saved my life more than once. I want to put another Best in Show on her."

"So does Tom," George whispered. "I'm betting he can't beat you."

"Betting?" Aleta questioned. "You mean money?"

"Sorta."

"I don't want anyone to lose money," Aleta cried.

"It's only a little bet." George explained. "This way I win no matter what happens."

Aleta chuckled. "You made the bet with Tom, didn't you?"

George nodded. "A little incentive."

"You are a sly one!"

George laughed, then said. "I appreciate the fact that you didn't even consider asking for this. That makes it a real gift."

"Mr. Sciretta, you've come a long way."

George changed the subject abruptly.

"You're going to Westminister, aren't you?"

"I won't be in any condition to show a dog." Aleta said.

"If you are, Tom said he would let you handle Maggie"

"If I am, I will," Aleta promised.

After the last group was judged, Harriet approached Aleta and asked her how she was feeling. Aleta's response was a raised eyebrow.

"Don't give me that look!" Her grandmother ordered. "You slept until after lunch today."

"I would say I am well rested then."

"Or just barely recovered," Harriet quipped. "However, the good news is Maggie doesn't run fast."

"I'm on Tank."

"How did that happen?"

"Tom's idea. George went with it. Tom said Tank would wilt if we switched handlers at this point."

"Nice gesture on George's part."

"He's betting on me beating Tom," Aleta remarked.

"There are five other contenders, you know," Harriet reminded her.

Aleta chuckled. "And one of them is Auggie."

"He's made it to the show two days running as has Stoney. Don't count either of them out," Harriet suggested.

Back in Tri-City Hospital, Dr. Cook approached Stanley's bed with a phone in his hand.

"I guess this is like the Kentucky Derby to you guys," he said. "Lyle arranged to give you a running account of the Best in Show competition. He says I should put it on speaker since both Aleta and Harriet are in, and he knows Grams would like to hear it too."

Stanley felt a warmth spread over him.

"Hi Guys," Lyle said. "Just tell me if you can hear me. I have to speak low."

"We can hear you, Lyle," Dr. Cook responded.

Lyle started.

"The dogs are filing into the ring. First one is that harlequin Great Dane that we've seen before. He's moving around the ring with great long strides. Behind him and matching him stride for stride narrowing the gap is Tank. Aleta is handling him. Don't know the details of the trade but George has a happy smile on his face.

"Next is Stoney. Boy, can that dog move! He looks great! Harriet is right with him. Boy, can she run!

"The individual examinations have started. Oops! The judge caught sight of a wayward foot on the Dane.

"Aleta is walking Tank into a stack. Perfect! Now Aleta is moving him. He practically floats over the ground. How can so big a dog be so light on his feet. I think the judge is impressed. He watched him all the way around the ring.

"Harriet is setting up Stoney. He's looking great. The judge is studying him too. He's done, but that's not unusual. He's seen him before. He's checking him quickly and asking Harriet to move him. I know what the judge is seeing. Stoney moves cleanly.

"He has moved onto the Border Collie. I think he's seen him before too. I didn't mean to dismiss Stoney as if he weren't in the running. He's a powerfully built dog. There's no way the judge wasn't impressed with him again.

"The Norfolk is showy. I don't know why he's not getting much of a look.

"Here comes Maggie. Guess what? Tom is showing her Aleta-style. And Maggie is responding. She's looking good. The judge is giving her a good look. Ah, there's a little tail wag.

"Tom is moving her now. You know, Stanley, she is an attractive animal. She has style. Your pup should do well if she takes after her mother.

"Here comes the table for Auggie. The Pug is impatient. He wants to be up on display. He is also getting a long look. Wouldn't it be a kick if it came down to the two dogs you own?

"That little guy sure knows how to show. I really like him. Cobby, sturdy, well-balanced, with a great headpiece.

"Chuck is moving him now. Clean. Jaunty.

"It's great to be last in such a competition, especially if you're good.

"Frankly, Aleta will have to pull a rabbit out of the hat to beat Tom and Chuck this time. And Harriet has Stoney looking magnificent.

"Judge Capoda is standing looking at the group. Now he's walking down the line. He passed the Dane. He's studying Tank's face. He's checking his chest. Tank is still a young dog, so his chest may not be as developed as it will be later. He's moved to the rear and is running his hand down his thigh.

"He's moved onto Stoney. Some attention to the head, chest and thigh.

"He's skipped over the other two and is down at the end of the line taking one more look at Maggie and Auggie. He's stepped back for one last look. Now he's going over to the table. Evidently, he's decided. And I haven't a clue which of the four it is."

There was a pause. Then Lyle began speaking again. "He still at the table."

Another pause.

"He has the rosette. It's a huge red, white and blue one. He's stepped in the middle of the ring. He's pointing."

The five in the hospital room held their breath.

"My word!" Lyle gasped.

"Don't have a seizure, Stanley," Dr. Cook ordered the man in the boat. "Lyle, out with it!"

"I don't believe it."

"Don't believe what?" Dr. Cook thundered. "Who won?"

"Did he pick the terrier after all?" Martha prompted.

"No. He picked one of the four," Lyle said.

"Which one?" Dr. Cook pressed. "You're not on TV. You're on a speaker phone. We hear the cheering. Who won?"

"Stoney!" Lyle cried. "Harriet won with her Chessie!"

Chapter 15

The hospital room was quiet for a few moments. Lyle's voice came over the phone.

"Hello? Hello. Anyone still standing? It shouldn't be a shock. It isn't as if Stoney wasn't one of those in contention. It's not as if he doesn't deserve it."

Martha's high-pitched voice broke it.

"You nailed it Lyle."

"Me? I was as surprised as everyone else." Lyle said. "Tank was commanding in presence. He was as showy as I've ever seen him. And Auggie was lively and I would have picked him if Tank weren't there."

"Showiness didn't win," Martha proclaimed. "The judge told everyone what the deciding factor was. You told us."

"Maturity?" Lyle guessed only his voice told everyone it was not really a question, but more of an affirmation.

"So Tank was the competition?" Lyle commented after a moment. "Well, well, well."

Martha spoke again. "How's Aleta?"

"For some reason, she's joyous," Lyle said. "It's written all over her face. I don't understand that either. She put her heart into that competition."

"Her grandmother won," Martha said.

"But she went all out," Lyle remarked.

"Which is why the win counts," Martha returned.

Stanley smiled inwardly. He was happy when he heard Aleta was showing Tank. It meant that he was put first.

He was unusually happy when Harriet won.

Aleta wasn't beaten by any of the pros.

The old lady quietly walked in and stole the show. What a marvelous bit of showmanship. She had the superior dog and she knew it. Stoney was a fully mature, superbly conditioned, outstandingly correct Chesapeake Bay Retriever showing under a retriever man, someone who would appreciate such quality in a breed sister to his own. Where was Lyle's head? He was so used to Aleta doing the impossible that he forgot her teacher was in the ring.

The part that Stanley found most satisfying, he let himself admit, was that he had won a Best in Show with Tank and Aleta hadn't. She hadn't matched his win. It was still unique.

A grunt from the nearby bed brought Dr. Cook over to it. He checked out Michael and removed the tube from his throat. Michael coughed and sputtered his anger over the use of it. Dr. Cook just groaned.

Martha kissed her husband and told him to be grateful. He calmed down. Michael knew full well the procedure had been called for.

Dr. Cook then came over to Stanley's bed and took his hand. "Don't even hope. The Atropine carries residual effects. Those worry me the most. You got such a heavy dose I can't believe you will escape them."

Stanley sighed inwardly. He squeezed Dr. Cook's hand once.

"Since the seizures appeared to have stopped and that heart-stopping performance by our redoubtable Chief Lyle West didn't inspire a new episode, I believe we've passed that stage so I'm going home to kiss my wife.

Stanley waved his hand as if he were writing and Dr. Cook gave him the pad and pen.

"Any med needed to stop psychotic episodes?"

"It would depend on what's happening. Some symptoms we can alleviate."

"Any urgency?"

"Why?"

"Stay home," Stanley wrote. "Have the nurse call you."

Dr. Cook turned and talked to Eunice who assured him she would call at any change.

When Dr. Cook came back to tell Stanley he was leaving, his grandmother asked if she could take Michael home.

Dr. Cook asked him a few medical questions and then agreed, but he told his grandfather that he had to rest.

"You aren't as young as you used to be. Give your body a chance to recover."

"Yes, Doctor," Michael said with apparent meekness.

"You aren't going to rile me are you?" Dr. Cook observed wryly.

"Two against one aren't my favorite odds."

"Grams, he doesn't come to the hospital before Tuesday, preferably Wednesday."

"He won't," Martha declared with a firmness that told everyone that Michael wouldn't leave the house for the next two days.

"Will you be okay, Stanley?" Dr. Cook asked. "You'll be here alone."

"I will be fine," Stanley wrote. "Eunice is here."

"And Lyle has the hospital locked down tight," Dr. Cook said. "So you should be safe."

Chapter 16

As soon as everyone left, Eunice settled at the nurse's desk, and Stanley let his mind ruminate about that day's events.

The men had been caught. They denied knowing the women.

She's got to be back here by now, Stanley reasoned. And she knows Chief West and Lieutenant French, his second in command, are both still at the show. On top of that, it's the weekend.

The men on guard duty will be green. Seniority will dictate that. The Co-ed Killer has got to take the fact that both doctors have left as a sign that I am getting better.

Stanley snapped his fingers. Eunice left her desk and came over.

"Call Chief Milani and tell him I need to see him," he wrote. Then he printed Tom's private cell phone number.

"What do I say to him?" Eunice asked.

Stanley underlined what he had written.

"It's Sunday night," Eunice protested.

Stanley rattled the paper. Eunice heard the heart beat on the monitor suddenly accelerate. That frightened her into yielding to his demand.

"Okay," she said, taking the paper. "Relax, I will make the call."

Stanley heard her on the phone. She identified herself and then read what Stanley had written verbatim.

"Did he tell you that it was an emergency?"

"No," Eunice said. "But when I asked for details, he became agitated."

"Go to the door and find out the names of the guards on the door," Chief Milani said.

Stanley saw Eunice go to the door, and he heard her talking to the guards. She returned a few minutes later.

"Mick Hudson and Bob Nivola," she told Chief Milani.

"Tell Stanley I will drop in on him in an hour," Tom said. "What are your orders?"

His query nettled her. What did he think her orders were?

"To watch him," she snapped.

"Don't take a break until I get there," Tom ordered.

"Is anything wrong?"

"Stanley never calls unless it's serious," Tom said. "But there are two good men on the door."

When Eunice hung up, she mumbled, "But he didn't call. I did. And you will blame me."

She picked her thermos and poured herself a cup of coffee. She stared at it with disgust.

I don't need coffee. I need coke, she thought. How long would I be gone? Ten minutes, tops.

She looked over at the man in the bed and called, "He's on his way."

She glanced at her watch. She'd better go now. Chief Milani couldn't find her gone. She left the room, breezing past the guards.

Eunice collapsed as she brushed past a nurse in the hall. The nurse turned and called to the guards. The nurse stayed by Eunice when she called to the guard.

"Help me carry her into this room," the new nurse called.

Mike Hudson didn't move, but Bob Nivola did. He ran down the hall and helped the nurse carry Eunice into the nearest room.

Together they laid Eunice on the bed.

"Thanks," the nurse said, opening her cell and turning her back to the guard.

"Dr. Brice, a nurse collapsed on the fourth floor. Send someone up with a gurney to bring her down to Emergency."

The nurse emerged alone from the room a few minutes later and went up to Mike Hudson.

"Eunice is worried about Mr. Praetzel," the nurse said. "I told her I would watch him until Jamara can get here."

"Where's Bob?"

"Watching Eunice. Dr. Brice is sending up an orderly with a gurney to take her to Emergency.

The nurse entered the intensive care unit and Mike Hudson radioed Chief Milani.

"Get into that room!" Milani shouted.

Mike turned, pushed open the door and had one second of clarity before losing consciousness.

The nurse then walked over to the bed. She had a knife in her hand. Her hand was gloved. A surgical mask covered her face.

The mask frightened Stanley the most.

"Write these words on that paper tucked under your arm," she ordered curtly.

Stanley picked up the soft felt-tipped pen and wrote her opening salutation.

"To Stanley Praetzel," he wrote.

Then he waited for her next words.

"You and your wife are to cease all activity for the next month."

The first thought that flashed into Stanley's mind is that she planned more killings. She had a list in her head.

He looked at her, waiting for her to speak.

The second thought that jammed itself into his brain was that she had learned to use a knife to throw the police off her trail until she finished. And she now was comfortable with using it. She could have just put more poison in his IV, but she wanted a bigger impact. She planned to stab him.

He held the pen poised, ready to write her words.

"You have a baby," she dictated.

As Stanley wrote the last words, he wondered why none of the prophets had foreseen his death.

Maybe I don't die, he thought. On the other hand, the prophets didn't foresee everyone's death. Good people died every day.

Tears sprang into his eyes. He didn't want to die like this.

The masked nurse took the tablet from Stanley's grasp and studied it.

"Don't think guards will keep you safe. They didn't this time. I have eyes everywhere."

The masked nurse walked around the bed and lengthened the restraint on his right hand. She took the note from the clipboard and placed it on Stanley's chest and put his right hand on top of the note.

"Hold it there," she ordered.

Stanley realized his right hand was still tethered. He was as helpless as before.

The woman played with the knife.

Fear rode on his next thought.

"Don't cut anything off," he begged silently.

He wanted every finger of his hand. He wanted the hand itself. He jerked his right leg.

The woman noticed the movement and quipped, "You trying to draw my attention to something you would rather give up than a finger?"

Stanley tried to pull his right hand out of the restraint, but the Velcro band held fast.

"I can do pretty much anything I want, can't I?"

Defeated, Stanley lay mute and still.

The nurse threw back the sheet and held up the catheter tube.

Stanley's brain went numb with fear as he felt his penis being raised.

"Oh, God, no," he prayed silently. "Anything else but that."

Suddenly, she thrust the knife through the flesh of his right hand, through the paper it was holding, deep into his side just under the rib cage.

Pain enveloped Stanley. His body which had been convulsing repeatedly for no apparent reason now refused to move. It froze as the pain shot up his arm and torso and exploded in his brain.

Stanley reflexively gripped the paper beneath his hand. That movement brought excruciating pain. He forced himself to lie still as waves of pain rushed one after the other to his brain.

"You thought I was going to cut it off, didn't you?"

Pain froze Stanley in place. He dared not move, even to reply.

"That was a warning," the woman snarled. "Cease all activity. I mean to finish."

A moment later, Stanley heard the door close. He was alone. The only sound he heard was the beeping of the heart monitor and the click of the clock marking the passing of the minutes. The pain was constant.

Stanley grimaced. He didn't dare move his hand or his body. Every breath told him to hold still. If he could have, he would have torn the breathing tube from his throat and held his breath forever.

Doesn't a person faint from pain, he wondered. Other people faint from pain. Why can't I?

The minutes dragged on. The big hand on the clock hit twelve.

I can't take much more of this, he thought. I can't take anymore of this.

Every breath brought a new stabbing pain. His feeling of helplessness overwhelmed him. It wasn't something one got used to. It wasn't something one learned to endure.

Each new onslaught made him cringe. Each new onrush of pain made him cry deep within his soul begging for relief.

At that moment, the Praetzel RV was weaving through heavy Sunday evening traffic on the western edge of Chicago when Aleta suddenly jumped up from the chair, took two steps to the front of the vehicle and told Hubert to signal that they were going to pull over. It took a few minutes for Hubert to find a space. Aleta watched Lyle pull over behind them.

"I need to go the rest of the way with Lyle," she announced, heading for the door.

The minute the RV was completely stopped, Aleta opened the door and jumped out without answering the queries that were thrown at her.

She climbed in the front seat of the police car and said, "It's Stanley. Something's happened. Get me to the hospital as quickly as you can."

The three in the RV saw Lyle pull out into traffic with lights flashing and the siren blasting. Cars squeezed into already crowded lanes to let the police car pass. Lyle blasted through intersections as cars entering his path screeched to a halt.

As soon as Aleta announced that Stanley was in trouble, Lyle called Chief Tom Milani.

"How did you know?" Tom asked. "I am in his room now. Stanley has been stabbed. Dr. Cook has arrived and is preparing to operate.

"Both guards are down. So is Eunice. The perp left a note. She made Stanley write it. It gives us no clue as to who is behind the attack."

"I am on my way," Lyle said.

That was the last word spoken in the car as it sped through the northwestern suburbs of Chicago heading toward the Tri-City Hospital in Arborville. It was not a time for chit-chat.

Aleta prayed briefly. It was a thank you. Stanley was still alive.

She hadn't had a vision of his death. She didn't understand why. Without such a vision, she wouldn't know what to do.

She leaned her head back, closed her eyes and waited. She heard the squealing of tires, the blast of horns, the siren above her head wailing, and the radio feeding Lyle information about events in Arborville. She muted those sounds mentally. And she concentrated.

After ten minutes, she sighed. She couldn't will God to tell her more. He had His reasons.

She protested silently, "I don't like working in the dark!"

Then she chuckled.

"As if I'm doing any work," she murmured.

Her own humor relaxed her. And she began to think.

Martha was right there, she thought. Why wasn't she told what needed to be done?

Because only I can do it, she concluded and then let her mind continue to muse over the situation silently.

So it's not a simple avoidance of an event that harbored death. It was something else.

I can understand people others can't, she thought. But I can't see that type of situation calling for racing through red lights in a police car.

Some of her grandmother's words floated into her thinking. Her memory refused to cough up the whole of it. Something about her power draining her, but she already knew she was tired after a vision. God knew it too. Besides, she had no control over the appearances of the visions. They just happened.

There was no way to prepare.

But this time I am suppose to prepare, she realized with sudden clarity.

Prepare? How?

She glanced at Lyle. While Stanley might have helped her reason through her confusion, Lyle wouldn't be able to. She knew this instinctively.

She turned away.

She prayed silently, "I need a hint God. Please!"

Suddenly, Lyle spoke. "Thanks for what you did for Lauren."

"The massage?" Aleta queried.

Her bewilderment doubled.

"That too," Lyle replied. "I am talking about your healing her shoulder."

Aleta's protest was instantaneous.

"I don't heal. I can't heal!"

"Harriet said you did."

"My grandmother told you I could heal?"

"Hubert said you helped Stanley Friday night," Lyle said.

"I calmed him," Aleta declared curtly. "That's all."

"You did more than that with Lauren. So whatever you call it, thanks for doing it."

"You're welcome," Aleta said, ending the discussion.

Even if that was it, there was no choice to be made. If she had the power to heal and Stanley needed to be healed, there was no choice. She would do it.

It was then she remembered. When she used her gift, Harriet had told her, it drained her. She remembered protesting that she felt fine. And then she had slept for sixteen hours. Her grandmother had insisted that Dr. Chesney check the baby's heart beat before she would allow Aleta to show in Group. Even when she had allowed her grandmother to dictate her actions, Aleta hadn't accepted her grandmother's reasoning.

She simply hadn't believed her grandmother--her grandmother, the prophet, her grandmother who was no more given to flights of fancy than she was, her grandmother who would never even consider curtailing her own use of whatever gift God bestowed upon her.

She hadn't believed.

And her grandmother hadn't once berated her for her disbelief. No wonder people have such trouble believing. She, who had not only received visions in concert with Martha Cook and her grandmother, had dismissed the message Harriet was delivering as inapplicable.

She stared at Lyle West. He always believed her. He trusted her.

My grandmother is even more trustworthy than I am, Aleta thought. So that's why I am in the car with Lyle.

Aleta laid her head back and closed her eyes. It was very clear. She had choices before her.

Choices? She pondered. Why had her mind used the plural?

Probably because life is replete with choices. But right now she was faced with just one.

It didn't seem like much of a choice. Stanley needed her. Afterward she would rest and the baby would again be nurtured.

She put her hand on her stomach to assure her baby, she would take care of him too. As she did so, she felt his distress.

"Lyle!" Aleta blurted out. "I can't choose!"

So startled was Lyle at the shout of anguish that he jerked the wheel and the car swerved. He recovered control quickly.

Aleta's reaction was verbal.

"You're a cop. You have the people yell at you all the time."

"From the back seat," he countered, "Out-of-control people."

"I am not out of control!" Aleta declared. "I am upset."

"It was abrupt," he replied speeding toward the hospital.

"I didn't choose when I would get upset."

"Okay, what's the problem?"

"You were right," Aleta proclaimed.

Lyle smirked, "And that's a problem?"

"It's what you were right about that's the problem," Aleta went on. "I can heal...well, that is... God sometimes heals through me."

"So?"

"It has a down side."

"You get tired?"

"It drains energy from the baby I'm carrying before it zaps my strength."

"As I see it," Lyle said, "All you need to do is ask God to tell you when to stop."

"And if He doesn't?"

"It's a reasonable request. Why wouldn't He?"

"I am not too good at listening," Aleta confessed a bit sheepishly.

"Then if I were you, I would practice that," Lyle said as he sped into the hospital parking lot and up to the Emergency Entrance.

Lyle took her straight to the operating room where Stanley's surgery was taking place.

"You can't go in," Lyle said. "We wait out here."

"Get me a gown and mask," Aleta said.

"The doctors seem to have everything under control," Lyle said, peeking through the small glass window.

"I'm going in with or without a gown," Aleta declared. "Your choice."

Lyle followed her into the operating theater. He stood just inside the door. Aleta approached the operating table.

"We're losing him," the anesthesiologist announced.

"That's not possible," Dr. Taekman shot back. "How?"

"His heart's failing. He's going into shock," Dr. Beck said.

Both surgeons stopped.

"That, Doctors," Aleta declared from the doorway, "is because he wants to die."

The doctor monitoring the anesthesia looked up.

"Who let her in here," he roared. "Get her out of here!"

"She stays," Chief West proclaimed.

Aleta moved to the head of the operating table.

"I'm here, Stanley," Aleta said as she put her hand on his bare chest near his heart.

"The heart rhythm is returning to normal," Dr. Beck reported.

"Stop the anesthetic," Aleta ordered. "It's not working."

"Of course, it's working," Dr. Beck contended angrily.

"Stanley says it's not," Aleta declared.

"I don't believe you," Dr. Beck spat out. "This is ridiculous. Dr. Cook, Dr. Taekman, aren't you going to do anything?"

Aleta turned.

"Lyle, Stanley says that if you help, he will owe you double the eight."

"Dr. Beck," Chief West ordered. "Out!"

"You can't order me away from a patient."

"The patient has dismissed you."

"The patient is unconscious."

"Evidently, he's not," Chief West said. "Now will you leave on your own or do I remove you."

Dr. Beck rose angrily, tore off his mask, threw it on the floor and stormed out, cursing.

Dr. Cook immediately took Dr. Beck's seat and checked the equipment.

Aleta felt a tiny movement. She put her hand on her stomach and could feel the warmth of it. It was a strange sensation but she knew she had responded appropriately.

"Now what?" Dr. Taekman said.

"Now you give a local and then work on his hand when it's numb," Dr. Cook said. "And you sit down."

A nurse was sent to get the necessary medication.

"You will have to endure a needle sting, Stanley," Aleta said. "But you're in control now."

Aleta turned and smiled at Dr. Taekman.

"Michael, he approves," she said.

Dr. Taekman sat down on the stool provided. "That's what Martha told me when I left. 'Sit and work.'"

"The wound in his side must be sutured," Dr. Cook said.

"I am going to heal that," Aleta announced calmly.

Suddenly, her face registered shock.

"What do you mean no?"

"What's his objection?" Dr. Cook asked.

"Harriet told him that...never mind...Stanley, I can do this—just this, no more..."

"Yes, I will obey your order." Aleta murmured. "No, I didn't know Dr. Taekman was sent here by Martha purposely to operate on your hand."

Aleta's voice cracked.

"Oh, Stanley, you can't take any more!"

Dr. Cook sent the only remaining nurse out of the room, then said, "Tell us what's going on."

"God can heal through me," Aleta explained. "However it drains me physically which wouldn't bother me, but I am pregnant. Stanley knows this. He claims that restoring his heart beat was all I should do for him."

"You mean you could heal his hand?" Dr. Taekman asked.

"Yes," Aleta said simply. "Only I didn't realize until now that God..."

"Did you heal his bone cancer?" Dr. Taekman pressed.

"I don't know. Dr. Cook, Stanley says you can suture the wound," Aleta said.

"The pain will be too much," Dr. Cook said.

"He says as long as you know about it, maybe you'll take fewer stitches."

"Don't you wish," Dr. Cook quipped

"Don't worry, Stanley," Dr. Cook added. "I can dull some of the pain with a local."

"Stanley," Aleta said with firmness, "I am staying. Don't tell me to leave again...And yes, I do intend to tell Dr. Cook when he's hurting you."

The nurses returned. Aleta settled down on the stool Dr. Beck had been using. The locals were administered. As the doctors waited for them to take effect, each watched the heart monitor. The beat was stronger than it had been before.

"Are you our new anesthesiologist," Dr. Cook asked. "You do know Stanley has to lie still."

"Stanley knows that. He can hear," Aleta said. "You can talk directly to him."

"Sorry, Stanley," Dr. Cook apologized. "Your heart beat is stronger than it's been since this began."

"I need a dry field, "Dr. Taekman said. He pointed to one of the nurses. "You handle the tourniquet."

The other nurse asked, "Should she be here?"

"Why are you here?" Dr. Taekman queried with a wry smile. It was directed at Aleta.

The nurse glanced at the doctor, puzzled by the question and the fact that it was asked of the interloper.

"I'm going to sit here and keep him from being lonely," Aleta responded. "Even though you're both half done, I know you doctors. You take an inordinately long

time to put in a few stitches. A seamstress would starve if
she were that slow."

The nurse gasped in shock.

Aleta chuckled. "Stanley says he's in no hurry."

Dr. Taekman asked, "Can you feel anything,
Stanley?"

"He says you can go ahead," Aleta replied.

"I am already working," Dr. Taekman said.

Aleta's voice was sharp. "What do you mean why
didn't I tell you? I'm not watching."

"Stanley, you will tell me if you feel anything when I
start, won't you?" Dr. Cook said.

"Wayne, don't be facetious," Aleta said. "Stanley
knows you've begun. He says the local made the pain a little
less but not much."

"That's because there's so much trauma to the
surrounding tissue," Dr. Cook said.

"No, Stanley, I am not telling him that! Now you just
hush up and be brave," Aleta said firmly. "I intend to tell
little Michael how brave you were every time he complains
about getting a shot...No, it won't scare him...I know what
boys need to know."

The two doctors smiled as they worked. Aleta was
better than music.

Aleta went on.

"You are so wrong, Stanley. Michael will need to
know what you were willing to do for him...Why? Because
he is our second son, that's why...What's not to follow?
How can you not understand my reasoning? Sometimes,
Stanley, you are so dense. I know you were an only
child...Yes, I know I'm the eldest and I'm a girl. What has
that to do with it? Jayline used to ask Dad if he wanted her
or just wanted me to have a sister...Oh, now you get it. Well,
I'm glad you have a few molecules of reasoning left...Why
does you're going through this prove you want Michael? ...If
you wanted a companion for Gerard, you'd have decided to
get Gerard a dog...I know Gerard already has two dogs.

That's not the point. The point is you don't just want another
baby, you want this one. Specifically, him...Well, I'm glad
you see my point. I'm so glad juries are quicker on the
uptake than you are...No, I am not clearer when I talk to
them..."

Suddenly, her voice softened. "Yes, I know."

Then Aleta was quiet. It was as if someone had shut
off the radio in the middle of a soap opera.

"So, Stanley," Dr. Cook asked, hoping to prompt a
new exchange, "Has Dr. Chesney confirmed the sex yet?"

"No," Aleta responded. "But little Michael is acting
like one...What do I mean? Stanley, you know what I
mean...All I can say is that if he is going to act like you, he
had better look like you. He can't look like me and act like
you. That would mix everyone up...Well, of course we're
different...You aren't like me at all...Well, for one thing, I
would have told Dr. Cook to just slap a butterfly bandage on
the knife cut in my side and let it heal jagged...Yes, I know I
had plastic surgery on my leg when I was shot. You like my
legs. You insist I wear very short shorts. I couldn't have an
ugly old bullet wound, now could I? I really do wonder
where your reason has gone...Why shouldn't you do the
same? ...Because it's hurting you to be stitched...Where is
your brain?

Suddenly, Aleta laughed. "Oh, Stanley, you are so
right...Okay, I'll listen."

The doctors thought they were destined for more
radio silence, but they were wrong.

"Stanley wants to know when you're going to take
this tube out of his throat. He says he's done needing it."

"Can we do one thing at a time," Dr. Cook responded.
"We're in the middle of operating and the tube is providing
Stanley with extra oxygen."

"There are less invasive alternatives," Aleta said.

"Stanley do you want me to stop and take it out right
now?" Dr. Cook charged. "Or can you wait?"

"Now!" Aleta said. "He wants to kiss me."

Both doctors stopped as laughter took over.

"No," Dr. Cook decided. "Not now, but we'll do it as soon as we're finished."

"And then he can go home?" Aleta asked.

"No," Dr. Cook decided. "You can stay here with him. There's no keeping you out anyway, but he has to stay here. We need to run tests. He needs rest. The minute he passes through the hospital doors the work 'rest' evolves into the word 'work.'"

"He can sign himself out, you know," Aleta said.

"If he's smart, he won't," Dr. Cook said.

"Stanley says we'll do it your way," Aleta reported. "He will stay."

Lyle West spoke up. His voice startled the people around the operating table. They'd forgotten he was in the room.

"We've instituted new guarding procedures," Lyle announced. "There won't be a repeat."

"Lyle, Stanley says that as soon as he can speak, he has some suggestions."

"Can't he tell me now?"

"He says he wants his suggestions to stay private."

That puzzled everyone in the room. A couple people glared at Lyle, but he said nothing.

Something was bothering Stanley.

If he didn't know better, he'd say the man was frightened.

Chapter 17

Stanley was moved to the two-bed room with the bullet proof glass because Aleta needed a shower in the room.

No one argued with her even after she told them she was going home to shower, change and pack.

One of West's men drove her home and back.

Meanwhile Lyle and Stanley began to talk, slowly at first because Stanley's vocal cords had been roughened by the tube.

"I read the note," Lyle said, starting. "Who do you think is behind this?"

"Co-ed killer," Stanley rasped.

"Are you certain?"

Stanley nodded. "Clever wording. You and your wife to cease from all activity. I hate to tell her."

"She was reading your mind."

"No," Stanley denied, coughing. "She could, but didn't."

"So tell me everything," Lyle requested politely.

Haltingly, Stanley told him all that was said and done by the woman with the knife. Stanley sensed that Lyle was both shocked and enraged.

Lyle's manner and voice, however, remained under control.

"So what are you going to do?" Lyle asked.

"Help you, of course," Stanley said. "But not overtly."

"That's not the way to go," Lyle stated.

"Why not?"

"Because she'll go after Aleta if you do." Lyle said. "And Harriet told me that the pregnancy is precarious."

"I see your point," Stanley said.

"Do I really get sixteen days?" Lyle asked abruptly.

Stanley nodded, puzzled.

"Good," Lyle said. "How are your eyes?"

Stanley raised a brow in query.

"Well, I can give you a body guard for a day or two because you were attacked, but if you stay on the case, I can justify guarding you as long as the case is active."

"What am I? Your think tank?" Stanley exploded, then started coughing.

"Your brain is what I value the most," Lyle responded. "That and the fact that you're one-legged."

"What?"

"You're unique."

Stanley growled. "I don't want to be unique!"

"According to Tom, we have a line of people who want to help that one-legged detective."

"Help me how?"

"Solve the crime."

"Cranks?"

"Some of them might be," Lyle said, "but for some reason the majority of the callers say that talking to you isn't like going to the cops."

"I am a dynasty?"

"We need leads, Stanley. You are a great listener."

"It would be a royal waste of time," Stanley protested hoarsely.

"That's why I wanted to be sure I had those sixteen days," Lyle said.

"You're going to order me to interview these people?" Stanley guessed.

"In exchange you get round-the-clock police protection for you and Aleta and your household."

"You would give me that anyway," Stanley stated.

"When can you start?" Lyle asked.

"Next week."

"Tomorrow will be fine. I will have Tom start lining them up."

"Tomorrow? I was just operated on."

"That's why tomorrow is perfect," Lyle said. "Justin will milk this big time."

"Let me repeat in case you went deaf suddenly. I was just operated on."

"I was there. Remember?" Lyle said. "Your voice is coming back."

Stanley held up his bandaged right hand.

"I will give you a tape recorder, Lyle said. "You won't need to write a word."

"I was stabbed in the side."

"Yes, that will play better." Lyle mused stroking his chin. "Dr. Cook will still have you confined to a wheelchair, won't he?"

"Doctor said 'rest', not 'work'."

"We'll rent a handicapped van so no one has to transfer you to the wheelchair, the kind with a platform that lowers you to the ground."

"No!"

"You aren't a side show freak," Lyle hastened to assure him. "You are a bona fide hero! You represent every man on the force. We cannot be intimidated. We cannot be threatened. We cannot be pressured into giving up."

"But I can," Stanley choked out.

"Don't be ridiculous."

"I have limits."

"Consider this," Lyle contended. "The person who did this to you threatened Aleta. Aleta can not be stopped. If ever she gets a vision of a girl about to be murdered, she will act on it. Your only hope of protecting your wife is to help us capture the woman who poisoned and then stabbed you."

Stanley sighed his acquiescence.

"Aleta did restore you to health, didn't she?" Lyle asked.

"As far as the residual effects of the Atropine, she did. I don't understand how she did it with one short touch. With my leg it's been so gradual."

"Maybe something else is going on," Lyle suggested.

"Like what?"

"A matter of timing," Lyle said. "God's timing. And maybe something else."

"Maybe He's protecting her," Stanley mused.

"I don't think it was healing Lauren's shoulder that drained Aleta and threatened your baby. Well, maybe it was, but her trip to bring you out of a convulsion would have drained her seriously first," Lyle explained, and then added. "I don't know why she is drained at all. But I do know you were right to stop her in the operating room."

Stanley smirked.

"Well, I'd hate to think I suffered for nothing."

"Aside from your two minor injuries, you are okay, aren't you?"

"They were hardly minor!"

"They weren't life threatening."

"I almost died."

"From the poison, not the stab wound, Lyle proclaimed.

"You win. Except for my stab wounds, I feel good. But, Lyle, they do hurt."

"Don't tell Aleta!"

"Why not?"

"She'll help you," Lyle said. "This time heal like the rest of us—slowly."

"Oh come on, Lyle!" Stanley retorted. "What do you think I've been doing?"

"Don't you see the problem?"

"Problem?"

"You're in the limelight," Lyle prompted. "As long as you're in the chair, no one knows how fast your leg healed. The fact that you aren't being fitted for an artificial leg just promotes the illusion that the leg isn't completely healed."

"Exactly what are you saying?"

"Don't you remember how it was when people first found out Aleta was a prophet?"

"We were inundated with people who wanted her to predict their futures," Stanley recalled.

Slowly, Lyle watched understanding appear in Stanley's eyes.

"If she were a healer," Stanley mused. "There would be no stopping people from seeking her out. At least with the prophecies, the three announced enough times that they could only foresee murders that eventually people stopped expecting anything else."

Lyle nodded.

"Thanks, Lyle," he said. "I can take it from here."

Half an hour later when Aleta reappeared, Stanley was ready.

At least that's what he thought.

She smiled at him, changed into pajamas and climbed into the bed which had been moved next to his. Most of the staff knew if they didn't do this, she would squeeze into bed beside Stanley.

"How much of what you and Lyle talked about aren't you going to tell me?" she asked.

"Can't I have a private conversation without telling you every detail?"

"Of course, you can."

"Good!" Stanley said, then waited for her next remark.

When it didn't come, he switched tactics.

"I am going to sleep now. Tomorrow we will talk. When my throat is healed."

"You've already made tons of decisions without me, haven't you?"

"Not tons. A few personal ones."

"Tell me."

"I will tell you one and then we sleep. Okay?"

"No," Aleta returned. "It's not okay."

"Okay, I'll tell you the two that affect you."

"You can't make decisions for me," Aleta protested.

"Oh, but I can," Stanley countered.

"You plan to order me to do something?" Aleta asked, puzzled. "Why? I don't intend to refuse any request you make."

"Remember when I first used the 'pillow' word?"

"Of course, I remember. You saved my life by keeping me silent. And afterward when you used it, it was always for my benefit even when I didn't see it at the time. But why would you use it now? There's just the two of us and you've never used it to keep me from asking you questions."

"That's not why I'm going to use it now. I want you to be silent until this time tomorrow night."

"Are you going to tell me what other decision you made regarding me?"

"Yes," Stanley said. "Pillow."

Aleta's face registered her bewilderment and her distress. Tears rose unbidden to her eyes and streamed silently down her cheeks.

Stanley took her hand in his and placed it in its usual place.

"Yes," he said. "I asked Dr. Cook to remove the catheter. I need a peaceful night's sleep which you're going to give me."

She curled her fingers around his penis and brushed the tears from her face with her other hand. Then she turned and laid her free hand on the bandage covering the stab wound in his side.

Immediately, Stanley felt the healing warmth of her touch. He gently removed her hand with his free hand and laid it on her stomach.

"Michael gets the energy you would give me," he said, lowering his voice to a whisper. "It is essential that the stab wounds heal slowly, normally."

Then he closed his eyes and said no more.

Lyle had told Aleta what the note said. She wanted to discuss the contents with Stanley. But more than that she wanted to know what else the attackers had said to him. That the visitor had threatened him Aleta was certain. It wasn't just the threat in the note.

She had been specific in a way that had terrified him. The man she had found in the operating room had given up.

What could possibly be worse than dying, Aleta pondered.

As she lay next to her husband and his breathing grew slow and even, she smiled. She felt the warmth of her hand on her stomach and knew that Michael was being healed. Stanley had been right to silence her. Their baby needed her. Evidently this healing power had consequences. Couldn't pregnant women heal without hurting their unborn child? Maybe it wasn't that general, she thought. Maybe it's just me.

Then why use me at all? Why not use my grandmother?

Maybe she was too old came the thought. Suddenly, she recalled a passage from Ecclesiastes: For he has appointed a time for every matter and for every work."

I will look that up tomorrow, she vowed. God will give me an answer.

Stanley groaned slightly as he slept. Aleta instinctively knew the wound in his side was bothering him. All she had to do was pull her hand away from its present location, slide it along his hip to his waist and then lay it ever so gently on the bandage. She knew that was all she needed to do.

She would just leave it there long enough to bring him comfort. Then she'd put it back where he had placed it.

She was given the power to heal, so why not do it? Why should he suffer more than he had already?

Surely a brief touch wouldn't hurt the baby. She would just slide the hand circling his penis up to the bandaged area. Her fingers uncurled and her hand slid over to Stanley's thigh.

He stirred.

"Aleta, put your hand back where it belongs," he ordered tersely.

Startled, Aleta did as she was told. She wanted to explain that he was groaning and that she could alleviate some of his pain, but she remembered that he had asked her again to fulfill her wedding vow. He had ordered her to be silent.

As her hand again found its special place, she felt his hand cover hers.

He hadn't done that before. Why now?

Her inability to question him frustrated her, but as she lay beside him, touching him, knowing he was alive, knowing that he wanted her near him, knowing he found pleasure in her nearness, all these things calmed her. She drifted into a dreamless sleep.

Stanley as usual woke early. He lay as he always did, rejoicing in Aleta's presence.

He had opted not to take any pain medication and both doctors understood his choice.

"The local anesthetic won't wear off for several hours," Dr. Taekman had told him. "If you fall asleep right away, you should have a good night."

Thus when Stanley woke, he was immediately aware that his hand hurt.

"Why couldn't my inner clock let me sleep in," he grumbled.

When he started to turn to look at Aleta, his side forced him to reconsider his objective. So he lay back and stared at the ceiling.

The hand throbbed as if he had used it when all he had done was move. At that moment, he realized he wasn't going to have the best day.

When he had told Lyle last night that his stab wounds hurt, he hadn't actually felt much pain. He was still numb from the locals.

His hand and side were no longer numb.

He rang for the nurse and asked if the doctor had left a note saying he could have a mild pain reliever.

She read his chart and said, "I can set up a codeine drip if you wish. Or I can bring you a couple of Tylenol."

"The Tylenol," Stanley said. "I am returning to work today."

She raised her brows in disbelief, but brought him his two pills speedily. Twenty minutes later the pain wasn't as intense.

He lay back and waited for Aleta to wake up.

But that didn't happen. Instead, at seven, Chief Lyle West entered, followed by Jamara.

Stanley was instantly upset.

Lyle got right to the point.

"Can you get Aleta to let go, so Jamara can bathe and dress you?"

"Now?" Stanley asked, shocked. "It's barely dawn."

"You've been up for over an hour. Has the Tylenol dulled the pain any?"

"Yes," Stanley admitted, then protested, "but Aleta is..."

"We don't intend to wake her," Lyle stated, as if declaring his intentions was all that was needed. "Now do whatever you need to, to disengage her so Jamara can get to work."

"Lyle, you're overstepping the bounds."

"What bounds?"

"Whatever bounds of decency there are."

"Oh, those," Lyle said casually. "You have an appointment with Justin and his cameraman at Willow Glen Station at eight. Justin has a deadline."

"I thought you were joking."

Lyle raised an eyebrow.

Stanley retracted his statement.

"Okay, so I knew you were serious, but I don't have any clothes here."

"Jamara, let me help you move these beds apart," Lyle offered.

"You will wake her" Stanley protested.

"Either get her to let go or give up a piece of your anatomy," Lyle quipped.

Stanley reached under the sheet and tapped Aleta's hand.

"Time to move your hand," he whispered.

To his surprise she released her hold. He took her hand and set it on top of her other one. The beds were rolled apart, Jamara drew the curtain and Stanley found himself being rolled up. He was handed a toothbrush, toothpaste, water and a basin. His electric razor was laid on the night stand.

Jamara placed towels at the foot of the bed and Lyle laid Stanley's clothes out on a nearby chair.

As she was preparing to bathe him, Stanley realized he wouldn't be taking a shower for a while. Minus one leg, with one injured hand and an injury to his midsection he couldn't manage on his own and he couldn't be helped by Paul as before.

He sighed heavily as Jamara rolled down his bed. "Sorry, I've been such a schmuck about being bathed."

"You be a private man. It be hard for you," Jamara said, and then observed, "You need clean hair today."

"It would be nice," Stanley responded.

"It might hurt your side a bit," she cautioned.

"Let's give it a shot," Stanley decided.

When she finished, he said, "Thanks for today. I think we can skip this part tomorrow."

Jamara smiled at him. "You be the boss."

Stanley returned her smile. "Tell me how your children feel about your job these days."

"Oh, they be liking this part."

"An emergency that calls for a nurse?"

"That be it."

"We won't mention the bath part, right?"

"They be too young."

Shortly afterward Lyle rolled in a hospital wheelchair.

"I can't go anywhere in that!" Stanley fussed.

"Sure you can. We'll push you," Lyle stated.

"A body guard can't push a wheelchair," Stanley groused.

"You want two body guards?" Lyle asked tongue-in-cheek.

"I want a motorized chair," Stanley declared, not noticing that Lyle and Jamara exchanged knowing glances.

"Can you drive one?"

"It's not a car."

"There will be pedestrians in your way."

"I'll honk."

"It doesn't have a horn."

"What doesn't have a horn."

"Your new wheelchair."

"When did I buy a wheelchair?"

"Last night after you went to sleep."

"What else did I do last night?"

"Well, you took my advice," Lyle commented.

"How do you know?"

"You're cranky. That means you're in pain," Lyle returned. "That means you told Aleta not to heal you."

"She be in God's service," Jamara cut in. "Ain't right you be telling her what to do."

"Don't fret, Jamara," Stanley said. "I can lay down all the rules I want, but ultimately, Aleta listens to God, not me."

The two helped Stanley move from his bed to the motorized chair.

"You look good!" Lyle said.

"Good? Missing a leg, one arm in a sling..."

"The sling is a nice touch," Lyle cut in.

"It's not a touch!"

"Boy you are really cranky!"

"I think I made a mistake not opting for the codeine drip. I should have just laid in bed with no pain for a couple of days."

"Then there would be no story!"

"You and your story!" Stanley snapped.

Lyle's face was suddenly solemn.

"I am trying to keep you from further attack," he said. "We can still return you to bed and get that codeine drip set up."

"And waste Jamara's hard work making me presentable?"

"Be nice to Justin and anyone else who's there."

"Who else is going to be there?"

"I did promise you had made a break through," Lyle admitted.

"You mean reveal that we're chasing a woman?" Stanley asked aghast.

Jamara gasped.

"You can't be funning around with this," Jamara chided, scowling. "Girls needs to know the truth"

"Exactly my reason," Lyle said. "We sat on this all weekend and we're nowhere."

"I will sound crazy," Stanley complained.

"Better you than me."

"No, not better me," Stanley objected. "I need my reputation."

Lyle pinned Stanley's badge on his coat which hung loosely over his left shoulder, its arm empty.

"Time to go. You're on the clock."

Stanley fiddled with the controls, backing the chair, turning it and stopping it, then commented. "You do remember you weren't going to use me during my work day."

"But I'm not. You're on sick leave from your job. No one expects you to work the rest of the week."

"I am supposed to be recovering," Stanley pointed out.

"What's so exhausting about sitting in a room interviewing?" Lyle said.

Suddenly, Stanley's eyes brightened and he began to laugh. "You don't have Cook's permission, do you? That's why the early morning interview."

"Let's just say I am assuming he'll be okay with this."

"You know he won't," Stanley said. "Let's hurry. He sometimes arrives early."

Chapter 18

Aleta woke a little before noon when Dr. Cook took her wrist to feel her pulse. She looked over at the other bed. It had been remade and was empty.

"Everyone was worried about where you were."

Aleta pointed at the other bed.

"Stanley left at seven-forty-five this morning according to Jamara's note."

Aleta raised an eyebrow.

"He didn't tell you not to speak, did he?"

Aleta nodded.

"I didn't sign him out. Chief Lyle West snuck him out. He's been on the news all morning," Dr. Cook reported.

Aleta tapped her wrist.

"It's almost noon. I was hoping to use you to interpret for me. I have an accident victim who's very agitated. No one can understand her. The driver of the car died."

Aleta wrote in the air.

"Yes, of course. You can write!" Dr. Cook exclaimed.

He handed Aleta a large metal thermos.

"Bertha sent this over."

Aleta took it warily.

"She said to tell you it has no liver in it."

Aleta sighed with relief.

"You are her boss, aren't you?"

Aleta waggled one hand as she began to drink.

"Sometimes?" Dr. Cook queried.

Aleta affirmed his guess with a nod, then pointed at the shake.

"She can tell you what to eat?"

Aleta nodded and patted her stomach.

"She pulled rank on you, huh?"

Aleta smiled.

After she dressed, Aleta followed Dr. Cook to the Emergency Department.

The woman in the hospital bed was barely thirty. She had dark hair and eyes and unintelligible words poured out of her mouth non-stop.

Aleta was introduced as someone who could interpret speech when others couldn't. The woman kept talking.

Aleta wrote, "She doesn't understand English."

"What does she speak?"

"Greek," Aleta wrote.

"How do you know that?" Dr. Cook asked.

Aleta shrugged.

"Do you know what she's saying?"

Aleta wrote a name and address and handed it to Dr. Cook.

"A relative?"

Aleta nodded, and then wrote, "She's pregnant."

Dr. Cook shook his head. The woman burst into tears. Aleta came over and put her hands on dark-eyed woman's stomach.

The woman grew wide-eyed. Aleta realized abruptly what she was doing. She understood now why Stanley had forbidden her to heal him. She had rushed forward with no thought as to the consequences.

The woman uttered a cry of surprise. Aleta withdrew quickly. Dr. Cook put a stethoscope on her stomach, listened and then nodded.

A string of Greek words poured forth.

Aleta ran from the room. Her guard, caught by surprise had to double-time it to catch up.

He took her home.

When Aleta walked in the door, Bertha met her and her face went from eagerness to share Stanley's appearance on television to concern.

"What's wrong?"

Jamara looked up from nursing Gerard. She had gone straight from the hospital to the house, told Bertha about Lyle's plans to use Stanley to generate new leads in the co-ed murders and shared her opinion that Lyle had more in mind than an interview with a reporter for the local paper. So the two women had turned the two television sets in the house to different news channels with a tape in each ready to record. They were rewarded for their foresight and discussed at length not only how well turned out Stanley was, but also what an agreeable manner he exhibited as well as his persuasive and logical presentation of the facts.

"He be really good," Jamara commented after the first interview. "He done pulled hisself together."

"Was he out of sorts this morning?" Bertha asked.

"He be snapping at the police chief the whole time."

"Chief West?"

"That be the one."

"What did Aleta say?"

"She be sleeping the whole time."

"That doesn't sound right," Bertha commented upon hearing that.

Her worry had prompted her to check with the hospital. She sent over a shake to press Dr. Cook into checking on Aleta. It had worked. She was here. Only she was in distress.

When Aleta didn't respond to her opening question, Bertha guessed, "He's done that silence thing again."

Aleta nodded, burst into tears and ran into her bedroom. Bertha sought out the officer that had driven her home.

"All I know is she visited a patient with Dr. Cook. I stood outside so I didn't hear much. First there was a lot of jabber, then crying and screaming, then happy shouts. Then Mrs. Praetzel ran out of that room as fast as she could go. Boy, that lady can run!"

Bertha called Harriet.

"We're practically at your drive. We were coming over to check on Keeper and the pups before we left on our hunting trip," Harriet responded over her cell. "Meet me out front. Keeper won't let us talk if I come into the house."

Bertha was waiting outside the front door. As soon as she could, she poured out her concerns and questions.

"Stanley did that silence thing again. He must have done it last night because Jamara told me she was sound asleep when Stanley left with Chief West. She slept through his complaining about everything while he was being dressed."

"He would resent that," Harriet remarked.

"I know," Bertha said, "But he seemed to have shaken that off. He looked great on television. It's Aleta I'm worried about."

"Take Keeper for a walk so I can talk with Aleta in peace."

"She doesn't like to leave her pups."

"I know. Just give me time to get into the bedroom."

A few minutes later, Harriet entered the bedroom. Aleta threw her arms around her grandmother and cried on her shoulder.

Harriet took a wild stab at the problem.

"You did something terrible to one of Dr. Cook's patients?"

Aleta shook her head.

"Well, then let's sit down and talk," Harriet suggested, "Although Stanley pretty much put a crimp on that, didn't he?"

Aleta nodded and then signaled her grandmother to wait. She hurried into the study and fetched her laptop. She returned, sat on the edge of the bed and began to type. Harriet sat beside her.

"Lyle told me that the stabbing of Stanley was a warning to me to cease all activity," she typed.

"You think she thinks you will prophesy about a murder and interfere?"

Aleta nodded.

"I won't risk Stanley's life," Aleta declared.

"You're bowing to blackmail," Harriet declared bluntly. "Stanley was just on television telling the world he can't be intimidated."

She left the conclusion of her thought unspoken.

"I am not Stanley," Aleta typed. "I am not so brave."

Harriet put her hand on her granddaughter's arm. "You've healed someone else, haven't you?"

Aleta nodded then typed. "I want out of the limelight."

"That is a wise choice at this time."

Aleta typed rapidly. "Stanley has forbidden me to heal either of his stab wounds. He says he's too visible right now."

"The stab wounds are minor."

"He is battling cancer, isn't he?" Aleta wrote. "I wasn't just healing his leg, was I?"

"You need to rest until he comes home," Harriet said. "Saving that baby drained you."

"How did you know I saved a baby?" Aleta wrote.

"I just knew," her grandmother responded.

Harriet took the lap top from her and called Bertha in. "Aleta is going to rest until supper. She needs something to eat first."

"A liver shake?" Bertha asked.

Aleta looked so woebegone, Bertha decided teasing wasn't appropriate.

"Or I could fix you an omelet with all your favorite toppings."

Aleta nodded her head vigorously.

"Take a shower," Bertha said, "otherwise you'll fall asleep before it's made."

Aleta nodded. She headed for the shower.

Bertha laid out her pajamas and then went to the kitchen.

Harriet couldn't help herself. She had to see the litter. Claude found her a few moments later. She was examining the pups.

"Which one is mine?" Claude asked.

"One of the boys," Harriet said.

"I already know that, but which one?"

"The one with the purple ribbon," Harriet said. "Aleta, Lauren and Beatrice agree that he's the pick."

"What do you think?"

"That they each have a good eye."

"They look alike to me."

"Hold out your hand," Harriet said.

Claude found himself holding the puppies one by one. First, he thought he was being told the biggest one was best, but it was something else.

"Substance," Harriet said. "That's what we're looking for."

"When can we take them home?" Claude asked.

"You can't wait, can you?"

"No."

"When they're three weeks old. I don't want to disturb Keeper's routine until they're ready to start on solid food."

"She's a paint-a-holic," Paul interjected. "She loves it in here. And she's nice company."

"Since you're taking such a keen interest in nursing mothers..." Harriet began.

She stopped when Paul eyed her coolly.

"Yes, I understand. They aren't human," she said, obviously discomfited.

She straightened up, "We will be back in plenty of time for your show."

Paul smiled. "I know you will, Mother."

"Will you have many pieces finished?"

"Once Paige suggested I could show work in progress, I finished several. She removed an inhibition I didn't even know I had. I kept thinking I had to finish certain ones. She freed me to finish the ones I was in the mood to work on."

"Do all artists work on so many at once?" his mother asked.

"I don't think there's a rule. I sketch when I see something that excites me. I grab at every inspiration."

His mother looked around. "Whatever your method, it's working."

"Bring us back a couple of ducks, Mother," Paul said. "Andrea and I are fond of duck."

Claude looked up. "Are we ready then?"

"Give me twenty minutes."

"I will air Stoney."

"See if Hubbs wants a duck to fix for Bessie."

Twenty minutes later, Harriet bid Bertha goodbye.

"I will have the ducks dressed in the field," Harriet said as she hugged Bertha good bye.

"I rather enjoy the task."

Harried chuckled.

"Okay, I'll bring yours back complete with feathers, beaks and feet.

"Never mind. You're right. I really won't have the time." Bertha said. "For a moment I forgot how bad off Stanley is. Jamara said he bit Lyle's head off repeatedly."

"Lyle's so glad Stanley's alive, he will take anything Stanley dishes out."

"Stanley looked good on television" Bertha said. "He was so persuasive when he explained his theory that I believed it totally."

"That took some doing," Harriet returned. "No one thinks of a woman as being capable of such cruelty."

"He has a good mind," Bertha said. "That came through all this intact."

"He will take care of Aleta. You take care of him."

"Jamara has that task. He's more or less assigned the work to her."

"So you'll have nothing to do then?" Harriet quipped with a twinkle in her eye.

"I packed you a lunch," Bertha said. "Claude has it in the RV."

"You put food in with my husband and dog?" Harriet exclaimed, openly unsettled.

This time it was Bertha who had a twinkle in her eye. "Better hurry or that nothing I am doing will disappear."

As Claude drove down the driveway, he said, "Harriet, you know I don't want you worrying the whole trip."

"I won't," Harriet said. "Stanley will watch over Aleta; Jamara will nurse Stanley; and Lyle and Tom will protect both of them."

"So you don't sense any trouble?" he queried.

"None," Harriet predicted.

That prediction lasted barely four hours.

Chapter 19

The interview with the Greek woman made the five o'clock news. Jamara was the only one in the house who saw it. She pushed the record button the second she heard Aleta's name.

She thought it was an interesting story and switched channels to tape another slightly different report.

"You needs to watch this," Jamara mentioned to Bertha.

Bertha was watching the report when Tank, Scooby and Harriet's two female Chessies began to bark. Bertha immediately perceived that there were people on the grounds. She ran to the master bedroom, charged in and drew the drapes just as a man with a camera snapped a shot through the window.

She glanced at the two lying in the bed. He didn't catch them in an intimate pose or without clothes.

The dogs continued barking furiously.

Paul emerged from his studio as television vans invaded the area around the house, ignoring the two guards at the front gate.

Bertha began to bark orders.

Jamara took Gerard to the nursery.

Keeper stood in her whelping box barking. Paul closed the gate securing the entrance to the family room and keeping Keeper inside the room. Bertha put Tank in with Stanley and Aleta. Scooby was assigned the nursery with Jamara.

Paul bolted the back door which led to the laundry room. King barked at someone lurking outside the guest bedroom and he was closed in that room.

Sirens were heard in a distance.

In the bedroom, Stanley woke up when Tank licked his face. The barking dogs, approaching sirens and closed drapes told him his privacy was being invaded and Bertha had tried to protect him.

A soft knock on the door was followed by a key in the lock. Chief West entered.

"There's been a development," he said. "Evidently, Aleta saved the unborn fetus of an accident victim at noon today. Dr. Cook couldn't understand one of the victims who speaks only Greek. The family heard her story and called the news media. They wanted to thank Aleta publically for saving the baby."

"How do we handle this?" Stanley asked.

"It's your call. It's your life."

Stanley looked over at his sleeping wife. "That's why she's sleeping so soundly. This morning's encounter depleted her."

Aleta opened her eyes.

Both men looked at her. She reached for a pad of paper and a pen on her night stand.

"Dress Stanley," she wrote. "I want him with me."

"You aren't going out there!" Stanley declared.

Aleta picked up the pile of casual clothes Bertha had laid out for her and disappeared into the bathroom.

Lyle radioed Chief Milani. "Aleta will have a statement in twenty minutes. Get the crowd under control or I am not letting her come out."

The three in the master bedroom could hear Chief
Milani bellowing through the bull horn.

Chief Lyle West fetched Jamara so she might help
Stanley dress which suited him perfectly. Jamara was very
careful of his wounded side and hand which were hurting
again.

Stanley was surprised Aleta wanted him with her. All
she had to do was ask him to release her from her vow or
write answers to the reporter's questions and have Lyle read
them. He didn't want to be redressed plopped in his
wheelchair and paraded out to be seen on television as his
wife's lackey.

Aleta, however, hadn't consulted him. She had taken
charge.

Strange, he thought, she would keep her promise to
obey him and not speak, and yet he knew that he had
relinquished the leadership role to her. It bothered him that
Lyle had witnessed it this time. It hadn't bothered him
before. Today it did.

He wanted time alone with his wife to tell her how he
felt.

Aleta breezed out of the bathroom dressed in jeans
and a simple pullover sweater. As usual she wore no make-
up.

"What took you so long?" he scolded. "I want to talk
with you about this."

"Can you drive that thing?" Aleta wrote.

"Yes," he replied. "But Aleta, I want to talk about
this."

She scribbled, "Why?"

"We can't face a bevy of reporters with no plan?"
Stanley proclaimed.

"You protect me," Aleta wrote.

"Protect you?" Stanley gasped. "How?"

"You're the chess master," Aleta wrote.

Then she put down her pad and pencil and strode to
the front door.

Stanley moved the lever that propelled the wheelchair forward. She held the door open for him. When he exited, Aleta put her hand lightly on his shoulder and he moved down the path to the picnic area. The TV crews scrambled to follow. When Stanley turned around, there was a jockeying for position among the cameramen.

Several reporters shouted questions.

Aleta stood silent. Confused, the reporters quieted.

"Gentlemen," Stanley said. "My wife cannot speak. If you will check with the accident victim whom she visited at noon today, she will tell you that my wife never spoke to her."

Justin was the first to affirm that.

"That's true. But, Mrs. Praetzel, did you restore her dead baby to life?"

Aleta shook her head.

A murmur of disbelief and anger swept through the crowd.

Stanley held up his hand and spoke, "Give me one minute and then ask your questions."

"One minute," Justin thundered.

The crowd quieted.

"Didn't Dr. Cook take you to a woman's bedside because no one could understand her speech?" Stanley asked.

Aleta nodded.

"Did he tell you she was pregnant?"

Aleta shook her head.

The crowd stayed still. He was not avoiding the issue.

"Did you tell Dr. Cook she was pregnant?"

Aleta nodded.

The press leaned forward, eager not to miss a word.

"She told you?"

Again Aleta nodded.

"According to the woman, Mrs. Antonopolous, Dr. Cook shook his head indicating that the baby was dead or was dying, correct?"

Aleta nodded. The crowd breathed a sigh of satisfaction.

"You then placed your hands on her stomach?"

Aleta nodded.

"Mrs. Antonopolous shouted something about the baby moving and you ran from the room."

Again Aleta nodded.

"Do you believe God healed that baby?"

Aleta nodded.

"Did you pray for the baby to be healed?"

Aleta shook her head.

"That's a lie!" A reporter shouted. "You were there. You put your hand on the woman's stomach, and the baby was healed."

Owen Haggard was a brash young reporter from a popular local TV news station.

More voices joined his. Questions poured out of angry mouths. Stanley tried to speak but went unheard as the anger of the crowd increased.

The sound of a gunshot ripped through the tumult commanding silence. It was obeyed.

"Stop acting like children." Stanley scolded. "Children who think they're being lied to when, in fact, they are being told the truth. I was not there. You were not there. All we have is the word of the two women who were there. So let's find out the whole truth, shall we?"

The crowd muttered its reluctant approval for Stanley to continue.

Aleta nodded.

"Did Dr. Cook do anything as far as you could tell?"

Aleta shook her head.

"What about Mrs. Antonopolous?"

Aleta shrugged.

"She might have prayed?"

Aleta nodded.

"And you placed your hands on Mrs. Antonopolous' stomach. Wasn't that a rather odd thing to do if you didn't believe you had some ability to help?"

"Yes! Answer that!" The brash reporter shouted.

Aleta shrugged.

"You are a prophet, are you not?" Stanley asked.

The crowd told Haggard to shut up.

Aleta nodded.

"You don't generate the visions. You simply receive them, correct?"

Aleta's nod was more definite.

"In the case of Mrs. Antonopolous' baby, you were the recipient of the healing power. In other words, God healed, not you."

Aleta nodded with a definiteness that spoke volumes.

"Can you heal anytime you want to?"

Aleta shook her head.

"Even if you wanted to very much."

Aleta affirmed that.

Stanley looked straight into the camera. "I know this is going to be difficult for most people to believe. But, first I am going to present a logical argument and then I am going to prove it."

Stanley heard the gasps from those who were not reporters. The reporters were raising their brows in query, which was more of a challenge than a question. Disbelief was the standard expression on the faces of those taking notes or focusing a camera.

"First," Stanley said, lifting his left knee, "You will notice I'm missing half a leg. Bone cancer. Don't you think I would have begged my wife to heal me? Don't you think she would have done it if she could?"

"Maybe you needed to pray," came a voice from the crowd. "Mrs. Antonopolous did."

Stanley smiled. "Oh, I prayed. Day and night for weeks. I am still praying."

The crowd grew silent.

"People are murdered every day, some right here in this town. The prophets only predict some of them. God chooses which they can forecast. They are surprised and dismayed when other people living here are murdered."

"Let's get on with it!" Owen Haggard barked. "Prove she can't heal."

"That won't do any good," someone else countered. "She will just not try."

"I have taken that into account," Stanley said.

"How?" shouted someone.

"If you'll all be patient and give me a moment to set the stage, you'll see."

"Set the stage?" Owen Haggard scoffed. "We don't want a production. Do it now without any so-called stage setting."

"I need a nurse to remove the bandage on my hand. The wound hurts like hell. I am guessing it's badly infected." Stanley said, turning to Chief Milani. "Tell Jamara I need her."

"This is a bunch of crap," Owen Haggard groused, pulling his knife from his pocket and opening it.

Several TV cameras followed Haggard's cameraman and focused on Haggard. Stanley, meanwhile was watching the door, expecting Jamara.

Suddenly, Haggard grabbed Stanley's hand, slipped the knife under the bandage and pulled. Stanley's shriek of pain electrified his audience.

"Haggard!" Justin shouted. "Are you nuts! He was stabbed in that hand last night!"

Owen Haggard stepped away, suddenly realizing that the rival news stations would have a field day with his heartlessness.

He hissed at his cameraman. "I want a close up of that wound. I want to be able to show that it's fake! You got me!"

Jamara was summoned and she emerged with a tray with medical supplies and sharp scissors. She set the tray down on the barbeque grill that Stanley was positioned near and began to cut away the bandage.

TV cameramen climbed up on picnic tables and used their zoom lenses to capture the process. Jamara gently laid back the bandage and gasped.

"It be infected!" she exclaimed.

The hand was swollen and red, the black stitches pulled taut. Red striations were evident halfway to his elbow.

Chief West called Dr. Cook on his private line and quietly explained the situation, adding, "If one wound is infected, won't they both be?"

He leaned over and whispered to Stanley, "Dr. Cook is on his way."

Aleta, meanwhile, was staring at Stanley's hand, tears streaming down her face.

Stanley held up his injured hand and bid Aleta take it.

She put one hand beneath his and he rested his hand on hers lightly. He grimaced as his hand met hers.

"Can God take away the pain?" Stanley asked.

Aleta nodded.

"Ask Him."

Aleta bowed her head.

"Pray so we can all hear," Stanley ordered.

Aleta spoke softly, "Please, don't hurt him. Thy will be done."

"That's not a proper prayer!" Owen Haggard yelled. "She's supposed to tell God to heal the hand."

Justin was the first to laugh.

"Tell God?" he questioned Haggard.

"Okay, not tell. But ask. She didn't ask." Haggard said. "And she didn't touch his hand. She needs to touch his hand."

"His hand is touching hers," Justin noted.

"But she's not touching his," Haggard claimed. "She needs to touch it."

Justin focused on Stanley, "Does she touch when she heals?"

Stanley was caught.

"Yes," he replied simply.

"Touch him!" Owen Haggard demanded. "I dare you."

Aleta shook her head.

"Why is she refusing?" Haggard demanded. "You said you'd give us proof. Her shaking her head isn't proof."

"Okay, Aleta. Repeat your prayer, and this time, touch my hand on the top," Stanley said. "Only please don't hurt me."

Aleta bowed her head and then stretched out her hand and touched Stanley's hand.

Owen Haggard couldn't resist the temptation to ascertain if there was a ray of energy coming from the sky like a lightning bolt. He waved his hand underneath Stanley's. The sensation of being stabbed caused both men to yell and instantaneously withdraw their hands.

"She stabbed me!" Haggard screeched.

Several cameras focused on Haggard's hand which showed no evidence of a wound of any kind. Other cameras stayed fixed on Stanley whose left hand was squeezing his right wrist as if to stay the pain.

Seconds later, all swung over to Aleta as she withdrew, her shocked expression proving to be the most convincing evidence of all. She could heal, but only if God wanted it.

She sank to the ground weeping.

Stanley was doubled over in agony. He couldn't speak. He couldn't move. He didn't dare let go of his own arm for fear the pain would escalate.

Lyle reached over and moved the lever that backed up the motorized wheelchair. Tom helped Aleta up and led her back to the house. Lyle followed with Stanley.

Dr. Cook drove straight up to the house, weaving around news vans, cars and trucks. Police were everywhere. He recognized units from Arborville as well as Willow Glen.

Chief West opened the door, ushered Dr. Cook in and pointed to the bedroom. Aleta was huddled on the couch weeping on Bertha's shoulder.

Dr. Cook took one look at her and hurried even faster into the bedroom. Jamara had only just begun to help Stanley change. She had removed his shirt by cutting it off. He wouldn't loosen the grip he had on his right arm.

"What in the world happened?" Dr. Cook asked.

"You aren't going to tell me I should have opted for the morphine drip, are you?" Stanley grunted.

"I wasn't planning to," Dr. Cook said kindly.

He took the arm and gently turned it.

"Bad, isn't it?" Stanley queried.

"You appear to be in more pain than you should be." Dr. Cook commented. "Did you fall on the hand or hit it against something?"

Stanley shook his head.

"The pain, Doctor, can you do anything for it?"

"Yes, but you need to stay in bed," Dr. Cook said. "You will be too dizzy to navigate, especially on one leg with one arm in a sling and an injured side."

"I am done being the hero," Stanley said. "Just make the pain stop."

And he did.

Chapter 20

When Aleta woke up the following morning, she rolled over and kissed her husband and announced she was taking the week off.

"You can't," he said. "I have a nine o'clock you need to take. We're hiring Kay Rivers. Dad set it up."

Aleta screwed up her face.

"I can't. Dad can hire her."

"We aren't folding under pressure."

"I already did."

"Get dressed," Stanley said. "You're going to work."

Aleta didn't move.

"Stanley, I can't face people yet."

"What do you think you did that was so bad?"

"I broke down and cried. Who wants a lawyer who folds like that under pressure?"

"Who wants a lawyer with a heart so big it burst when she inadvertently hurt her husband? I'll tell you who. Everyone," Stanley proclaimed vociferously. "Aleta, you weren't a wimp. You were a woman who had no power to heal put in a position where you wanted to do that with all your heart. Aleta, you honored me and now you are going to honor God."

She pushed herself upon one elbow.

"By going to work?" she asked, utterly confused.

"Staying home might send the message that you are upset because your power failed you on national television."

"I have no power," Aleta said.

"Exactly!" Stanley declared. "That's why you're going to work. You said you had no power. God proved your claim."

Aleta frowned.

"That's what I don't understand," Aleta said, confused. "You got hurt. God doesn't hurt people, but He hurt you."

"I wasn't expecting it. I can't explain that."

"I need it explained," Aleta insisted. "I was praying the whole time."

"So was I," Stanley said.

"That's not something you do," Aleta charged.

"I needed help," Stanley admitted.

"Were you praying for me not to heal you?"

"I was hoping for that. I was praying for guidance and help."

"Just that?"

"I am sure my heart had a few more requests that piggybacked onto that prayer. I wanted the pain to go away. And I wanted somehow to punch out that smart aleck reporter Owen Haggard."

Aleta chuckled. "I wonder if his hand still hurts."

"Are you ready to get dressed now?"

"I was looking forward to a lazy day in bed with you."

"Give Kay a couple good cases. Make her feel welcome," Stanley said. "Don't accept too many cases. I won't be returning to work for several days, although I must admit that I am feeling pretty good. I wonder what Dr. Cook gave me in that shot."

"Something to give you a good night's sleep so the antibiotic would have a chance to kill the infection," Aleta responded. "And he said you would be out for at least a week. Second, I don't take cases for you. Third there won't be a line unless it's a line of people wanting me to cure them."

"I am feeling much better, thank you," Stanley said.

"I know you are," Aleta affirmed, smiling. "But you aren't well."

A little before nine, Aleta took the elevator to the second floor. The line of people stretched out into the street.

"Didn't Tim weed out anyone?" Aleta asked Alice. "I have a nine o'clock appointment with Kay Rivers."

"I had her fill out the forms," Alice said. "She arrived at eight-thirty. Was I presumptuous? She had this note from Mr. Praetzel."

"A note from Stanley?" Aleta asked, puzzled.

"His father. She was told you had the final say, but..." Alice stammered.

"Oh, Alice, you will never get in trouble obeying a directive from Stanley or either of his parents."

"Yes, Ma'am," Alice said. "And Tim already sent home a bunch of people."

"Have Kay and Tim join me in my office," Aleta ordered. "We're going to walk the line."

Five minutes later, Kay Rivers and Tim Jordan accompanied Aleta as she greeted the people standing in line.

She glanced at the people and turned to Kay. "The woman with the child is yours. Give her this card and have her see Alice for an appointment time. Alice will have her fill out a data sheet. Your earliest appointment will be ten. After you send them to Alice, rejoin me."

"Am I hired then?"

"You will be by ten," Aleta said. "Ten percent over what you were earning at your former firm."

"That is acceptable," Kay said formally.

"If it's too low, I will raise it later." Aleta said.

"And if it's higher than any other associate?" Kay asked.

Aleta smiled impishly. Kay realized she probably knew exactly what she had been making. What Kay didn't know was what Praetzel, Locke and Praetzel Associates made.

"Thank you for hiring me," Kay said.

"Thank you for applying," Aleta returned. "We need you, but not as a criminal lawyer. We don't take criminal cases."

Aleta turned to Tim. "Give the first old man in line one of Roland Chin's cards. Write emergency on it. Give the second old man in line one of Nigel Oliver's cards. Not an emergency."

The two broke away from Aleta and the three she singled out made their way to the front desk. Aleta, meanwhile, told the next three that she wasn't interested in their cases. All three protested, but Aleta moved on. When Tim returned, the three turned to him.

"I am sorry," he told each in turn. "Mrs. Praetzel has the final say."

By the time Tim and Kay caught up to Aleta, she had dismissed two more cases.

Kay wondered if she was going to accept any more cases as she rejected three more with the simple words, "I'm not interested."

Tim's job seemed to be one of soothing ruffed feelings and quickly dispatching those who'd been rejected. Aleta looked down the group on the stairs.

"Tim," she said. "Have that old woman with the cane at the bottom of the stairs use the elevator and give her Oliver's card. Dismiss the woman in the wheelchair who's behind her. Tell her I can't make her walk."

"She said she had a legal problem," Tim said.

"She has money," Aleta said. "She's not waiting in line for legal help. Send the old man behind her to Oliver."

She turned to the next person in line.

"Divorce?" she asked.

"Custody," he replied.

"Tricky?" Aleta asked.

"Very."

"Were you hoping to enlist the services of Mr. Praetzel?"

"Yes."

"Why did you wait in line?"

"I knew he was sick and I figured anyone on his staff would be good."

Mr. Praetzel will be back next week; however, he has a home office, so he might be able to talk with you before then. In fact, tell Alice that I recommend that she see how soon he can see you. Mr. Praetzel cleared his calendar in advance of his surgery so he has time to take on a complicated case right now."

She handed him Stanley's card.

Then she turned to the next man in line. He was a sixty-year-old black man dressed in a worn suit.

"Your case interests me," Aleta said.

"It's not so important as the others," the man said politely. "I only need a little advice."

"It's important enough for you to stand in this line," Aleta said kindly. "Tell Alice your appointment with me is at ten today. She will have papers for you to fill out. There will be no charge for the initial consultation."

"Thank you," the man said fingering the card. "If I need more legal help, maybe we can exchange services."

"I think that will be to our mutual advantage."

"You don't know what I do," the man said.

"You're a farrier," Aleta said. "Hubbs says you're the best in the business."

Aleta rejected four more with a cursory "Not interested", and Tim escorted them out. By now Kay's mind was brimming with questions. Aleta had listened to only a word or two before deciding which clients to accept.

Kay's puzzlement must have been obvious because Aleta said, "I sense triviality without a lengthy interview. I also sense an underlying evil purpose. And some of them are people I just don't like."

"Aren't you afraid of turning away someone who needs a lawyer."

"We aren't the only lawyers in town."

"You aren't afraid people will stop coming?" Kay ventured. "You turn away so many."

"We give good service and we always take referrals."

"I think I'm worrying about my own security."

"We already have enough cases to keep us all, including you, busy until the end of the year. We have two huge clients that will send us as much work as we want."

"Why do you accept every old person that comes?"

"Seniors need help."

"I can help with them," Kay offered.

"You will be too busy," Aleta said. "You are about to be assigned three new cases."

"Really? How do you know?"

"I like the next three people in line," Aleta said.

"That's it?" Kay asked. "You don't know what kind of cases they have."

Aleta grinned. "It's the way it's done here."

"What do I do?"

"You escort your three clients to Alice's desk. She will guide you from there."

"Do I have an office?" Kay asked.

"Alice will show you around while your clients are filling out forms. Alice is very organized."

"My contract?"

"Alice will have that factored I," Aleta commented. "I am available any time I am not with a client."

With Tim trailing behind, Aleta excused the next five people without hearing more than a few sentences from each one. She stopped at an older man.

"Thought you'd ship me off to one of them staff people you got handling old folk."

"Only ordinary old folk go there," Aleta said. "I take the special ones. Dr. Schwartzmann sent you, didn't he?"

"How'd you know?"

"You carry his mark."

"Mark? What mark?"

"Self-assurance. Sense of humor. Intelligence."

"Whoa! Where'd you get that?"

"Dr. Schwartzmann wouldn't send me a client without some of those traits. Your first words told me you had all of them." Aleta said, handing him her card with instructions to give it to Alice.

"Do I get a rate?"

Aleta raised a brow.

"Oh, okay! Herve said not to fool around, but God knows you don't need the money."

"Doesn't Herve know anyone who isn't tightfisted?"

The old man grinned.

"We run in packs."

"Apparently."

Aleta picked out two more cases for Kay and sent the rest away.

At ten o'clock LaVerne Brown was shown into Aleta's office.

"I'm sorry you had to wait," she said to the sixty-year-old black man whose hands were those of a laborer and whose well-worn suit attested to the fact that he was well-muscled.

"My beef is a small one. I hear you got two fine Afro-American lawyers working here."

"Yes, we do. And we have two of mixed blood as well."

"Anyone of those be fine," he said politely.

"Good," Aleta said. "Now tell me your problem."

"So I don't get none of those?"

"You got the best one of those—according to my husband, at least. Of course, he's pretty prejudiced."

LaVerne laughed, "You got me."

Aleta chuckled. "I think it's the other way around."

"I got serious problems with vandals at my place. It used to be just once in a while, but no more. Now it happens too much."

"What did the police do?"

LaVerne smiled. "You're right. I called them each time, and they caught them couple of times. The judge let them off with some community service."

"So what do you want?"

"I want them to stop mostly," LaVerne explained. "They don't steal nothing big. Little stuff. Batteries from the remote. The electrical cord from the microwave. Bulbs from all the lamps. Stuff like that."

"What else?"

"They make a mess," LaVerne said, digging in his pants pocket.

"The cops gimme copies of pictures they took. They don't like this no more than me."

He shoved the pictures across the desk. The floor in the living room was littered with books, DVD's, magazines and newspapers with paint splattered on everything.

"They ruined your stuff!" Aleta exclaimed. "Did you get any compensation?"

"Some. But it was a hassle. I want it to stop."

"The cops who respond to your call--are they the same ones?"

"Pretty much. Why?"

"I have an idea," Aleta said. "You live in Oakwood, right?"

"The cops do work at tracking down the kids," LaVerne was quick to explain. "The chief came out time before last. They took fingerprints and everything. He promised they'd catch them and he did. The judge let the boys off with community service. It's a new bunch each time."

"We need to make it too expensive a prank. We need more teeth in the punishment."

"Jail time?"

"No. More creative community service," Aleta said. "And maybe a little peer pressure."

"How are you going to do that?"

"I need to set it up first," Aleta said. "Give me the rest of the day. Meanwhile, I'm going to ask the chief to post a man at your house."

"That's pretty heavy."

"You do understand why, don't you?"

"So they won't bother me?"

"Partly," Aleta replied. "Mostly to set the next boys up. It may take two or three times to get the lesson across. But I think you'll be happy with the results."

"Um," LaVerne hesitated.

When Aleta waited for him to speak, he did so.

"I hate to say this, but you could make it worse for me if you go too far. The dads all see this as a harmless prank. If you come down too hard on their kids, they'll go after me personal."

"I intend to walk that tight rope with you and have neither of us fall off," Aleta said. "I intend to use white power to stomp out this budding racial hatred."

"Not black power?"

"A Swedish study showed that when the white community found prejudicial acts against blacks unacceptable, they pretty much wiped them out."

"No violence?"

"None," Aleta promised. "We want people to disapprove of what is happening to you."

"You gonna tell me your plans."

"If you can wait a bit longer, you can be in on my conference with Chief Peets," Aleta said. "At this office, we serve lunch if you're here at noon—roast beef sandwiches."

"I got a horse shoeing appointment at eleven."

"Come back at noon for lunch. We will eat and talk."

"Do I tell the lady at the front desk?"

"Yes. If you want something other than roast beef, she'll order it. It's free."

Alta answered her intercom as Brown was leaving. Alice told her Kay Rivers wanted to see her and Mrs. Cook was coming over at noon."

Brown hesitated at the door, closing it slowly.

"Call Martha Cook back, Alice. 11:30. Take her lunch order. Mr. Brown has a twelve o'clock appointment with me. And send Kay in."

LaVerne Brown closed the door the rest of the way. He approached Alice smiling.

"Mrs. Praetzel said I could order from the menu," he said.

"Anything you like," Alice said, handing him the menu.

"This is from Alfredo's," he commented.

"That's who does our lunches," Alice said.

"I hear he has great lasagna. Can I order that?"

Alice nodded and took down his choice of soup and beverage.

"Dessert too?" he inquired.

"Yes," Alice said. "It comes boxed so you can take it with you for later."

"Thank you, Ma'am," LaVerne said. "I'll be able to eat it all. Chocolate cake."

Alice wrote it down and Mr. Brown left.

Martha Cook left the elevator at two minutes before her appointment time. Alice buzzed Aleta who came out to meet her.

"Mr. Maxwell," Martha said, extending her hand toward the gentleman who exited with Aleta. They shook hands and she turned to Aleta.

"I can wait until you finish your business."

"Papers need to be drawn up. I will need to sign them before I go. Mr. Maxwell will review them with one of my associates, so we will be uninterrupted until Chief Peets and another client arrive at noon. I expect you to join us for lunch. You might have some good ideas."

"Before I get to that," Martha said. "How are you doing, my dear?"

"Stanley was wonderful, wasn't he?"

"Did he take the heat off?"

"Only two petitioners in our line this morning."

"It was an effective demonstration," Martha observed. "Pretty hard on you though. You looked so bewildered and upset."

"I was," Aleta admitted. "Stanley didn't give me a clue as to what he planned to do."

"You convinced me and I know the truth."

"He's been through so much," Aleta said. "I wanted to heal him, but those are minor wounds. How I wish I could give him back his leg."

"You gave him back his life twice that I'm aware of. I think he feels singularly blessed."

"God did that," Aleta said. "He said God told him to let go of his leg."

"Michael said it was a wise choice," Martha said and then added, "Poor Michael. He had a bad few days before I was convinced he had done the right thing."

"So I heard."

"I'm old and set in my ways," Martha said. "He shouldn't have married me."

"I think that all the time," Aleta said. "I'm no easier to live with than you are."

"We do have some special men."

"I agree. Now tell me what you need."

Chief Peets joined Martha and Aleta for lunch. LaVerne Brown entered the office while the lunches were being distributed.

The talk turned immediately to LaVerne's vandalism problem.

"Sounds like it's taking a lot of police effort and the punishment is no deterrent," Martha said.

"I suggest a change in the time and type of community service," Aleta said.

"To what?" Martha asked.

"Right now the boys are doing community service on Saturdays and maybe one day a week. What if we made it less convenient and less enjoyable?"

"What's enjoyable about cleaning graffiti off school walls?" Chief Peets asked.

"Save that for the graffiti artists," Aleta said. "Suppose every week day, the vandals have to stand guard at Mr. Brown's house from two o'clock until seven, from eleven to four on Saturday and nine to two on Sunday. That's five hours a day seven days a week. That's thirty-five hours a week."

"Too much," Peets said. The judge would never go for it."

"There are two of them. Two days on two off. If one is sick and misses a day, he starts from scratch.

Peets grimaced. "You're out for blood."

"Ok, there's more. They are responsible for any vandalism on their days whether or not it happens when they are there. Their punishment will be double for a second offense unless they turn in the offenders."

"They'll stand guard forever!" Peets said.

"It will get boring after a while. No radio. No IPOD. No cell. No talking while on duty."

Peets scowled as he considered the punishment.

"They'll hate it," he concluded.

"Then it might work," Martha put in.

"Next, they or their parents pay for all destruction. Your cops take the inventory. Mr. Brown is put up in a motel suite. A cleaning crew restores his house the next day. The parents reimburse the city for all expenses resulting from the vandalism."

"The city hasn't spent any money up to now. They won't want to either," Peets said.

"It goes into a fund," Aleta said. "Mr. Brown is never going to clean up his house again."

Martha stared at Aleta. "I'd heard you'd become a victim's advocate. I guess the rumors are true."

"I'm not happy with the precedent," Chief Peets said.

"There is no precedent," Aleta said. "Mr. Brown has been a victim of the junior high school boys for years. It's almost as if it's considered a tradition. Well, that's a tradition that needs to be broken."

"It won't work if we can't catch the kids," Chief Peets said.

"We're going to set up surveillance equipment at the house," Aleta said.

"I'll pay for that," Martha said. "It's expensive."

LaVerne opened his mouth to protest, but Martha stopped him. "One citizen helping another anonymously."

"I understand." LaVerne said.

"Are you making any headway on the latest attack?" Aleta said.

"We have prints that aren't Mr. Brown's on the remote that was tampered with, the door that was jimmied and the broken dishes that were thrown on the floor.

"Cheap stuff." LaVerne Brown said. "I put my wife's good china in the basement after the first attack."

"We can't print a minor without parent's permission." Peets said. "Most of these boys don't have juvie records."

"How about the thumb prints on driver's licenses?" Martha asked. "And, if they're local, we did the fingerprints of every child in the Tri-City area for identification purposes about seven years ago. It was a part of a child identification program. To help us track down lost children."

"We've got prints from at least two other attacks," Chief Peets said.

"The old chief didn't do anything," LaVerne Brown stated. "His men found a couple of the vandals but nobody took any prints at the beginning."

"I don't suppose Mr. Brown that you have any records of what was destroyed the other times," Aleta asked.

"We have photos from several old attacks," Chief Peets said. "That should help some. I saved all of them even though the statute of limitations has run out."

"Oh, Peets, I love your thoroughness!" Aleta exclaimed.

"You still have to convince the judge to take the cases seriously," Peets said.

"I know," Aleta said simply.

Dr. Michael Taekman knocked and then entered Aleta's office.

"I'm looking for my wife," he said. "I was going to treat her to lunch, but I see she's been fed."

"I thought you weren't supposed to be walking around yet," Aleta observed.

"You were there when I operate on Stanley," Dr. Taekman remarked.

"Special dispensation," Aleta noted. "You woke up and found Martha gone and...and that's what Stanley will do with me gone."

"What?" Martha asked.

"He'll wander," Aleta said.

"Not in his condition," Dr. Taekman remarked. "Wayne says he won't leave his bed for three days at least."

Chief Peets and LaVerne Brown eased themselves out of the room. Their business was finished. Each had jobs that needed doing.

"I think God healed Stanley's side," Aleta said when she was alone with the Taekmans.

"He thinks Dr. Cook gave him a particularly powerful drug. He can move without pain."

"You touched him?" Michael asked.

"He was moaning."

"That I have to see!" Michael exclaimed.

"Not his hand," Aleta put in.

"That's even better," Michael said. "We have to call Wayne."

"He's busy," Martha said.

"He's always busy," her husband replied, "but I know what type of interruptions doctors like. Trust me."

"Oh, that I do," Martha said.

Michael leaned over and kissed her gently on the cheek.

"You are a love," he said softly. "I am a lucky man."

"It's silly to worry about what people will think," Martha declared.

"Don't you dare!" Michael exclaimed. "Not one cent. Do you hear me? Is that why you're here?"

He paused.

"Martha, you aren't listening," he said, exasperated. "Martha, I'm rich!"

"I am in your will," she argued.

"That's because you're my wife...wait, that won't fly," Michael said. "Scratch that! Oh, Martha, it's so important to me that you never have a moment's doubt that I didn't marry you for your money."

"You wanted a wife who burns toast?" Martha quipped.

"If she is you, I do," he said.

"I burn oatmeal and rice and biscuits too," Martha pressed.

"I don't like oatmeal or rice," Michael replied. "And I can live without biscuits. That is, I... Oh heck! What can I say to undo whatever comment you overheard?"

"You're doing it," Martha said quietly. "I love your passion."

"You know I didn't marry you for your money, don't you?"

"You are a very rich man," Martha said. "The one thing you don't need is money."

"You had me investigated?" Michael asked.

"I was afraid my desire was clouding my judgment," Martha said.

"You desired me?" he asked, dumbfounded. "I thought you had decided that...never mind what I thought."

"You thought I married you for your money?" Martha asked slyly.

"Well, no," Michael hedged, and then studied his wife's face. "I am putting my foot in it, aren't I."

"Oh yes, you are," she grinned. "I am looking forward to this evening."

"You fox, you!"

Chapter 21

Later, Martha Cook accompanied her husband and her grandson to the Praetzel Farm to check on Stanley. Martha stayed in the kitchen and talked with Bertha while Dr. Taekman and Dr. Cook were shown into the master bedroom where Stanley was resting. After the two doctors had examined Stanley's side and his hand, and found the one healed and the other not, Stanley stopped them before they left to discuss the matter privately.

"I think Aleta can rid me of whatever cancer is left," Stanley said. "But I have a dilemma."

"I don't see one," Dr. Taekman said.

"Healing drains her of energy," Stanley said. "It affects the baby most of all."

"How can we help?" Dr. Taekman asked.

"I can't very well ask you to come over every time I want to check the baby's heart rate," Stanley said. "I want you to teach me how to use a stethoscope."

"Do you even have one?" Dr. Cook asked.

"I will after one of you gives me yours," Stanley smiled.

"It's not that easy," Dr. Taekman said.

"All I need to know is what's normal for this baby," Stanley explained. "I am not comparing different hearts. I am only going to listen to one heart beat, one baby's heart beat. I need you to tell me what changes I should worry about."

"We can't do that, Stanley," Dr. Taekman said.

"Why?"

"Suppose you miss something," Dr. Cook said.

"I am not going to sue you, if that's what you're worried about," Stanley said. "Besides you teach parents with sick children how to monitor their symptoms all the time."

"This isn't the same."

"Sure it is. Michael is simply an unborn child."

"Why not let Jamara listen to the baby's heart?" Dr. Cook said.

"She's not always here."

"Monitor it when Aleta touches you," Dr. Taekman advised.

Stanley raised an eyebrow.

Dr. Taekman backed down. "I just thought she...well...I thought you could feel it."

"I can," Stanley said, "but, I can't always stop her. I mean, I have been told not to."

"By whom?" Michael asked.

"Your wife's boss."

"Oh, Him."

"Afterward Aleta feels fine," Stanley said. "I need to know how Michael feels."

"Oh, what the hell!" Michael exclaimed. "Retirement doesn't look all that bad. Let's start with Wayne's heart."

"Mine? Why mine?"

"Because you have one and it's beating." Michael said.

"Yours is beating too," Wayne shot back.

"I want him to listen to a healthy heart."

"What's wrong with yours?"

"You heard the slight murmur, didn't you?"

"So your heart is aging," Wayne observed.

"Stanley needs to start with a normal heart," Michael contended. "Now take off your shirt."

Aleta walked in as Stanley was listening to Wayne's heart.

"Close the door!" Wayne said. "Grams will think I am sick."

Aleta shut the door.

"I meant with you outside," Wayne said.

"What's going on?"

"We're teaching Stanley how to use a stethoscope," Dr. Taekman said, "so he can monitor the baby's heart beat."

"Go put on a sweat suit," Stanley said. "We need to listen to Michael's heart beat."

Aleta stared at Dr. Taekman who laughed.

"Your Michael, Aleta. Not me."

Bertha entered as Aleta was changing in the bathroom. "Where's Aleta?"

"You may as well stay," Dr. Cook said.

By the time Aleta emerged from the bathroom, four people were waiting for her.

"Is this a class in monitoring?" she snapped. "Because it's not necessary. I would know if anything were wrong."

"You healed me last night," Stanley said, "And then you spent a busy morning at the office, and I want to know how Michael is."

"He is fine!" Aleta declared. "And I am fine!"

"Lay down," Stanley ordered. "I want him to be fine so I have a basis on which to judge when he's not."

"Not with everyone here!" Aleta protested.

"Everyone isn't here," Stanley exclaimed. "And you aren't undressing—not completely anyway. Now lay down. That's an order."

"Oh for heaven's sake!" Aleta groused as she laid down on the bed. "This is so unnecessary. I feel good."

Dr. Taekman listened first. Without comment he handed his stethoscope to Dr. Cook. When Dr. Cook straightened up, Stanley scooted over in the bed, sat up and put the stethoscope on his wife's bare midsection.

"I don't like the sound," Stanley announced.

"Well, I might be a little tired," Aleta admitted reluctantly.

Bertha asked for a stethoscope and Stanley handed her his. After a few minutes, she straightened up.

"Neither do I," Bertha agreed.

"Maybe a bit more than usual," Aleta confessed. "But I don't feel sick."

"She needs to stay in bed and rest for a full twenty-four hours," Dr. Cook announced. "I will be back tomorrow afternoon."

"I am just a little extra tired. It was a tough day. I will bounce back with a good night's sleep," Aleta insisted.

"I would advise no more healing," Dr. Cook said.

"You can't order that," Stanley objected.

"Why not?"

"Because God wants her free to do that."

"Then think about this," Dr. Cook said. "If she heals, she does no other work for at least forty-eight hours."

"Why so long?" Aleta asked.

"It's been twenty-four hours since you healed Stanley and your baby is still in jeopardy."

"But I worked all day," Aleta protested. "If I had rested, I would have been okay in twenty-four hours."

"We will talk tomorrow," Dr. Cook said. "You two have some decisions to make."

"I will tell Robert we're staying the night," Bertha said. "Oh, and as long as we're staying, can Paul put in a couple extra hours?"

"Sure," Stanley agreed. "Neither of us is leaving the bedroom tonight. Dr. Taekman, can I go to work tomorrow?"

"There's no keeping you two down, is there?"

"I think the reason Aleta is so tired is because she cleared up my infection as well as healing my side."

"The arm stays in the sling for ten days," Dr. Taekman said. "And that hand can't handle the weight of your body for four months."

"No crutches for four months?" Stanley gasped.

Aleta heard the anguish in his voice.

"You're basically wheelchair bound for that long. And you can't use the hand to lift yourself in or out of the wheelchair," Dr. Taekman added firmly. "You need someone with you every time you make the transition."

Stanley's response was a groan.

"If you follow my instructions, you can work half a day the rest of the week."

"Only four hours?"

"Take it or leave it." Dr. Taekman declared.

"Four hours of work," Stanley reiterated. "I will take it!"

Dr. Cook snickered.

As the two doctors left the room, Michael put his hand on his grandson's shoulder.

"What am I missing?"

"I have no idea. Those two create new ways to circumvent each order I give. Stanley gave in too easily."

"Four hours is four hours," Michael stated.

"I suspect he spotted a loophole," Dr. Cook said. "Do you want me to tell you tomorrow what it is?"

"I'm not sure," was the response.

"You want to believe he obeyed you implicitly?"

"I think that's what I want."

"I will call you when I find out." Dr. Cook promised.

When they were alone, Stanley took his wife's hand and kissed it. "Thank you for what you did for me. My side feels great. My leg feels great. My hand is better. But, please, stagger whatever it is you plan to do."

"Don't try to save the whole world in one day?"

"Precisely."

"And you aren't going to give me any orders?" Aleta asked.

"No."

"And you will wait to be healed until the baby is born?"

"Aleta, I am alive. You saved my life. I can handle four months in a wheelchair."

"What about the cancer?"

"Michael comes first," Stanley said. "He is a special baby."

"Are you going to trust me on this?"

"God said to let you work," Stanley said.

He paused, thought for a minute and then added, "Aleta, I know what you're thinking."

"No, you don't!"

"You know when you put your hand on your tummy that you can heal the baby, but the energy will come from you."

"Better me than him."

"He won't live if you die!" Stanley exclaimed. "And I won't want to."

"I feel the same about you, you know," Aleta said. "Something's got to give."

Their talking stopped abruptly when they heard the rattle of dishes. Bertha and Robert brought in two trays with short legs on them and set them down over their legs on the bed.

"You were expecting me to be bedridden today?" Aleta quipped.

"Getting two made sense," Bertha said tartly. She sensed a scold in Aleta's tone.

"Don't mind her, Bertha. She's upset because she was wrong," Stanley revealed.

"No, I'm not. I was joking," Aleta protested.

Stanley frowned at her. "When did you start disguising your feelings behind so-called jokes. Apologize."

"I am not a child," Aleta declared, irked.

"You're being petulant like one," Stanley remarked.

"Eat everything on your plate and I'll forgive you," Bertha said.

"You agree with him?"

"You're in a bad mood. You aren't all-knowing, you know."

"I know that," Aleta snapped.

"Aleta!" Her father countered. "Stop it! You wore yourself out. Exhaustion dulls the senses."

"But I am carrying the baby. I should feel his need," Aleta protested.

Stanley cut in.

"How do you expect to do that when you're busy denying your own?"

Aleta paused thoughtfully. These three weren't blaming her. They accepted her drive to charge ahead with her self-appointed tasks and ignore her own fatigue.

"I hate the truth sometimes," she declared peevishly.

Stanley reached over and took her hand. "We all love you."

She pulled her hand away.

"I am not sure that helps. I almost failed my own child. I could have killed him."

"That's why God gave you me and Dr. Cook's handy stethoscope," Stanley remarked lightly.

"I should probably wear it around my neck so anyone can check me anytime."

"That's a great idea," Bertha shot back.

Aleta glared at her.

"It is not," she declared so vociferously that everyone laughed.

"We have to go eat with Paul or he won't stop working," Bertha said. "If we put a bit of weight on Aleta, the baby will gain too."

"It doesn't work that way," Aleta proclaimed.

"Indulge me," Bertha ordered.

Aleta looked at her plate.

"I am not sure I can."

"Robert," Stanley said as the two were leaving. "I will be coming to the office at ten tomorrow."

"That will give you only two hours," Aleta inserted.

"I will be leaving around four."

"That's six hours!" Aleta declared.

"One hour for lunch, one hour for visiting, four hours of work," Stanley returned, smiling.

"You never visit," Aleta pointed out.

"I will tomorrow. I need to talk with Kay Rivers and see how she's doing. I need to chat with my dad. I need to call my mother and..."

"You can call her from here."

"If I call her from the office, she will believe I am okay."

"She will be in court," Aleta said.

"I will leave a message that says I can be reached at the office until four."

"That would do it," Aleta said. "Are you going to be well enough to be there that long?"

"Yes."

"Who will check on Michael?" Aleta asked.

"You will be in bed all day and Bertha will be stuffing you with food," Stanley grinned. "Tomorrow I am not worrying about Michael for one second."

Stanley fell asleep almost as soon as Bertha took away his tray. His last comment to Aleta was that she had to decide what God wanted her to do and be willing to give up the rest of it.

Stanley was sound asleep when her hand found its usual place. He felt the warmth of her touch and memories of that being usual lulled him into deep sleep.

Aleta, finding that Stanley didn't object to her holding him in the usual way turned slightly sideways and placed her other hand on top of his bandaged hand held next to his chest by his sling.

He had fallen asleep without removing it and Aleta took the proximity of the hand as a sign. In her mind she sensed that to heal his hand would drain her completely.

"How many days1?" she asked silently.

The answer came and she sighed. Then she placed her hand on top of her husband's and lay awake as the healing power of God flowed through her and restored Stanley's hand to full strength.

He will be upset because I will have exposed myself again, she realized. But he will also be deeply grateful.

She had seen his anguish at the thought of spending months in a wheelchair because his hand would be too weak to support him on crutches. It wasn't the sitting in the chair that bothered him as much as not being able to move into and out of it at will. That was a level of helplessness that would gnaw at his spirit.

"Did I disobey, God?" Aleta asked. "He didn't give me the order not to heal him directly, but he did make it clear that he wanted me to put Michael first."

Suddenly, she smiled.

"I didn't heal him. You did," she murmured. "Can you help me remember that?"

Chapter 22

Stanley woke at dawn as usual. He realized at once that he felt amazingly good. He felt Aleta's hand in its usual place and loved the gentleness of her fingers as they curled around his member. That was one of the reasons the threat of its removal hit him so hard. It wasn't a major reason, but it was something that was truly irreplaceable. He didn't want to be without this pleasure.

It took several minutes for him to realize that the hand in the sling felt unusually heavy. He glanced down. His eyes confirmed what his senses had already told him. Aleta's hand was not only on top of his, but there was no pain accompanying her touch.

She healed me, he thought. He flexed his fingers and he didn't even feel a twinge of discomfort. He placed Aleta's hand on her stomach, removed the sling and peeled off the bandage.

"There's not even a scar," he murmured, surprised.

He stretched his fingers and squeezed them into a ball. He grabbed hold of his half-leg and lifted it. He pushed himself into a sitting position and realized his hand could handle the pressure. It was healed completely.

As he sat there staring at his hand, his eye caught sight of the stethoscope.

Suddenly he remembered.

He grabbed the stethoscope and crawled over to Aleta. He set the metal bell on her mid-section and listened. The beat was faint but regular.

Aleta opened her eyes.

"He said two months."

"Two months?" Stanley questioned.

"In exchange," Aleta murmured weakly. "I think. I don't understand at all."

"What does that mean?"

"He asked and I agreed," Aleta whispered. "Maybe it's a penance."

"God doesn't expect penances anymore. Not since Jesus."

"My power to heal has been withdrawn. I can't heal Michael."

"Is God angry with you?"

"No."

"With me?"

"God took away all your cancer," Aleta declared.

"What's going on?"

"All I know is that I am to be in a comatose state for two months. I am to be completely obedient to His will."

"I don't understand," Stanley rejoined.

"I need rest," Aleta breathed. "Don't wake me."

Then her eyes closed.

Stanley's fingers moved the bell of the stethoscope to her left breast.

Startled, he yelled for Bertha. Within seconds Bertha burst through the door.

Unable to speak, Stanley held out the stethoscope. Bertha took it and listened to the baby's heart.

"Faint," she said, "but regular."

"Aleta," he choked out.

Bertha moved the bell to Aleta's breast.

"I will call Dr. Cook," she said and rushed off.

A knock on the front door caught Bertha as she was leaving the bedroom. A siren could be heard in the distance. The door was opened by one of the guards and Dr. Cook headed straight toward the bedroom.

Stanley looked up, startled.

"Martha called me. She said Aleta was dying," Dr. Cook announced. "I came right away."

Stanley blanched.

"She healed me while I slept. She said she would be well in two months."

Dr. Cook examined her quickly.

"Not without intervention," he declared. "She's near death now."

"She didn't tell me that. She said she just needed to rest."

The ambulance siren brought Robert from the bedroom and the dogs began to bark full force. The baby woke and began to cry lustily.

Bertha ignored the baby. Robert came in as Dr. Cook was telling Stanley there was no way Aleta could be cared for at home. Her condition was too critical.

Stanley turned to Aleta's father.

"She healed me while I slept. Not just the hand, but the cancer. I told her I could wait. I meant it."

"It's Aleta who couldn't," her father said. "That's the way she is."

The paramedics rushed in and Dr. Cook began issuing orders. An IV was started. Aleta's eyes remained closed. She didn't even twitch when the needle was inserted.

The paramedics folded her arms across her chest as they lifted her onto the gurney.

"Robert," Stanley said. "Help me dress so I can go to the hospital."

The paramedics avoided the wheelchair as they wheeled the comatose young woman to the waiting ambulance. Dr. Cook climbed into the back with them.

Bertha told her husband that Aleta had said she would be well after two months of total rest. Then Bertha went to the nursery to care for Gerard who was still crying lustily.

Robert suggested Stanley dress for work.

"I need to get to the hospital" he responded.

"You aren't going to sit by her bedside day and night for two months or even for one day. She's in the middle of several cases. You can't drop these people."

"We have associates," Stanley argued.

"Aleta never takes a case an associate could handle and your father has a full load as do I. In fact, all our associates have heavy loads. Hubert is hoping Kay can find time to help him. We absolutely need you if we don't have Aleta."

"I want to be with her," Stanley declared. "I don't want her to wake up and me not be there."

"You can't stay by her side day and night," Robert declared. "The hospital will call us when she wakes."

"My brain says you're being reasonable, but my heart doesn't want to listen."

"Well, we're going with your brain," Robert proclaimed. "I made you a stool for shaving. I want you to use it and tell Aleta about it tonight."

"Tonight?" Stanley asked, flabbergasted.

"When you visit her."

"I am going over this morning."

"Okay. I'll drive you there as soon as you're dressed. You're going to tell her you are going to pick up her cases and for her not to worry."

Stanley grew thoughtful.

"She will worry, won't she?"

"And that will rob her of energy."

"But if she feels abandoned, that will sap her strength too."

"Not if she has family visiting her every two hours. There's Andrea and Bertha, Jocelyn and Lettie, Paul and me, Harriet and Claude, Martha and Michael, Lyle and Lauren,

Hubert and Lydia and then there's you. Give us all a chance to show our love."

"You win," Stanley said. "that is a better way. Where's the stool?"

"I will get it," Robert said. "Do you have your crutches?"

Stanley pointed under his bed.

Robert chuckled. "I remember Bertha complaining about them being there."

"Why? They're out of the way."

"Not when she vacuums," Robert retorted.

"She knows too much about me," Stanley quipped.

"Well, if she does, she doesn't share it. I only get the uninteresting stuff. I get more out of Hubbs than my own wife."

"He's hardly ever even in the house." Stanley protested.

"I know more about the peculiarities of your horses than you do."

Stanley smiled happily. They hadn't been talking about him.

When Stanley and Robert left the hospital, Stanley reiterated. "She told me it was an exchange. Then she said that maybe it was a penance. She wasn't sure. All she knew is that I wasn't to try to wake her. Her agreement to stay in this state was important. Two months of absolute obedience."

"Maybe she didn't really know."

"You mean that was as close an understanding as God could give her?"

"Something like that," Robert guessed.

"How can you be so calm?" Stanley charged.

"She said she will be well in two months. That's the hope I am clinging to. I don't dare entertain any alternatives."

"She is a prophet," Stanley mused.

Then he brightened as he realized something else.

"More than that, Martha sent help. God only does that when He wants to save people."

They were met at the office by Justin and the TV camera crew that responded every time he called. Justin still had one foot in the newspaper business waiting for a solid offer from one of the TV networks.

"How does he find out what's happening so fast?" Robert asked, his eyes locked on Justin.

"I think he holds markers," Stanley replied.

"Markers?"

"Chief West owes him. Justin evidently sat on some juicy stuff."

"Should I send them way."

"Actually no," Stanley said. "This could work to our advantage. You get out the wheelchair. I will take it from there. Thanks for making me dress for work."

A few minutes later, the cameraman locked on Stanley using crutches to exit the van and lower himself into the wheelchair.

Justin shoved a microphone in his face. "Did Aleta heal you?"

Stanley tucked his crutches into the holder at the back of the wheelchair and then held up both hands. He turned them around. The camera man focused on them.

"Where's the scar?" The cameraman hissed at Justin.

"There's no scar," Stanley said. "God healed more than my hand and my side."

He patted his left leg. "Bone cancer took this leg. I still had cancer. God cured me of cancer as well."

"Through Aleta?" Justin probed.

"Yes, He used her," Stanley said. "There were consequences."

"We hear she's dying," Justin said.

"She's in a coma," Stanley said solemnly. "She told me she would be well in two months."

"Is she faking the coma?" Justin asked.

"She told me something else," Stanley said. "She told me the power to heal was gone. She couldn't even save our baby. Those were her last words."

"Was she admitting she had the power?"

"She never denied that God used her. All she is saying is that God is no longer going to use her."

"Did she bargain with God for your recovery?"

"God doesn't bargain."

"Did she make a pact with the devil?"

"No!" Stanley declared adamantly. "Historically, prophesying has exhausted her for a day or two. I believe this encounter took her to death's door. She didn't know it. It was another prophet who sent the doctor and the ambulance to save her."

"She can't cure herself?" Justin asked.

Stanley smiled. "She can't cure anyone, especially herself. And God has chosen not to use her anymore."

"Why are you here? Why aren't you at the hospital?"

"We just came from there," Stanley said evenly. "Other family members will keep my wife company while I take care of her special clients."

"Some will accuse you of putting money ahead of your wife. How will you answer that charge?"

"Those who would level such an accusation are reflecting their own priorities, not mine," Stanley said calmly. "Such people do not deserve a response."

Having said that, Stanley extended his hand. Justin shook it and turned to the camera to summarize the startling revelations Stanley had made.

Stanley entered his building and took the elevator to his office and told Alice to call a staff meeting immediately.

The group assembled quickly in Stanley's office. Several had seen Justin and the TV crew set up at the entrance to their offices. They were waiting for someone. All guessed it was Aleta.

As soon as everyone had gathered, Stanley stood on his crutches and moved to the front of his desk and pushed on the edge of his desk. His movement pushed the group back into a wider circle. Maya's wheelchair was moved to the front of the semi-circle.

"Aleta is in a coma," Stanley announced. "Sorry, Dad, there was just no easy way to start."

The groups silence was the product of their shock.

"Last night while I was asleep, Aleta elected to heal me, that is, she asked God to do it and He did. As some of you know, when Aleta makes a prediction, she's worn out for several days. Healing is even more draining," Stanley explained.

He paused briefly and then went on.

"I didn't ask for this. In fact, I asked her not to. Be that as it may, the effect has taken every ounce of strength from her. Before she lost consciousness she told me she would be well in two months. She also said that the power to heal was gone. I know some of you wonder why she didn't cure the cancer in my leg before this. I could say it was because I didn't tell her about it and that is the truth. But a more profound truth is that I prayed and took the course God chose for me. I do not understand that anymore than I understand why Aleta has been stricken. She has prophesied that her coma will last two months. That is all I know and what I believe."

Stanley paused and took a deep breath.

"Intake will be suspended for two months except for seniors and children. I understand Hubert needs help on a couple of big cases. In addition, we have two big clients-- The Tontine and the City of Willow Glen who will send us more work if we but ask. But I see us struggling to emerge from Aleta's penchant to take every interesting case she comes upon. So our job is to get caught up so when she returns, we will have room for the cases she will draw in."

"As for Aleta's cases, I will be taking those over. She did manage to assign me a tricky custody case her last day on the job."

"I will be working pretty close to full-time," Stanley finished. "Are there any questions?"

"What about the baby?" Maya asked.

"She is still pregnant. He is weak but still alive." Stanley responded. "Anything else?"

Robert spoke up.

"At my suggestion, Stanley is allowing friends and family to take his place at his wife's side. He is scheduled for evenings only."

Stanley then turned to Kay and said, "Stay a few minutes after everyone leaves."

He turned to his father, "You too."

After the room emptied, Stanley said to Kay, "I know Aleta meant to help you on your first cases. You can come to me or to Hubert. And Hubert, Kay can sit second chair on any case you choose."

"I have this divorce case," Kay began.

"We don't take divorce cases," Stanley said.

"Mrs. Vashi came in with a complex situation and Aleta decided divorce was the woman's only option. Her demented husband has decided to leave his wife impoverished. Aleta had a plan and while I can carry out most of it, I need advice."

"Dad?" Stanley asked.

"Since I am getting her help on my cases, I can advise her on that one."

"On the other," Stanley said. "See me."

"I will be in later," Kay said. "Say eleven?"

"Tell Alice," Stanley said. "She keeps my schedule. Tell her how long you need."

Kay left. Hubert lingered.

"I'm so sorry about Aleta," Stanley's father said.

"Lauren is scheduling the visits because Lyle needs to give his men a list. You won't be allowed in at any other time."

"How healed are you?"

"The infection is gone; my hand is good as new; my side doesn't even have a scar; and Aleta told me the cancer is gone."

"Did she do too much?" His father asked.

"God healed me," Stanley said. "Aleta was involved totally, but she didn't do the healing."

"It seems as if..." Hubert began.

"I know it looks as if her collapse resulted from her involvement in my healing. But it's something else. Aleta was confused. She used the terms exchange and penance."

"Penance? For what? Is God angry?"

"I asked. The answer is no. That's when she told me the cancer had been eradicated," Stanley related.

"Well, that's no penance," his father said. "Does this mean you will be fitted for a prosthesis?"

"No," Stanley said. "Not until Aleta wakes up. She hates change."

"But she's always changing things."

"If she makes the change, it doesn't count as a change. It's considered progress."

"What if...sorry."

"Robert and I talked about that. Neither of us can deal with the alternative right now. If our faith in her words proves to be futile, we will deal with it then. Right now, she's alive. So's our hope."

"Mine too, Son. Mine too."

Chapter 23

A short time later, seated at Aleta's desk, Stanley opened the first file on her desk.

"Now, let's see what my dear wife got us into."

He opened the file marked "Newton Maxfield."

"We have power of attorney for another one," he muttered. "Herve has got to stop sending us clients."

The light on the phone flashed. Stanley picked it up.

"Newton Maxfield is here," Alice said. "He's very upset."

"He's not the only one," Stanley quipped. "Send him in."

The old man hobbled in, deep despair only barely hidden by his angry visage.

"Which one are you?"

"Stanley Praetzel," came the terse response. "How may I help you?"

"You're sitting at her desk, and you're pawing through my file. Who gave you the right?"

"I am the Senior Partner," Stanley said.

"You're a child advocate."

"Yes, I am."

"Can you handle adult cases?"

"I am a regular lawyer. I happen to like working with children."

"Because they won't know that you're no good."

"Because they can see through bullshit which is what you're spewing a lot of. If you want to change lawyers, you have only to ask."

"Doesn't her signature bind your whole firm to represent me?"

Stanley paged through the documents.

"Only the partners are empowered to act on your behalf."

"I heard she was dying. How can a healthy woman die so fast?"

"She's in a coma," Stanley said. "I expect her to live."

"She liked me," the old man said suddenly.

Stanley smiled. "She has excellent judgment. We all respect her decisions. We will be happy to represent your interests."

"Do I have to go over it all again?"

"Her notations are quite clear," Stanley said and then read them all aloud.

"She's sharp! Didn't miss a one. Can you do it?"

"Yes, I can."

"You aren't going to fall over as soon as I leave, are you?"

"Not if I stay in this chair," Stanley chuckled as he backed the wheelchair away from kneehole and rolled it around the desk.

"Come with me. You need to meet our other partner."

"When did you lose 'er? Your leg, I mean," Maxfield asked.

"Nine days ago," Stanley replied as he headed toward Robert's office.

"Accident?" Maxfield asked.

"Bone cancer."

"You going to die too?"

"Mr. Maxfield, if you're terribly worried, you may cancel your power of attorney. I will refund your money and you can look elsewhere."

Stanley tapped on Robert's door and entered with Newton Maxfield. He introduced the two.

"Stand up!" Maxfield ordered.

Bewildered, Robert rose.

"Walk over where I can see you," Maxfield demanded querulously.

"What's this all about?" Robert asked, noting Stanley's nod to obey.

Stanley responded, "Mr. Maxfield is upset because he heard Aleta is dying, from Herve I would assume, and he just found out I lost a leg to bone cancer, and he's given us power of attorney, both medical and financial."

"Maxwell surveyed Robert. "You look like you'll last couple of years. Your eyesight okay?"

"It's fine," Robert said, swallowing a smirk.

"Aleta wrote out all my preferences. Will you do what she wrote?"

"We all respect Aleta's decisions," Robert said.

"I could come out dead, you know. I don't want to be hacked up into pieces and distributed anywhere. I want to be buried in one piece."

"We will follow your directions," Robert said.

"And you'll see I get good care, even in the long term?"

"Yes, we will.

"I don't trust all my kids. Two of them is too weak to stand up to the bully and he don't care about me. Oh, he'll make all the right noises, but, he won't make good decisions. Herve told me what Aleta did for him. That's why I'm here."

"Mr. Maxfield," Stanley said. "You are talking to Aleta's father. She is a reflection of him."

"Begging your pardon, but she is a reflection of nobody. She's a single—one of a kind."

The two men exchanged glances.

"We will follow her directions to the letter."

"Okay then. I guess I can go get that damned tumor removed. Dr. Taekman says I'll be fine, but I'm not sure he's got all his marbles. Rich guy like that marries a woman that's ninety. That makes no sense at all."

"If you met her," Stanley said, "it would make a lot of sense. She's a lot like Aleta. She's one of Aleta's best friends."

Maxfield stroked his chin thoughtfully. "So you're telling me Taekman has got all his marbles?"

"He's a fine surgeon," Stanley said. "He's operated on Aleta's head four times and she's fine."

"Who cut off your leg?" Maxfield asked abruptly.

"Dr. Taekman," Stanley responded, "but he doesn't remove heads even if the tumor in them is cancerous."

"You sure?" Maxfield asked.

"If he does, we'll sue him," Stanley said. "You'll make a fortune."

"I'll be dead."

"But you'll be rich," Stanley quipped.

"You mean you'll be rich," Maxfield retorted.

Robert cut in.

"Stop dreaming you two. Michael isn't going to chop off anyone's head."

"Okay, I'm satisfied," Maxfield said. "Herve was right."

"Right about what?" Stanley pressed.

"Tell you some other time. My time's up. Aleta said I'll be charged one hundred dollars for every quarter hour. I'm coming up on thirty minutes."

"That's for Aleta's time," Stanley said.

"She plugged that loophole," Maxfield said. "That's why I signed on. She's sharp."

"When do we go to the hospital?" Stanley asked.

"You mean you aren't just going to fax over the paperwork?"

"Aleta wouldn't," Stanley said. "With her clients we do things her way."

"Didn't her note say, 'no charge for initial hospital visit'?"

"Was that what she told you?" Stanley asked

Maxfield took the measure of the man in the wheelchair.

"No," he admitted reluctantly.

"She didn't offer you a cheaper second-class rate?" Stanley asked tongue-in-cheek.

"She said there was only one rate," Maxfield countered. "I am almost over my thirty minutes. You lawyers will talk me poor. One o'clock this afternoon."

"I will be there," Stanley said cheerfully.

"So will my kids."

"I can handle kids."

"They're grown-up."

"I guessed that," Stanley said. "Better hurry."

"Why did you keep him?" Robert asked when Maxfield left. "He's going to take all your time."

"He was Aleta's client," Stanley said. "I am doing it for her. Besides he's a challenge."

"He's belligerent, complaining, suspicious..."

"And he has a brain tumor."

"As I said, let's give the man a break."

Back in Aleta's office, Stanley opened the file folder marked Daniel Wallace. Stella Woodbridge recommended him. Spousal abuse. Three children: Becky, 4, Jennie, 3, and Scott, 2. Safe House.

"Safe house?" Stanley muttered. "What safe house?" He flipped through the pages and found nothing.

"Aleta, where did you put him?"

He flipped the intercom. "Alice, do you know where Daniel Wallace is?"

"A safe house."

"Where?"

"Mrs. Praetzel didn't tell me. Martha Cook knows."

"Martha?" Stanley asked. "Get hold of her for me.""

While he waited, Stanley scanned the next file marked LaVerne Brown. He read two notes.

"Martha will hire Ed to do surveillance," one said. The other said, "Peets will run point."

"My stars, Aleta! Why did you call in favors from such powerful people on a simple vandalism case?" he muttered. "What am I missing?"

The phone light flashed. Stanley picked up the receiver.

"Martha," he said. "I need help. Aleta left some cases on her desk."

'Why are you working?" said the familiar high-pitched voice.

"She told me she would be well in two months."

"Why aren't you there?" Martha insisted.

"She predicted the coma," Stanley explained. "I am taking care of her clients for her."

"So you want to know about Mr. Brown?"

"The file is sketchy, but it looks like she pulled out big guns for a case of juvenile vandalism."

"Repeated acts of vandalism," Martha explained.

"That's not uncommon."

"Black man in white neighborhood."

"Now I understand Peets' involvement," Stanley responded. "What don't I know?"

"The pattern is the same. Aleta suspects someone directing the attacks. Peets caught one pair. Juvenile judge let them off with community service. Aleta has a new plan."

"Tell me about it," Stanley said.

And so Martha did.

When she finished, Stanley told her he would handle Aleta's end.

"I think she was planning on asking you," Martha told him.

"I need to find another client, a man with three small children."

"They were in Tonia Morales' old house," Martha told Stanley. "A couple bombs intended for Mrs. Morales were found."

"I saw the news. So Daniel Wallace was the father with the three kids on the news," Stanley said. "But where is he?"

"I don't know." Martha said. "The house has been searched and cleared. Daniel Wallace hasn't come back."

"Give me the number of the supervisor of the Home."

When Stanley called the number, the man said, "I'm sorry, I can't give you any information about any of our residents or former residents."

"Get a message to him," Stanley said identifying himself. "Tell Mr. Wallace to call me. I'm handling his case while my wife is in the hospital."

"Your wife can tell him."

"My wife's in a coma."

"Sorry, I can't help you," the man said and hung up.

"Can't or won't," Stanley muttered.

He worked on completing what Aleta had begun the day before. He finished with enough time to call Peets and tell him Martha had given him the rundown on the LaVerne Brown problem.

"You can count on me to uphold Aleta's end," he finished.

"How is she?"

"No change."

"I am surprised you're working."

"Aleta predicted this coma. She said it would last two months."

"Really?" Peets asked, wonder coloring his tone.

"That's the shortened version, distilled by repetitious replies to that particular query," Stanley replied. "I am taking over all of Aleta's cases."

Alice appeared at his office door.

"There's been another murder at the college. Chief Milani wants you over there now."

Stanley's police body guard stepped into the room.

"Chief Milani wants me to escort you there ASAP."

"Alice, I have to be at the hospital at one today. I won't be back. Tell Kay to take one case to Roland, one to Andrew and one to Hubert. Tell her I am sorry."

"Your lunch?" Alice said as the elevator doors began to close.

"Have Tim bring it to the surgery waiting room," Stanley directed as the doors closed.

The elevator began its descent. When it reached the bottom, Alice was half way down the open stairway. Stanley called over his shoulder.

"After one o'clock have Tim deliver it personally."

"Yes, Mr. Praetzel," Alice said as he disappeared through the door with his police escort.

Chapter 24

The scene at the dormitory was chaotic. TV newsmen and cameramen were scurrying around from terrified student to terrified student compiling unrehearsed, panicky statements. The police were drawing their share of criticism. They were being generally castigated for their ineptitude in failing to protect the college's young women.

Chief Lyle West met the Willow Glen patrol car carrying Stanley.

"I have to be at the hospital at one," Stanley said.

Suddenly, a microphone was shoved in Stanley's face and questions began raining down upon him.

"No comment," Stanley said repeatedly as Lyle cleared the way for him.

Before he reached the door to the three-story red brick freshman girl's dormitory, the questions progressed from curious to biting to vitriolic, the sole purpose being to get a useable sound bite from the man in the wheelchair.

When the question thrust upon him accused him being more interested in seeing himself on television than in sitting unnoticed by the bedside of his dying wife, Lyle shouted, "No comment!"

Then he waved at the guard to open the door. The
chief personally pushed Stanley through the door into the
hallway. The guard closed the door and stood in front of it.

"Thanks," Stanley said. "They were hitting below the
belt."

"Only one victim this time," Lyle said. "The coroner
says death occurred between nine and ten."

"The coroner is here?" Stanley asked, surprised.

"That's why the rush to get you here," Lyle said.

"I have a one o'clock appointment at the hospital I
can't miss."

"I will see you make it," Lyle promised.

"It's not Aleta," Stanley said.

"Peets told me what she predicted," Lyle said as he
led the way down the hall.

Stanley saw the police around an open door. His
stomach did a flip. He was grateful he hadn't eaten
breakfast. The emergency with Aleta had closed all thought
of food from his mind until Alice mentioned lunch and his
memory of being poisoned warned him to make
arrangements he could trust.

No amount of assurances would persuade him to
touch food or drink at the hospital until this serial murderer
was in jail.

"Chief," Stanley said, turning toward Tom Milani.
"What was the routine for checking the rooms?"

"All who went to class signed out. Immediately after
the first class started, the officer knocked on the door of
everyone who hadn't checked out."

"He never actually went inside, correct?" Stanley
asked.

"No, but he had to get verbal confirmation."

"Can I speak to the officer on duty when this took
place?"

"He's upstairs typing up his statement," Tom said.
"He was pretty shaken up and those reporters outside would
have eaten him alive."

"I need to talk to him," Stanley said.

Tom sent one of his men to fetch him.

Stanley turned his attention back to the crime scene. He tried not to look at the girl on the bed. The coroner would tell them if there was anything unusual. Forensic Chief Hawkins Monroe was already at work. He glanced up when Stanley's wheelchair was rolled into the doorway, nodded a greeting and went back to work.

Stanley immediately noted several differences in the array of clothing dumped by the bed.

The girl's night clothes were nowhere in sight. There were also no underclothes. The clothes dumped beside the bed were a bad combination of colors. That bothered him. He studied the large poster on the wall. It showed the girl bigger than life, sitting on a stone near a lake, the same shoes on her feet as were sitting askew near the bed.

He studied the preciseness of the pose in the poster. The orderly array of books on the shelves and then the neatly stacked sweat shirts on the closet shelf. The stack had been disturbed.

The perp had matched the shoes and jeans in the blow-up photo but not the sweat shirt. She had evidently looked for the matching shirt and finally settled for a similar one. Why had she wasted time with doing that?

Then Stanley realized that she didn't know that he knew she wore the victim's clothes. The killer had entered the dorm room expecting her target to be dressed or at the least have laid out her clothes. When she found out her target hadn't done that, the killer tried to match the clothes in the photo.

The young cop who had been on duty arrived. Stanley recognized Cole Weldon who had guarded him and Aleta on numerous occasions.

"Could a person have snuck in while you were checking the rooms?"

"I locked the door to prevent that," Cole said. "I know it's against fire regulations, but the doors have push bars that automatically unlock them from inside."

"So no one could get in."

"Not without a key."

"Okay, Cole, I need to know how this girl answered when you knocked."

"The first time she said she couldn't open the door because she wasn't dressed."

The first time?"

"At eight-thirty. I check approximately every hour," Cole said.

"So what did she say at nine-thirty?"

"She didn't answer, but I heard the toilet flush and so I figured she was okay," Cole said.

"Between checks, where were you?"

"On the door. Some girls have late classes. The building is pretty empty by ten. I started my last check at quarter after ten. I found her at ten-thirty-five."

"Okay, this is important," Stanley said. "Did you hear any phones ringing early this morning?"

"How did you know?" Cole responded.

"What time?" Stanley pressed.

"Six-thirty." Cole said. "Someone had their cell turned up."

"What room?"

"I have no idea," Cole said.

Lyle and Tom took Stanley aside. "What's up?"

"I think our serial killer got a call from the hospital telling her Aleta had been brought in comatose."

"So she felt safe to move again?" Tom asked. "I don't like the implication."

"Look you guys made me out to be a super sleuth. Don't complain if you were believed."

"What else?" Tom asked.

"Our perp has a key to the building. Maybe even to the rooms." Stanley said.

"I will have Cole hunt down the phone call," Tom said. "He needs an important assignment right now. And I will get a warrant to hunt for a key to the outside door."

"Our perp won't be one of the girls on the inside at eight-thirty," Stanley said.

"That widens the field," Tom grumbled. "You're suppose to help us do the opposite."

"Eliminate every girl in class between eight and ten. Check that first," Stanley suggested. "Our perp may figure we will concentrate on the girls in the dorm since the doors were locked."

"I will put French on it," Lyle said.

"Carradine too," Tom put in. "Two heads are better than one."

Stanley turned away and watched the removal of the body. He called to Hawk who joined him at the doorway.

"I don't know much about what you can do in the lab..."

"According to CSI on TV, I could do more," Hawk stated ruefully. "But no scene is so pure that a minute investigation will spit up only one flake of skin or hair," Hawk stated ruefully.

A tall man, he had to lean over to keep the conversation low-key.

"Suppose I narrow the field?" Stanley offered lowering his voice to a whisper.

"How?" Hawk whispered leaning a bit lower.

"She surprised the victim before she dressed. She hadn't laid out her clothes," Stanley whispered.

"How do you know?"

"The stacks of sweat shirts is disturbed."

"I noticed that."

"There's no underwear."

"Noted that also."

"The outfit matches the photo."

"Almost. Top is different," Hawk said.

"Not only different, but wrong," Stanley corrected.

"You're an expert I women's fashion now?" Hawk questioned, brushing his long hair back. It was an old habit. Since he married Paige, she saw to it his hair never covered his eyes when he was looking at a person.

"The shoes don't match," Stanley said. "And there are matching shoes in the closet. Our perp was following the poster. She found the shoes first."

Hawk turned and stared at the jeans still lying undisturbed on the floor. Natsumi had just finished photographing the room.

"Those legs are too narrow to pull over another pair of pants," Hawk assessed aloud.

"She slipped in the bathroom afterward," Stanley said.

"I noticed that too," Hawk agreed. "You think she left blood on the inside of the knees."

"She would have noticed that," Stanley reasoned. "These jeans were not worn by our victim. They were worn by her killer."

"So no blood," Hawk puzzled. "Do you think extra skin cells might have been rubbed off in the fall?"

"This perp leaves almost no clues," Stanley said. "It might be worth the manpower."

"She's the kind of killer who gets away with it," Hawk said. "Ed's been working on some sort of connection, but there doesn't seem to be any."

"There has to be! These attacks are vicious! If not these girls themselves, then they remind her of someone."

"If we knew who she was, then we might be able to uncover a motive, even a twisted one," Hawk said.

"Tom is getting a warrant to search the rooms for the key to the outside door," Stanley told him.

"She will have it on her," Hawk predicted.

"Maybe not," Stanley said.

"I wish I could go with whoever does the search."

"Do it," Stanley said. "I'd go, but this wheelchair makes it impossible for me to look over anyone's shoulders."

"It's a long shot," Hawk observed as he straightened up.

"You're good at suggesting where things might be hidden."

"Get them to look where I want to look?" Hawk asked.

"I knew our minds were in sync," Stanley said. "I am sorry I'm getting credit for any progress we're making."

"I'm not," Hawk said. "They've singled you out for vilification. Paige would be so hurt if the press attacked me personally."

"Glad to be of service," Stanley quipped ruefully.

"You might get fired if we fail."

Stanley reacted with surprise.

"Fired? I am a volunteer!"

"Someone's head will have to roll."

Stanley's face underwent a change of expression. "Lyle set me up!"

"Maybe he thought you would succeed," Hawk said. "But either way, he's protecting his police force."

"I was poisoned!" Stanley lashed out. "I almost died!"

"I am sure that wasn't part of his plan," Hawk remarked. "He likes you."

"He set me up!"

"Oh, come on. Except for the poisoning, you've enjoyed the challenge. I know I have."

Stanley scowled.

"I will get back to you on that. First, I need to ream out Chief Lyle West."

He spun his chair around and wheeled over toward the two chiefs. "Lyle, drive me to the hospital," he demanded.

"My man will do that," Lyle said.

"No, you will! I have a bone to pick with you."

"You're still wearing that badge," Lyle reminded him.

His voice demanded respect.

Stanley took a deep breath and backed off.

"Okay, Chief, I will do it your way. The report will be on your desk as soon as I finish taking care of my client, but later, when I am a civilian again, I am going to ream your ass."

"Deputy Praetzel, come with me," Chief West ordered brusquely.

"Now you've done it," Tom murmured loud enough for Stanley to hear.

West led the way to the last room on that floor. He opened the door and ushered Stanley in.

"This is trespassing," Stanley noted.

West ignored him. He shut the door.

"How dare you threaten me in public!" Lyle raged.

"How dare you set me up for public humiliation," Stanley shot back.

"Who says I did that?"

"I say that. You're as smart as I am, maybe even smarter. Why call me in except to be a fall guy in a hopeless case?"

"Where is Aleta when I need her to knock some sense into you?" Lyle moaned. "Stanley, you are smarter than me. Maybe not a lot, but you rank right up there with Hawk. This is the kind of case no police chief wants in his district. Tom suggested I ask you to help."

"He did?"

"He said you had a more analytical mind and this case called for that," Lyle said. "He wanted both you and Aleta, but I nixed using Aleta. There are some things a woman shouldn't see."

"She saw the old woman who was raped and murdered," Stanley mentioned.

"She insisted on coming along as I recall."

"You aren't using me as a patsy?"

"No. If you fail, we all fail."

"Insist Hawk accompany Tom's men when they search the rooms. Tell them to look everywhere he suggests," Stanley said, calming down and testing the waters.

"You're working on something."

"The motive," Stanley said. "Or anything that will link these women to one another."

"There is none," Lyle contended. "These are random slayings."

"I'm sure there's a connection," Stanley asserted. "It's simply eluding us."

"I will follow your suggestion."

"Lyle, I'm sorry. I was out of line."

"If you were one of my regulars, you would be suspended or fired," Lyle quipped.

"It won't happen again," Stanley said. "I really am sorry. How about ten days? It's your last shot at me with no more dog shows in my future."

"A pittance," Lyle retorted. "Your conduct was outrageous."

"Twenty?" Stanley offered.

"I am feeling a bit more like forgiving you."

"You are a hard man," Stanley said. "I will give you a year. Just leave me enough time to practice being a lawyer."

"Can I loan you out?"

"The year is yours," Stanley said. "I am profoundly sorry."

"I have never had so great an apology," Lyle acknowledged. "I am at a loss for words."

"You could say that it's too much," Stanley suggested. "I could be argued out of it."

"You don't want me to do that."

"Try it and see." Stanley urged.

Lyle extended his hand.

"I accept your apology."

"And my servitude," Stanley added morosely.

"That too," Lyle grinned.

Chapter 25

In the end Chief West drove Stanley to the hospital.

Tom Milani couldn't believe the change in West's demeanor.

How had Stanley worked the miracle, Tom wondered. He had never seen West so furious.

Stanley had been equally incensed. West had taken him into the farthest room on that floor. He would have taken him outside were not the building surrounded by reporters.

There had been an initial loud exchange of words muffled by the door and the distance, and then apparent silence. The two had emerged, both again in full control of their emotions, their anger dissipated, their friendship apparently still intact.

When they reached the hospital, Lyle and Stanley separated. Stanley found Milani's man again attached to his hip.

He wheeled himself into pre-op a few minutes before one. Mr. Maxfield was undergoing the first of the IV needle insertions. A nurse was preparing to shave the area to be operated on.

Stanley told Mr. Maxfield that he was going to see his family in a few minutes.

"Tell me which, if any, you want with you now."

"You mean in here?" Newton asked.

"Family can be with you until you are taken to the operating room."

"I want you."

"Hold on," Stanley told him. "I will tell them and I will be right back."

"Promise?"

"See that clock on the wall." Stanley said. "If I take larger than five minutes you get one hour of our time free. If I take longer than ten you get two."

"Starting now!" Maxfield said excitedly, his eyes merry.

Stanley arrived in the waiting room and glanced at his watch. He looked around.

"I need to speak with Newton Maxfield Junior, Kimberly Altman and Candace Cohen," he announced.

Three people separated themselves from the group.

"Your father does not want any of you with him at this time. I will ask him about the period following his operation."

"Why you?" Newton Junior snarled.

"Because I have his power of attorney and therefore I can speak for him."

"You can't bar us from our father," Candace said.

"He has the right to choose," Stanley said.

Kimberly began to cry. "He needs us."

"He doesn't need your blubbering," Junior snapped. "Dad didn't tell us about you. I want to talk to him."

Stanley glanced at his watch. "Not now. I will be back shortly and explain everything. Right now I need to go back to your father and see if he has any last minute instructions."

"I am going with you," Newton Junior declared.

"No, you are not. You are going to go back to your seat and wait until I return."

"No, I am not," Newton Junior said, planting his foot in front of the right wheel of Stanley's wheelchair.

Stanley glanced at his watch. "You are on the clock at four hundred dollars an hour starting now. If you leave that foot there, it's eight hundred."

Junior removed his foot, but moved himself in front of Stanley. "I said I am going with you."

"Me too," Candace declared moving next to her brother.

"And me," Kimberly sniffed, wiping her eyes.

"Mr. Praetzel," said a male voice. "May I help?"

"My lunch!" Stanley exclaimed. "On time. Thanks, Tim."

He took the lunch and set it on his lap.

"Tim, when you go back to the office tell Alice to bill Newton Maxfield Junior four hundred dollars for legal services."

"What services?" Junior blustered. "You haven't done anything for me."

"You're talking to me. Lawyers can bill for that." Stanley said. "Mrs. Cohen, Mrs. Altman, if you sit down and wait, I will ask your father to explain his reasoning and then I will consult with you free of charge. I need to be with him now, so please excuse me."

"Maybe we better wait," Kimberly Altman said, plucking her sister's sleeve.

Candace hesitated and then followed her sister to the chairs lining the walls of the waiting room.

"You don't get rid of me so easily," Newton Junior proclaimed.

"Do you have a lawyer, Mr. Maxfield?"

"Yeh, I got one."

"I would call him if I were you and ask him how many laws you are breaking by detaining me."

"If I was breaking laws, he would arrest me," Junior sneered nodding at the police officer.

"Evan's under orders not to leave my side," Stanley said.

"Good," Newton Junior spat out. "Now I'm going with you to see my father. And you can't stop me."

"He doesn't want to see you at this time." Stanley said moving away.

"Then you're not going either," Junior declared, stepping in front of Stanley's wheelchair so abruptly Stanley's foot hit Junior in the shin. His lunch tumbled from his lap and fell on the floor.

Junior kicked it across the slick floor. It was stopped by the wall. The box folded and one side opened up.

Stanley turned his wheelchair and headed for his lunch.

Junior rushed past him. The two sisters yelled at him to stop, but, as Stanley was reaching for the box, Junior's big foot smashed the box flat. The potato salad container spewed mayonnaise-covered potatoes in a wide arc around the white box while the sandwich flattened by the huge foot spit out the tomato, onion, pickle and dressing onto the sides of the squashed box.

"Arrest him" Stanley ordered. "Call for backup to book him."

Evan pushed Junior against the wall and ordered him to put his hands flat on the wall and spread his feet. Junior protested and twisted away. Evan grabbed Junior's arm and rotated it behind his back.

The click of the first cuff made a distinctive sound. Surprise made Junior hesitate briefly. His other arm was pulled behind him and the second cuff was attached to that wrist.

"You can't arrest me. I haven't done anything."

Evan talked into his radio and called for backup.

Stanley stared at his lunch. Bits and pieces clung to the spokes of his wheelchair. An orderly rushed up and offered to help.

"Get someone to clean up this mess," Stanley ordered. "Evan come with me."

"I will take you," the orderly offered quickly.

Evan pushed Junior into a sitting position in the nearest chair.

"Stay there," he ordered as he rushed between Stanley and the orderly.

"Let's go," Stanley said.

Evan glanced back at Junior. He was struggling to rise.

"You move and I will charge you with resisting arrest," Evan called back.

"It's been over ten minutes," Maxfield said as soon as Stanley entered.

"Your son's a piece of work," Stanley said.

"Can you keep him away from me?"

"Yes, I can," Stanley said. "Your daughters want to be with you."

"He'll finagle a way of accompanying them," Newton Maxfield said.

"I can stop that today," Stanley assured him. "Would you like to see your daughters now?"

"Without him?"

"Yes." Stanley said as he turned his wheelchair around.

Evan stepped up. "Mr. Praetzel, you can't go back."

"Tell whoever's there that Mrs. Cohen and Mrs. Altman can come here to see their father."

Stanley turned back toward the old man. "Your son's a bully."

"I know."

"Has he ever hit you?"

"Yes."

"Do you have anyone who can testify to that?"

"My daughters, but they're scared of Junior."

"Anyone else?"

"Herve knows, but I don't want him hurt. He's been a good friend."

"I am beginning to understand the terms of your will," Stanley said.

"Your wife is a shrewd woman."

"I had your son arrested."

"He will sue you."

"You can't harass a man in a wheelchair and get away with it. Not in this state."

The two daughters rushed into the room. Newton Maxfield held out his hands and each took one.

"We love you, Dad," Candace said.

"Why didn't you want to see us?" Kimberly asked, wiping the evidence of tears from her cheek.

"Your brother," Stanley interjected.

"Oh, Dad," Candace cried. "He's been arrested. He would want to be here. He loves you too."

"Tell them the truth," Stanley urged.

"I didn't want to see him," Maxfield said.

"You can't mean that!" Candace cried.

"I don't want to ever see him again," their father told them.

"Just talk to him," Candace entreated. "I know you can work things out. You're the only one who can handle him."

"He's fifty-six years old," Maxfield said. "He's been a bully since he was five. He likes bullying people."

"I am sure that's not true," Candace countered.

"I think maybe it is," Kimberly put in timidly. "He says he likes it when people are scared of him."

"He would never listen," Maxfield remarked.

"He will be so angry that we got to see Dad and he didn't," Candace said. "How will we ever explain that?"

"Listen to Dad," Kimberly said. "He just told us Junior never listens to him. There's nothing we can say that he will accept."

"You have my permission not to explain my actions," Newton Maxfield told his daughters. "All you need to do is listen to my lawyers. I spelled everything out for them. Please love me enough to let them take care of me."

"But we want to do that, Dad," Kimberly said.

"Neither you nor Candace can protect me from Junior. And I don't want you to even try."

"Dad, you're going to come out of this operation just fine," Candace stated decisively.

"Candace, if he hits me during my recovery, he could kill me," her father stated bluntly.

"We won't let him," Candace avowed with determination. "We love you too much."

"That's not true. Your fear of him overshadows your love for me."

"I won't accept that!" Candace declared.

"You've seen him hit Dad," Kimberly charged. "What did you do?"

"It was never very hard," Candace answered defensively. "And he was always sorry. He won't hit Dad when he's sick."

"He was never sorry," Kimberly said, sniffling.

The orderly came to take Newton Maxwell to surgery. The two women reluctantly let go his hands.

"Dad, we need you!" Kimberly cried. "Don't die!"

"Don't say such a dumb thing," Candace scolded.

"Don't treat Kim like that," her father admonished as he was moved onto the gurney. "Be kind."

"But she...she shouldn't have said that!" Candace declared.

"It showed she cared," her father said.

"I care," Candace cried as the gurney was rolled away.

"I love you both" he called back. "I won't die, Kim."

The double doors swung shut and Candace broke into tears.

"He doesn't think I love him," she sobbed.

"Let's go back to the waiting room and talk," Stanley suggested.

"Sorry, Sir," Evan said. "I haven't been cleared to let you leave here."

Stanley sighed. "We'll talk in here."

Unknown to Stanley and the two sisters, Newton Maxfield Junior was no longer in the waiting room.

The orderly had led him to a service elevator.

Anxious to avoid being booked, Junior was eager to escape and consult his lawyer. He was hoping to get the charges dropped.

The elevator doors opened and Junior stepped inside. The orderly handed a plastic bag with Stanley's crushed lunch inside to a burly man dressed in scrubs and wearing a surgical mask.

The doors closed. The elevator descended.

Newton Maxfield Junior left the hospital through the morgue entrance. By the time he was shoved in the back of a van, he had been blindfolded and his mouth had been taped shut.

He was returned to the hospital two hours later, his hands still cuffed behind him. He had been beaten and his right leg knee-capped.

To his utter amazement he was treated like a criminal, not a victim. He was rearrested. His hand was cuffed to the gurney and he had a police guard.

He discovered his sisters had accused him of assault and elder abuse. A restraining order had been issued that forbid him to come within a hundred feet of his father or his father's lawyer, Stanley Praetzel.

Junior's lawyer, Rodney Schulman, arrived before Junior's operation on his knee was scheduled to take place. Chief West met him, briefed him on the altercation between

Junior and Praetzel. He had no leads on who attacked Junior. He told him that Praetzel had been under constant police surveillance so the attack hadn't been instigated by him. Chief West shared a few other things with Junior's lawyer.

As a result, Rodney Schulman told Newton Junior he needed a criminal lawyer and walked away from his former client with one parting piece of advice.

"Obey the law and leave Stanley Praetzel alone."

Chapter 26

After Stanley was told that Newton Maxfield Junior had been arrested, he left the sisters in order to check on his wife. The array of monitors shocked him. There were so many. And she was lying so still. He wheeled up to her bed, picked up her hand and began to talk to her.

"Oh, Aleta, there is no way I should be taking your place. What were you thinking?"

He paused for a moment just in case she would answer and then he answered his own query.

"I know. You were thinking of me. I won't ever say I am not grateful to be well. I am grateful beyond measure. You do know your two months of celibacy is my two months of celibacy. It's going to be a long two months."

He was quiet for several minutes then spoke in a lighter tone. "You know, I think I'll visit the sperm bank, maybe more than once. In fact, maybe I'll visit several, just in case one burns down."

His jocularity ended as he laid his head on her limp hand and let his tears flow.

"Here you are," a cheerful voice said.

Stanley stirred, hastily wiped his tears away with the edge of the sheet.

"Straight from Alfredo's," Lyle West said. "I even brought coffee."

"You've got two boxes," Stanley noted.

"I charged them to your account," Lyle said. "You don't want to eat alone. Besides I told Dr. Cook I would tell you what he wants to do. I told him you wouldn't get angry with me."

He opened his box and signaled to Stanley to do the same.

"They want to put in a feeding tube, don't they?" Stanley said, unwrapping his sandwich.

"She's pregnant. She needs more nourishment than they can give her in an IV."

"Why is he afraid to tell me that?"

"It is something they do when they know the coma is going to be long term."

"Not always," Stanley argued.

"She's pregnant," Lyle repeated. "He also thought you would need to talk it over with someone who's not a doctor."

"Isn't an anesthetic dangerous?"

"Yes, but..." Lyle left the remainder unspoken.

"He's not going to risk anesthesia?"

"He says it's a quick procedure. They'll give her a local. That will help a little."

"I don't want her hurt."

"She wouldn't want the baby hurt," Lyle countered. "The baby's barely hanging on as it is."

The two ate their lunches in silence.

When Stanley finished, he asked. "What's Cook's idea of quick?"

"Under thirty minutes."

"That's not quick!" Stanley snapped.

"It's your decision," Lyle said.

"Tell him yes."

That night Stanley was back at his wife's bedside.

"You know, Aleta, I've been thinking. You can't lie still for two months and still have good muscle tone. I'm going to learn how to exercise them and do it for you every night. It'll be our time together."

He rose out of his wheelchair and stood on one leg next to the bed and pulled down the sheet. As he talked with her about his day at work, he took one leg at a time and moved it gently into various positions. He repeated the motions several times and then moved to the other leg.

He spent a lot of time trying to figure out what motions would exercise what muscles.

He was sitting on the bed flexing her ankles when Dr. Cook entered.

"You know Jamara knows a lot about therapy for coma patients," Dr. Cook mentioned.

"When's her surgery?" Stanley asked.

"Tomorrow morning. I brought the authorization for you to sign."

"You'll do it quickly, won't you?"

"Once it's in, she'll know the pleasure of a full stomach and her intestines will be asked to work normally."

Stanley stopped massaging Aleta's foot and signed the paper.

"Now, how are you holding up?" Dr. Cook asked.

"The family has pretty much arranged my life for the next two months. Robert and Bertha have moved into the guest room; Andrea is taking care of Jocelyn and Lettie; Paul is painting into the night; Jamara and Bertha have taken over Gerard's care so I can be here nights. Days I'm at the office."

"I heard you don't trust hospital food," Dr. Cook said.

"Not yet," Stanley admitted.

"Are you any closer to catching the Co-ed killer?" Dr. Cook asked.

"We have some fresh leads," Lyle said.

"I think the college is planning to shut down," Dr. Cook revealed.

"I don't want anyone else killed," Stanley said. "But if they close down, the investigation will screech to a halt."

"Have you really narrowed it down?" Dr. Cook asked.

"We need a week," Stanley said. "And, yes, we are close."

"If you come up with a fool-proof plan to safeguard the girls, my grandmother will get you the week," Dr. Cook promised.

Stanley scooted to the edge of the bed and stood on one leg. He leaned over and kissed his wife.

"Aleta, I need to leave," he said.

Then he settled into his wheelchair.

"She probably doesn't know you're here," Dr. Cook said.

"I know."

Dr. Cook was still writing orders when Stanley returned.

"Lyle suggested we meet here," Stanley said. "We are going to iron out a plan to safeguard the girls. We'd like you to sit in on our planning session."

"I was going home, catch a snack and go to bed," Dr. Cook sighed.

"Tom's bringing cake. Lyle's bringing coffee. Peets is bringing himself."

"I hope it's a big cake." Dr. Cook said sitting down. "So how are you holding up?"

"You asked me that before."

"And you told me your family had a schedule worked out. But, you didn't tell me how you are doing."

"God healed me," Stanley said.

"So, not well."

"I didn't say that."

"I can read between the lines."

"There weren't any lines. I uttered three words."
Stanley snapped.

"She's going to live," Wayne said kindly.

Stanley slumped a bit in his wheelchair. "I know.
And that should be enough, but..."

"You know one thing Jamara will tell you is that
Aleta needs an all over massage with body lotion. You could
do that. I can schedule you in from nine to ten every night.
Total privacy."

Stanley flushed.

"I am not taking advantage of a woman in a coma,"
he declared.

"You are her husband," Dr. Cook said evenly.
"Women like to be caressed. I think it might be good for her.
We don't know how aware people are in a coma, but..."

"Nine to ten is fine," Stanley said quickly to cut off
further discussion. "Would it be possible to lose some of
these monitors?"

"She's not asleep, Stanley. She's in a coma." Dr.
Cook said kindly, but firmly. "I need to keep track of her
vitals."

"How important is that hour I'm with her?"

"I will show you how to turn off the monitors in
here."

"I want the next step."

"You want to remove the patches?"

"Yes."

"The tubes will have to stay in."

"I realize that, but the beeping and the bouncing lines
are too much.

Dr. Cook nodded, "I will arrange it."

"Thanks for the suggestion."

Tom arrived with the cake first. In less than fifteen
minutes the three police chiefs, the doctor and Stanley were
eating cake and tossing out ideas about how to protect the
women in the dormitory.

Over the next half hour, various plans were proposed and in each case one of the men could see a problem.

Aleta moved her hand. The movement startled Stanley who was sitting next to the bed.

"She moved," he announced loudly.

Silence dropped over the group instantly.

"Open," Aleta said clearly.

Dr. Cook rose and examined Aleta while everyone sat silently expectant.

"No change," he reported. "Slight movements are not uncommon. Coma patients have been known to utter a few words. Neither are necessarily indicative of a truly conscious state."

"Can I at least try to ask her a question?" Stanley asked.

"She can't respond," said a high-pitched voice from the bedside of the comatose woman.

"Grams!" Dr. Cook exclaimed. "How on earth did you get in without our knowing it."

"I have a message for Stanley," Martha said, ignoring her grandson's query.

Chief West glanced over at his fellow chiefs.

"We now have two Harriets," he whispered.

They understood that another of the prophets could pass unseen past their guards. None of them mentioned that this one could enter a room and sit down and listen to their conversation without them being aware of her presence.

"There is a time for every matter under the sun," Martha said.

"I know that passage," Stanley said. "It's about opposites. A time to be born and a time to die. A time to weep and a time to laugh. A time for war and a time for peace."

"A time for silence and a time to speak," Martha said. "But this isn't that time."

"I shouldn't ask her questions?"

"No."

"But..."

"She entrusted you with her care," Martha reminded him.

"But..."

"She said 'open,'" Martha remarked.

"Does that mean the surgery should proceed?"

"What else could it mean?" Martha questioned.

Lyle spoke up. "You know. We've been talking about how to close these girls up in their rooms to keep them safe. What if we did the opposite? What if we opened all the doors?"

"Open the doors!" Peets exclaimed.

"Anybody could go anywhere," Tom said. "We'd invite chaos."

"Our perp has a pattern," Lyle went on. "What if we insist no doors are closed at any time."

"They won't do it!" Tom announced.

"Remove the doors," Martha said.

"They need privacy to dress," Tom said.

"All doors," Martha said. "No privacy. Just safety."

"Okay, Martha, give us the details," Lyle said.

"A police woman is assigned to each floor and she patrols the entire floor continuously during the early morning hours when girls are showering and dressing. Her male partner stands at the end of the hall monitoring her reports. He reports continuously to headquarters."

"This could work," Tom put in. "It would only take seven officers a shift. We would have every girl under almost continual surveillance."

"It would force the perp to rethink her pattern."

"You are sure we should take off the bathroom doors as well?" Tom asked.

"She might just switch to the bathroom," Lyle said. "She killed one girl in the bathroom already."

"You need to institute the plan tonight," Stanley said.

The chiefs left immediately and finalized the plan as they rode down in the elevator. They all planned on meeting at the college to institute the plan.

Martha had said she would call the president of the college and tell him the police were instituting a new plan that would guarantee the safety of the girls living there.

The president herself met the three police chiefs at the dormitory. The fire alarm was sounded and the police checked every room on all three floors, then guarded the entrances to the dormitory.

The janitorial staff joined the police in removing the doors. The girls standing outside were given envelopes to put their valuables in as soon as they were allowed to return to their rooms.

Chief West addressed the students and answered their questions.

Someone asked him how close the special investigator was to finding the person responsible.

Chief West looked around and then made a startling announcement.

"Mr. Praetzel has asked for one more week. That's how close he is. We don't want to risk another life in that week. He and his wife helped us devise this to protect you until then."

Lyle took Tom aside. "Stanley should have two men on him at all times. I just made him a target."

"I heard," Tom said. "You're counting on the prophets, aren't you?"

"Yes."

"Aleta's in a coma. Harriet's on a hunting trip. Jocelyn appears to be limited to prophecies about horses which leaves only Martha," Tom burst out.

"I gather you're worried," Lyle said

"Stanley's only got one leg," Tom growled. "He's a cripple for God's sake!"

"I will warn him."

"I think Justin will do that."

"What are you saying?"

"Justin has his TV crew here."

Lyle looked around. "Where?"

Tom pointed toward a cluster of trees.

"He's dressed in black!"

"Burgundy, I think."

"Same thing. It makes him invisible at night."

"Should I arrest him for being invisible?"

"He didn't see Justin?" Peets inquired quietly.

Lyle jumped at the sound of the deep voice. "Don't sneak up on me!"

Tom chuckled, "Especially when he's upset. He just dangled Stanley in front of our perp as bait and now he's having second thoughts."

"Do you need another man?" Peets asked Milani. "I can loan you one to help guard Stanley. I need Stanley alive and well for our sting operation."

The two chiefs spun toward the tall, black chief.

"What sting operation?" they chorused.

"It's Aleta's plan and it's a humdinger!"

"That's what we get? It's a humdinger?" West spat out.

"You've been busy with the attacks at the college and at the hospital."

Lyle charged back. "That reasoning doesn't hold water. I am your boss!"

"It's a small matter," Peets said. "But Stanley is the key that will make it work."

"You aren't going to tell me?" West asked.

"Out here?" Peets responded.

West bowed to his reasoning.

"Later," he grumbled.

Chapter 27

When Jamara arrived early Thursday morning, Bertha handed her the baby and told her that Stanley wanted to change their daily schedule. Jamara sat at the table. Gerard waited for her to open her blouse.

"He wants us to be Aleta's primary caretakers," Bertha announced as she set the plates on the table. The bacon was sizzling on the grill alongside the hash browns.

"She be coming home?" Jamara asked, her mouth watering. Gerard began to nurse.

"No, we are to go there," Bertha said. "Did you watch the news last night?"

Jamara nodded as she adjusted her blouse and Bertha set her breakfast in front of her.

"The hospital has nurses," Jamara said, taking her first forkful.

"Stanley doesn't trust the hospital staff." Bertha explained. "He's ordering private nurses for Aleta round the clock. You are one. Eunice is the other. As for me, he wants me to prepare all her meals here."

"They be putting in a tube," Jamara remarked.

"I am going to cook the food and puree it and take it all the way to the room personally."

"To me?"

"Breakfast and lunch," Bertha said. "I will pick up the breast milk at noon and at five."

"The baby, he likes to nurse," Jamara noted.

"Let's ask Stanley about that," Bertha said.

"He be sleeping?" Jamara asked.

"Dressing. He showered earlier."

"He be well enough?"

"Apparently Aleta healed him completely. He can use crutches. His hands are as strong as yours."

"Too bad she not do his leg."

"He says that wasn't part of God's plan for him."

"He be alright with that?"

"I don't know."

Stanley entered the kitchen via the hallway door. He never used that door with the wheelchair.

"Gerard, he likes to nurse," Jamara stated abruptly.

"You're talking about my changing your duties, aren't you?" Stanley asked.

"That be so."

"My wife needs the best nurse I can find. She also needs a nurse I can trust. I know Gerard may suffer a little for a week or so, but, his mother's life takes precedence."

"She be in danger?"

"Chief West told the whole world that Aleta helped formulate our new plan to protect the girls."

"This killer, she be the one what poisoned you."

"We think so," Stanley said.

"I be taking charge of feeding Mrs. Praetzel. Gerard, he be okay."

"Dr. Cook said you know what kind of exercise Aleta needs to keep her muscles from atrophying."

"That be so."

"Aleta is being operated on at eight. I want you there when she is returned to her room."

"I needs to get my uniform." Jamara announced.

"Go," Stanley said. "Gerard's done, isn't he?"

"He don't think so."

"Give him to me, Stanley said.

"You be dressed for work," Jamara objected.

Bertha held out her arms. "Come on, little guy, tell me your troubles."

Jamara rose, her breakfast only half eaten.

"I will bring you lunch and coffee," Bertha told the hefty, black woman before she reached the door.

Chief Lyle West was waiting for Stanley at his office. As soon as Stanley was seated, he set a stack of photos on his desk.

"I told you I don't remember what that nurse looked like," Stanley protested, guessing the purpose for the stack of photos.

"Pick out the victims," Lyle said.

"You know who they are," Stanley declared.

"It's a test." Lyle announced.

"Why are we testing me?"

"Humor me."

Stanley sorted through the photos and set aside five photos.

"Where did you get these?"

"Student photos, taken during Freshman orientation." Lyle replied. "Now pick out quickly anyone whom you are certain was not the nurse who poisoned you."

Stanley began sorting. Soon the pile of not possibles contained more photos than the other pile.

"You were a big help," Lyle said.

"There are fifteen photos left," Stanley noted.

"You eliminated three with weak alibi's."

"Tom's men have narrowed down the suspects?" Stanley inquired, his interest piqued.

"Eight have weak alibi's," Lyle said. "Five are still in your pile of possibles. We're getting down to a workable number."

Stanley began to study the photos that were left. He took out five.

"What are you doing?" Lyle asked.

Stanley picked up the photos one at a time.

"This one. Eurasian. At first glance she looks like the nurse, but I would have noticed a person of mixed heritage."

"Go on."

"This one. Two front teeth are slightly buck. I would have noticed that."

Lyle nodded.

"This one. Hair is too curly. Even pulled back it's frizzy. There was nothing unusual about the nurse's hair."

"How come they weren't considered not possible before?" Lyle asked.

"Similar face shape and even features. Remember I was racing through the photos," Stanley explained. "Number four has braces. I didn't notice that before. She's barely smiling in the photo."

"And the last one?"

"Eyes are too light," Stanley said. "Now what are we down to?"

"Four with weak alibi's" Lyle said. "You eliminated one more possible. We can investigate four."

Stanley studied the ten photos that were left. "Investigate all ten I picked out. Double check their alibis."

"Not concentrate on just four with weak alibis?" Lyle asked.

"No. You came here today because you were worried. That we might have eliminated the killer somehow. While I didn't notice her enough to pick her out, I did notice her enough to know who she wasn't."

"You make sense" Lyle said. "We'll expand our investigation to your final ten."

"Did Hawk turn up anything?" Stanley asked.

"Ask him. You have a nine o'clock appointment with him." Lyle told Stanley.

Stanley pressed Alice's button. "Do I have a nine o'clock with Mr. Monroe?"

"Yes Sir. He's here now."

"Send him in." Stanley said.

"He doesn't want me here," Lyle commented, rising.

"Hawk wouldn't do anything illegal."

"He thinks he's crossed the line," Lyle said. "You are his lawyer."

Lyle began to gather the photos. Hawk walked in and Stanley put his hand on Lyle's.

"Leave them. I will get them back to you."

Lyle greeted Hawk and left immediately.

"Give me a minute," Stanley said taking a pen and putting an 'S' on the back of each of the ten photos he had first selected.

Hawk started right in when Stanley put down his pen.

"I think I know who the killer is, but I have no proof," Hawk announced.

"Did you get DNA off the clothes?"

"Yes, but I have only the victims' DNA on file."

"Does all the unknown DNA match?"

"Yes. The last samples are being run now, but I expect those results will match as well."

"Did you find the key?"

"No, but I found masking tape under one of the drawers. The key had been hidden there. It was gone."

"Which room?"

"207."

Stanley flipped through the piles checking for the room number marked on each photo.

"One of the ten," he announced. "She has a good alibi."

"The piece of tape I found might not have held the key we're looking for," Hawk put in hesitantly.

"Anything else?" Stanley asked.

"A sixth-grade class photo in a book in a drawer. I can't say I saw it in plain sight."

"School photos in any other room?"

"Family photos, boyfriends, vacation photos, pets. No grade school photos."

"What book?"

"<u>Crime and Punishment,</u>" Hawk said. "Trouble is we can't get a warrant on the basis of a piece of tape."

"West is researching ten women I tentatively identified as the nurse who poisoned me. She is in that group."

"We can't get ten warrants." Hawk said, his attention on the group of ten. "We searched for the key and came up empty."

"A good defense attorney will throw out the DNA evidence unless we get it with a court order."

"It'll take a couple days to run and match the DNA. We have no probable cause for arrest. We don't want to spook her," Hawk said.

He began studying the photos in both piles. He picked out seven.

"I recognize these," he said.

"Four of those were victims," Stanley said.

"Never saw them alive." Hawk responded. "Pretty women."

"The other three?" Stanley pried.

"Must have seen them on campus," Hawk said, dismissing his own observation as immaterial.

Stanley, however, wouldn't let go.

"You saw half the women on campus. You picked out seven and you selected the one victim we figured was in the wrong place at the wrong time."

As Stanley was speaking, Hawk was arranging the photos on the desk as one would a puzzle. Once he finished, he sat back, satisfied.

The photos were not arranged in a row or even in several rows. The spaces between the photos were uneven. "They were in the photo," Hawk announced triumphantly.

"None of these girls had the same home town, even for a short period," Stanley protested.

"They were younger in the photo," Hawk went on.

"West checked out the backgrounds of the victims. There were no ties," Stanley insisted.

"I studied that photo because the children looked familiar," Hawk said.

"Look alikes?" Stanley asked.

"That might be true for us looking at a flat photograph," Hawk said. "But in real life a person's character comes from within and defines him or her."

"Are you suggesting their attitudes triggered a long buried hate?" Stanley ventured.

Hawk was stunned by the conclusion the two of them were reaching.

"You think our killer tortured and killed look-alikes?" Hawk ventured, his voice barely louder than a whisper, his eyes staring in utter disbelief at the photos. "Look-alikes?"

"Yes," Stanley declared. "And at least three more are slated for death."

"Didn't you say she had an alibi?"

"Yes," Stanley replied. "She's in the group because she was one of the ten who looked like the nurse that I believe poisoned me."

"Then we have West start with the alibis," Hawk decided. "We can't get a warrant if her alibi holds."

"We can't tell West which girl we suspect," Stanley cautioned. "You and I are basing our conclusion on a theory derived from your discovery of a photograph."

"I can't let on that I know who the killer is, can I?"

"Nor can I," Stanley replied.

"She could destroy the photo," Hawk worried.

"Consider it destroyed," Stanley advised. "Its existence can't even be alluded to."

"I understand."

"Tell West we want to be there when he questions the ten girls," Stanley said.

"What reason do I give?" Hawk asked.

"I want to hear her voice," Stanley said. "And you are going to be certain I don't go by any other criteria."

"Suppose you don't pick out our suspect?"

"I will only be eliminating the ones I'm certain aren't the nurse who poisoned me."

"I am never present during police interrogations," Hawk contended. "Let me get back to my work."

"You need to be at the interrogation," Stanley said.

"If you think it's that important, I will be," Hawk promised.

"Ask me if I'm sure," Stanley said. "And I will explain. Don't let me excuse our killer. Tell me to listen longer."

"We can't do that," Hawk said.

"You will think of something," Stanley assured him.

Chapter 28

The Willow Glen police headquarters was housed in an old brick building, the top floor of which formerly housed the forensics lab. The lab was now located in an adjacent modern brick building.

Hawk, who used to charge down the stairs to enthusiastically announce every breakthrough in a case, still charged into Tom Milani's office with any significant find.

That was the reason that when Stanley was ushered into Chief Milani's office, Hawk was there. It was Hawk who greeted him.

"Good! You're in time. I was just going to tell Chief Milani and Chief West what I've found."

"Don't let me stop you," Stanley urged.

"She cut herself," Hawk announced.

He stared at the blank faces.

"Don't you get it? She cut herself! I have her blood type."

Some comprehension began to appear on the three faces in front of him.

"Her blood type is in her medical file at the college clinic."

"Which is guarded by privilege," Lyle noted.

"How do you know she cut herself?" Stanley asked.

"There was a smear of blood on the neck band on the sweat shirt of the last victim. I tested it. It was a different blood type from the victim's."

"How did it get there?" Tom Milani asked.

"My guess is she picked up the garment to toss it next to the bed and didn't realize that some of the blood on the label was hers." Hawk explained. "It's fresh blood. And it's on the label."

"So we arrest someone with a cut on her finger," Tom concluded.

"Or her wrist or arm," Hawk added. "A minor cut because she didn't notice it. And it's probably healed by now."

"It's a good find, Hawk," Stanley inserted. "While we figure out how to get to the medical records, let's go with the voice recognition test now. I need to be at the courthouse at two-thirty."

"Are the girls all here?" Lyle asked Chief Milani.

"Yes. We told them we needed to talk with them about their alibis," Tom said.

"I would like to watch," Hawk said.

Chief West eyed Hawk curiously, but nodded his approval.

When Stanley and Hawk were ushered into the observation room, Lyle put a blindfold over Stanley's eyes and said, "As long as Hawk's here, we will let him record your take."

"I am ready," Stanley said.

The girls were ushered in. The one with the slight lisp and the one with the slight foreign accent were let go immediately. The one with the high-pitched voice was excused after a minute; the one from the deep south and the one whose voice reminded him of his mother's voice, after three minutes. Five were asked to wait.

Two of the five had weak alibis.

Stanley peeled off the blindfold when the two chiefs re-entered the observation room.

"Is it one of those five?" Tom asked.

"Yes," Stanley replied.

"Are you sure?" Hawk asked.

Lyle glanced at him with curiosity.

Stanley didn't reply immediately. It was important that no one else know that he and Hawk knew who the killer was. The police had to find her through regular channels. It was important she not escape retribution as the result of a technical foul-up.

"One of those five served me the poisoned coffee," Stanley declared finally.

"And stabbed you?" Tom pressed.

"Everything was a blur and my fear shut down my brain," Stanley related. "I couldn't speak or move. I was more aware on the day of the autopsy."

"We'll check their alibis for the day you were stabbed," Tom said.

"Can you hold them?" Stanley asked, thinking of Aleta.

"Not for very long," Tom replied.

"So we're down to five," Hawk concluded.

Chief Lyle West had been studying the exchange between the three men. His suspicions were aroused initially by Hawk's singular interest in the interview process. Hawk had never involved himself in this aspect of police work before. Inconsistency was a marker West used to foresee a problem.

What neither Hawk nor Stanley knew was that they had been videotaped. As soon as this session was over, West planned to review the tape.

Stanley's police guard got him to the courthouse by two-thirty.

During the ride to the courthouse, Stanley tried to shake the last hour from his memory, but to no avail. Hawk had the blood type. Stanley wanted to wrestle with how to get the medical records from the school legally. In order to introduce the photograph, everything leading to its discovery had to be by the book.

As his wheelchair was unloaded, Stanley was glad he had brought the manual one. It was an honest presentation of exactly where he was in his recovery. Dr. Taekman had ordered limited use of crutches despite Stanley's protestations that his hands were fine.

Aleta had give him his health back. He instantly corrected himself. God had healed him.

For some reason I am supposed to be in court in Aleta's place, he thought. I am to do something she wouldn't.

"Mr. LaVerne Brown," Stanley murmured. "Let's see what God has in mind."

He took LaVerne into a private room and talked with him at length about the vandalism and then about Cooper Egan.

"You need to let me speak for you today," Stanley finished. "I may not be as flamboyant as my intrepid wife, but I believe I can represent you with dignity."

Stanley wondered briefly how that word had found its way into his statement.

LaVerne Brown nodded and smiled.

"You picked the right word," he said. "You do that and it don't matter if I win or lose."

"Yes it does," Stanley declared. "You were wronged."

"There be lots of wrongs in this old world," LaVerne remarked. "You planning on righting all of them?"

Stanley smiled. "One at a time, Mr. Brown. One at a time."

After Stanley led Mr. Brown to their seats, he noticed that the old man was trembling slightly.

He leaned over and whispered to LaVerne, "You're not on trial."

LaVerne replied in a soft voice. "A black man is always on trial.

"Not today," Stanley declared. "Not in this courtroom. Not with me. You may be in deep water but I am an experienced lifeguard who's got a firm hold on you. Relax and let me do the swimming."

"Do you know where the shore is?" LaVerne asked in a normal voice.

Stanley smiled. The voice had lost its hesitancy.

They stood with the others when Judge Norma Jacobi entered the courtroom and sat down. Hers was an informal courtroom setup, but the judge herself was not casual in her decisions. Stanley had appeared in her courtroom as a child advocate in every instance until now. Usually he sat at the defense table with the child, occasionally, in the chairs behind when the contending persons were the child's parents, sometimes with a child beside him, sometimes alone. Never before was he seated beside an adult.

Having read a brief summary of the case, Judge Jacobi instantly recognized the aging black laborer as the victim. Her face still reflected her surprise at Stanley's presence. There were numerous reasons why he shouldn't be there, the main one being that Aleta was in a coma. Then she realized that this was Aleta's client.

Stanley would not be prepared, she thought sadly. Too bad.

When everyone was seated, Stanley remained standing. His one hand was resting on the shoulder of the black man.

Elias Finch turned to follow the judge's gaze and did a double-take. What the hell was Praetzel doing here. The man had just lost a leg. Elias could tell from where he sat that Stanley was standing on one leg. On that basis alone, he remained silent.

Stanley spoke. "Your Honor, I have a brief to present to the court requesting that this child be tried in adult court as this is a hate crime."

"Approach," Judge Jacobi said waving the attorneys forward.

Stanley lowered himself into his wheelchair and rolled forward. Elias was impressed with the smoothness of his movement. He acted as if his disability were of no moment. Elias wondered if he could do the same.

Norma Jacobi, her plump face with its crown of dark curls displaying her displeasure at this proposal, immediately asked why this request was being presented now.

"The defendant's parents wrangled an immediate hearing. I was caught off-guard and I apologize," Stanley said with the right degree of respect. "I will understand if the court feels that I am out of line."

"In the time you took to prepare the brief, you could have taken the proper steps."

"I did not prepare the brief. Aleta did. She did not have time to tell me much before she slipped into her coma."

Elias Finch cut in.

"All this notwithstanding, the fact remains that Cooper Eagen is only fourteen years old and he is charged with vandalism, not murder."

"I am going to review the brief," Judge Jacobi declared.

"Don't you want me to prepare an argument?" Elias asked, surprised.

"Not necessary," the judge declared. "Court recessed for fifteen minutes. Stay seated, Mr. Praetzel."

Elias turned to Stanley. "Adult court? You?"

"It's a conspiracy, Elias. The leaders are adults."

"But you're a child advocate!"

"Today, I'm not. Today I'm a victim's advocate."

The Assistant DA, Shannon Taylor, a slender, young woman who had worked with Aleta in the past, interrupted with a query.

"How is Aleta?"

"Doing well."

"Tell her I wish her well," Shannon said, then her face registered her sudden awareness of what she had said.

"I talk to her," Stanley said kindly. "She may even hear me."

Shannon nodded silently, and then motioned Stanley aside. "Why didn't you tell me you were going to do this?"

"The brief was handed to me just before I entered the court. I haven't even read it," Stanley said. "And my client is jumpy."

"But everything else is still in place?" Shannon asked.

"Except that if Jacobi decides this is a hate crime, she can beef up the punishment markedly," Stanley responded.

"His loss is under three hundred dollars," Shannon pointed out.

"No, it's not. He's had to hire an attorney to see if he could get those vandals to stop. We cost a lot."

"You want attorney fees?"

"Yes. Stanley said. "And Cooper Egan sprayed paint not only on the walls but an oil painting. It cannot be trashed as valueless. His deceased wife painted it. It must be restored. The one estimate he got was eight hundred dollars."

"Does your client want to testify?"

"No. He's afraid."

"Let's see if I can get him a little satisfaction," Shannon said.

Meanwhile back at the Willow Glen police headquarters, Chief West and Chief Milani were reviewing the video tape of the interviews. One girl had discarded her can of root beer in the trash. The smoker had left her cigarette in the ash tray. They could recover DNA from both. Hawk was called and rushed over to recover the can. He bagged the cigarette stub as well.

"How did he miss that?" Tom asked Lyle.

"That was when Lyle told Tom about Hawk's appointment with Stanley."

"He found something not covered by the warrant," Tom guessed. "Does Stanley know?"

"I don't think so," Lyle said. "He only knows that Hawk knows."

"So that's why Hawk was at the voice line-up," Tom concluded.

"And that's why he didn't zero in on the root beer can or the cigarette our only smoker left behind," Lyle reasoned. "They weren't important."

"If we ask those two to volunteer for blood tests," Tom said, "it would be reasonable. We have their DNA. It would eliminate them faster."

"We do this without Stanley or Hawk," Tom said. "Stanley's in court, isn't he?"

At that moment Stanley was sitting beside LaVerne Brown as Elias Finch and Shannon Taylor presented their arguments. The facts were not in dispute, just the motivation and the intent.

Judge Jacobi turned to Stanley after the two sides had finished and asked him if he had anything to add.

"I do, Your Honor," he replied. "May I remain seated?"

"Please do," the judge said.

"Cooper Egan is fourteen years old. He says he doesn't know Mr. Brown. Mr. Brown shoes his sister's horse. But I will give him that one. Tradesmen are often invisible to those they serve," he began.

"Cooper Egan denies the attack was based on Mr. Brown's race. He claims it was a foolish, prank and the house was picked at random.

"Mr. Brown has been targeted by vandals for almost four years. No other house on that block has been vandalized during that same period. No other house on that block is the home of an African-American.

"While I believe the attacks are orchestrated by an older boy or group of boys, I am going to speak only to Cooper Egan's claim that his was a random selection.

"Cooper Egan just entered Tri-City High School. Two of his classmates have been arrested and prosecuted for vandalizing Mr. Brown's house. Both these boys are friends of his."

Stanley paused a moment to give Judge Jacobi a moment to reflect on his opening statements. Then he switched his approach.

"When he decided which house to vandalize, he didn't eliminate that house because that house had been targeted twice. He also didn't eliminate that house from consideration because the man living in that house was a peace loving Afro-American. What he decided was that he wanted to tear apart the home of a hard-working American. What he decided was that he wanted to give him a miserable couple of days, not because he did anything to him personally, or to anyone he knew, but because his ancestors were African."

After Stanley spoke, the judge recessed until nine the next day.

"What's that mean?" LaVerne asked.

"It means she's thinking over what I said."

"Is she going to let him go?"

"No." Stanley said. "I will meet you here tomorrow at nine."

"It won't take all day, will it? I have to work."

"You will be out of here by nine-thirty," Stanley said. "I am sorry."

"It's not you that's making my stomach knot up. It's those kids. They have no idea how hard it is to walk into the mess. The money I get doesn't give me back the hours I spent cleaning up what they left. It doesn't erase the anger that eats away inside of me for weeks afterward. Then just as I think it won't happen again, it does. I thought this would help somehow, but it doesn't."

"Mr. Brown, we can't do anything about the misfortunes that life sends our way. Frankly, I think you're handling them superbly. I am not sure I could."

"You?" LaVerne gasped shocked. "You're hopping around on one leg as if it's no big deal. I couldn't handle that!"

Stanley chuckled. "I guess that's why you and I have different loads to carry."

"My wife used to talk like that," LaVerne said.

Suddenly, Stanley didn't want to face Lyle.

"How would you like to go out for supper?" he asked.

"Don't you have a family?" LaVerne queried.

"This is more important right now," Stanley said. "I need to talk to someone. Don't you?"

"Yes, I do," LaVerne said," but I don't take charity."

"I'm not offering any. I know this great place and the owner owes me a couple of meals."

"What about your guards?"

"They're here to keep me alive," Stanley said. "I am not supposed to distract them."

"Who's after you?"

"Several people," Stanley said.

"What did you do to them?"

"Nothing."

"Just like me, huh?"

Stanley paused.

"Pretty much," he said finally. "Let's go eat."

Alfredo set the two up at a table in the back corner. The police guards took positions as inconspicuously as possible, but Alfredo was still pressed into explaining their presence to his customers. He finally gave up and told them a version of the truth. The police were guarding a famous lawyer on an important case.

The two men talked. Stanley asked LaVerne about the early days of his marriage. LaVerne talked about his wife in loving terms, the move to the house on Beach Street nostalgically, and his work as a farrier with joy. The talk turned to Hubbs and they compared notes about his idiosyncrasies and his way with horses. LaVerne had known Hubbs a long time. Stanley listened raptly to his stories.

"Hubbs has a girlfriend, you know," Stanley said.

LaVerne laughed. "Who'd love that beat up old stick of a man?"

"The artist, Bessie Dobbins."

"The one what's selling her paintings for a fortune now?"

"She comes over on weekends and they exercise the horses riding bareback around the place."

"No wonder I'm shoeing them all."

"Don't all horses wear shoes?"

"Not those that no one rides," he explained. "They gonna get married?"

"I think they're both happy in their situations and neither want to make a change."

LaVerne chuckled. "That old goat!"

Stanley smiled. "She stays at the house when we're gone and watches the pup for me."

"Hubbs can cook, you know," LaVerne confided. "He could've gotten a job as a cook. He told me he likes horses too much."

"He has full use of the kitchen when we're gone."

"He's got the best of both worlds," LaVerne said. "He loves to cook for people."

"Was your wife a good cook?"

"One of the best" La Verne reminisced. "Luanna used to bake cookies for the whole neighborhood when our kids were little and she kept it up until the Shacklefords moved in. That was a year before she died. I'm glad she never lived to see the vandalism. It would have broken her heart."

"Tell me about your kids," Stanley urged.

Two desserts and three coffees later, LaVerne Brown and his lawyer left the restaurant.

Parked next to the curb in front of the entrance was
the Arborville Police Chief's car. Leaning against the side of
it, waiting, was the owner of that car.

West approached the pair, focused on Stanley and
asked him bluntly, "Are you avoiding me?"

"LaVerne Brown, may I introduce you to Chief Lyle
West who is obviously peeved at me."

Lyle shook LaVerne's hand.

"How did it go in court today?"

"The judge went home," LaVerne said.

"That could be a good sign."

"That's what Mr. Praetzel says."

"One of Chief Peets men will follow you home,"
West said. "He ordered a guard posted at your house
tonight."

"You think I'm in danger?" Brown asked.

"You talked to Stanley. He's contagious," West
responded tongue-in-cheek.

"Lyle, be serious!" Stanley snapped.

West glared at the man in the wheelchair.

"I amend my statement," Stanley said. "Mr. Brown,
the police in our towns take their jobs seriously. They sense
that you may have angered some irrational men today."

"What did I do?" LaVerne asked.

"Nothing," Stanley returned. "Racists are irrational
men. Any action can incite them."

"Like my breathing?"

"Like that."

One of the men escorted LaVerne Brown to his truck.
Lyle opened the front door to his car.

"Am I riding with you?" Stanley asked, not moving.

"You're on duty from now until nine," Lyle told him.

"Suppose I have things to do?" Stanley asked.

"Like what?"

"Things."

"You can do them later."

Stanley shrugged. "You win."

He rose, hopped two steps and sat down in the passenger's seat. His guards folded his wheelchair and slipped it into the back.

Stanley heard Lyle giving the men instructions. It didn't matter where they went. Lyle somehow sensed that Hawk and he were holding out on him. He couldn't approach Hawk, but he had a hold on Stanley. When Stanley was on duty, he was under Lyle West's supervision. Lyle would demand to know what was going on.

Lyle climbed into the car.

"Where are we going?"

"You're going to the hospital to guard your wife," Lyle said. "I am really short-handed."

"Do I get a gun?"

"Yes."

"Is this legitimate?"

"Yes." Lyle responded. "You didn't need to hide from me. You and Hawk have your reasons for keeping us in the dark. You will be glad to know we got blood samples from the two with no alibi. Both are A positive. Our killer is AB negative."

"That leaves only three suspects," Stanley commented.

"I picked you up to see if you could remember any jewelry she was wearing. I could probably get a search warrant if I had something like that."

"She had a gold watch. One with an expansion band."

"When we get to the hospital, I will have you describe it to me. I will sketch it."

"It's a common watch."

"But we only have three suspects."

"But all have good alibis."

"Tom's working on those."

"I have something for Peets," Stanley said. "The Shacklefords who live on Brown's street had an altercation with Luana Brown a year before her death."

"She was white, you know," Lyle said.

"She was light," Stanley corrected.

"Are you saying theirs wasn't a mixed marriage?"

"Yes," Stanley returned. "If the people behind these attacks on LaVerne Brown are people who want to keep the races pure, then the leader of the vandals has been operating under a false assumption."

"That would explain why Brown is a target and the two black families on the next block haven't been targeted," Lyle said.

"I was puzzled by what made him different."

"Peets must have known."

"I think there are some things Peets doesn't share."

"It's still a hate crime," Stanley declared.

Twenty minutes later, Stanley was installed as the guard assigned to his wife's room. Both police chiefs had been summoned to a meeting at the hospital and Lyle was busy sketching the watch Stanley remembered seeing on the nurse's waist.

When Chief Milani and Chief Peets arrived, each brought a man to stand guard while they joined Stanley and Chief West in Aleta's room. The nurse was told to take a break until ten.

"This meeting needs to be over at nine," Stanley said as the three chiefs settled in chairs around the room.

"Why exactly is it we're meeting here?" Tom asked.

"Because the only place Stanley won't leave is this room," Lyle responded. "And we need to run our ideas by him."

"We've never needed to do that before," Peets observed, staring at Stanley who was sitting beside his wife's bed holding her hand.

"We've never had one of our men know who the perp is and not tell us," Lyle contended, knowing that Peets was sensitive to Stanley's pain.

Peets jaw dropped. "You know?"

Lyle replied for him. "Both he and Hawk know but for some reason they can't tell us. My guess is that Hawk found something when he was helping Tom's men search for the key, but since it wasn't covered by the warrant and it wasn't in plain sight, he had to let it go."

"That makes no sense," Peets said. "If he had opened a drawer to look for a key and saw whatever it was, that's the same thing as being in plain sight."

"I have a feeling it's a more complex issue than that," Lyle said. "So far neither has panicked as we've progressed in our investigation and we've narrowed it down to three suspects. Blood samples from the two without alibis leaves us with three with alibis. We can't move until we break those alibis."

"So why are we here?" Peets asked.

"Tell him, Stanley," West ordered.

Stanley, relieved that they were on to other business, said, "About five years ago the Shacklefords moved into LaVerne Brown's neighborhood."

"I talked to all the neighbors," Peets said. "They all checked out."

"Luanna Brown had a run in with Mrs. Shackelford five years ago that upset her deeply," Stanley went on. "Did you know Luanna Brown wasn't white?"

"Yes," Peets replied evenly.

"I don't think Mrs. Shackleford did," Stanley said. "According to her husband, Luanna never told anyone."

"That could explain why the other two black families in the neighborhood were never hit," Peets said.

"Surely you considered this possibility," West said.

"One of many," Peets responded.

Aleta mumbled something but the word was short and unintelligible.

Stanley shrugged and then explained.

"Dr. Cook told me that people in comas sometimes speak, but they aren't necessarily reacting to their surroundings or to questions put to them."

"She said 'missus'," Peets said and then went on. "Her speaking reminded me of something. Stanley, didn't you say that Luanna Brown had an altercation with Mrs. Shackelford?"

"Yes."

"I will start there."

"Moving on," West said, handing Tom the sketch of the watch. "Stanley said the nurse that served him the poisoned coffee was wearing this watch."

Tom studied the photo.

"This is an ordinary watch."

"But we have a good chance that only one of our suspects owns one," West said.

"We would warn them they're suspects," Tom pointed out.

"They know that already," Lyle said. "None of the final five had an alibi for the period Stanley was attacked."

Stanley broke in. "What about the alibis for the latest murder?"

"Those are holding," Tom said. "Two students verified Rene Carow's alibi. She was with them. They are standing firm. A professor was meeting with Valerie Snow. The professor said she didn't stay long, but she was on time for the meeting. It was on his calendar. Linda Ellis was in the library with her boyfriend. He says she was never gone for more than ten minutes. He cut out for almost twenty, but another friend says that Linda waited for him to return which he did."

"Any suggestion on those alibis?" West asked Stanley.

"Have Ed investigate the professor and the two students," Stanley said. "Double check the time on the library alibi. See if another student can verify the story."

"Which first?" Lyle prodded.

"I can't tell you that," Stanley said.

No one spoke for several minutes.

"We ignore the watch," Stanley said. "It's too obvious."

"I say we get a warrant to search the girls' rooms for the watch," Tom Milani argued.

"We will be warning her," Stanley said. "I think she has set up a patsy."

"If she's as smart as you say she is, she knows we're on to her," Peets put in. "She could get away."

"She's not going to spook. She thinks she's smarter than us," Stanley countered, "but the decision is yours, not mine."

"I say we get a warrant to search each girl's room and arrest whoever has the watch," Tom Milani proposed.

"Following Stanley's reasoning," Peets said, "If our killer is really smart, she wouldn't be caught with the watch in her possession."

"She might not have noticed she was wearing it," Tom argued. "Her attack on Stanley couldn't have been planned."

This woman is devilishly clever," Stanley asserted. "Even if she forgot she was wearing it when she walked into my hospital room, she would have noticed it after she walked out; however, I contend that she wore it on purpose."

Before Tom could reply, Lyle spoke up.

"Tom, your arguments are sound, but you remember the reason we asked Stanley to work on the case was because he would view it differently. Because he did, we know we're after a woman. His insight changed our whole approach. We're on the verge of nailing a serial killer, thanks in good part to his input," Chief West expounded. "We will do as he suggests and hold off on getting a search warrant for the watch."

"I can focus on the alibis," Tom resolved.

"It's nine o'clock," Lyle announced.

The three chiefs filed out of the room silently.

Stanley rose from the wheelchair. He turned on his one leg and gazed at his sleeping wife. He started removing the patches attached to the monitors. He worked slowly, talking softly as he allowed his hands to caress her body. He told her about his day and as he did so he reminded her again that they were married and it was okay for him to be touching her like this.

"Do you like to be caressed by your husband?" he asked as their hour was coming to a close.

Her response was a slight arching of her back.

He couldn't believe what was happening.

Dr. Cook had said that people in comas sometimes responded to various stimuli. Until this moment he believed all her senses were dormant. Now he wasn't sure.

Her coma is not a usual one, he told himself. Immediately, he reminded himself that not much was known about comas because people who emerged from them woke with little memory. Hers could be very ordinary.

What wasn't ordinary was Aleta. She never fit the mold. Why would she fit it this time?

"You are a delightful woman," he purred. "You send me indications of your love even when you're practically removed from this world."

He continued to let the touch of his fingers tell her he was with her and that he loved her.

Perhaps, he thought, her ability to be reached was limited to the kinesthetic.

He dismissed that thought. He knew she could hear him. He didn't know if what he was saying was filtering into her memory, but he believed she was responding not only to his touch but to his voice.

At ten o'clock, dressed and back in his wheelchair, Stanley took Aleta's hand and removed the ring. As he did so the hand curled slightly.

"I will marry you again tomorrow night with a ring you can keep," he promised.

Chapter 29

At nine o'clock the following morning, Stanley and LaVerne Brown were settled in Norma Jacobi's courtroom. Neither spoke. Both were too apprehensive for idle chatter. If LaVerne had been a child, Stanley might have taken his hand.

Judge Norma Jacobi didn't keep the litigants waiting. Stanley rose on his one leg when the bailiff asked all to rise. His leg, tired from all the standing he'd done the night before, objected to his rising, but he ignored its protest.

The judge noticed Stanley's gesture of respect. It pleased her.

The courtroom quieted quickly in anticipation.

Judge Jacobi, whose written judgment lay before her, began to speak.

"It is not the intention of this court to incarcerate this boy as punishment..."

A sigh of relief from the parents was quickly squelched by a look from Elias Finch.

"The court, however, finds him guilty of criminal trespass and destruction of the property of another. The latter act calls for restitution. The court awards Mr. LaVerne

Brown full restitution for all damaged property plus
attorney's fees. In addition, the court awards Mr. LaVerne
Brown ten thousand dollars in punitive damages..."

Groans from Cooper's parents told the judge, she had
hit the mark.

"It is the opinion of the court that hate drove Cooper
Egan to vandalize Mr. Brown's home. The hate may have
been born in someone else's heart, but Cooper Egan did not
stop it from entering his own and ruling his actions.

"While you as his parents will bear the financial
burden of your son's lack of understanding that not only does
breaking the law have consequences, but also that this
country will no longer tolerate one race subjugating another.
I hope that as parents you will now teach your son these
lessons so that he never sees the inside of a courtroom as a
defendant again."

Cooper Egan sat relaxed as his parents were being
scolded. They would in turn yell at him, but that had
happened before. He only had to say he was sorry and his
mother would persuade his father to forgive him. He
predicted that he would be grounded.

The judge addressed Cooper by name. Elias Finch
hissed at him to sit up.

"Cooper Egan, you will serve two hundred hours of
community service."

Cooper's jaw dropped.

"It is double what is ordinarily given. A hate crime
allows me to stiffen the penalty. Moreover, the court is
going to dictate your particular service. From two o'clock
until six each weekday you will stand guard outside Mr.
Brown's house and report any attempts to vandalize his
property. If any vandalism occurs, you will be considered a
co-conspirator and again come under the judgment of this
court.

"You will stand guard without benefit of head
phones, hand-held games or any entertainment device. You
will not do any homework at this time. You will not talk on

your cell phone or in person to anyone while you are on guard duty."

Cooper's father objected before Elias could stop him. "But he's on the freshman football team."

"He also has an honors math class last period," his mother piped up.

The judges face grew stern. "Your son broke the law, Mr. and Mrs. Egan. Mr. Brown has paid dearly for Cooper's so-called prank. It is Cooper's turn. I cannot give back to Mr. Brown the hours lost in cleaning up and repairing the damage to his home, nor can I compensate him for the despair he felt when he opened his door and found his home in a shambles. Biblically, the punishment would be an eye for an eye, but the law doesn't allow me to mete out that kind of punishment. The closest I can come is to take away some hours from your son's life in exchange."

"Finally," Judge Jacobi said and paused as moans were heard from all three Egans.

"Finally, Mr. Brown, you have suffered egregiously at the hands of this young boy. The court wishes to thank you for bringing this crime to the attention of the police despite early dismissals of your suffering as minor. I do not believe that this violation of your rights had been previously addressed by the court as seriously as it might have been. I wish to tell you that your forbearance and your choice not to retaliate in kind are in the eyes of this court the hallmarks of an honorable man."

Court was then adjourned and the judge left the room.

Elias Finch came up to Stanley. "I told the Egans not to fight the judgment. It was a little on the high side, but Cooper refused to give up whoever planned this. I told his parents that Cooper could have wound up in Juvenile Hall. That shocked his mother. I told them the award for the next boy who doesn't cooperate will be higher. That settled the father down. Innovative community service idea. Smart move, by the way, showing up with Mr. Brown. And that stunt with the leg even had me rooting for you."

"It wasn't a stunt."

Elias grinned. "That's why it worked."

"The absence of my leg shouldn't enter in," Stanley protested.

"Stanley, everything enters in," Elias said.

Elias' words bothered Stanley. Fortunately for Stanley, LaVerne Brown's mind was absorbing the judge's words, and, so steeped was he in the word honorable, that he was oblivious to Elias Fish's patter and to Stanley's defensive posture.

By the time they had exited the courtroom, LaVerne was again in control of his thinking.

"We won, didn't we?" he asked.

"You won," Stanley said. "The punishment was severe enough to make an impact, but not so outrageous as to invite an appeal."

"Will the vandalism stop now?"

"Chief Peets has arrested another vandal," Stanley said. "He will need you to stand strong."

"I don't understand."

"I believe we need to do this once or twice more."

"Can you go without me? I hate to lose all that work time."

"Maybe I can fix that," Stanley said. "What Chief Peets wants is to convict the adults behind these attacks."

"So what do I do?"

"Don't do any bargaining on your own."

"Who's going to try to bargain?"

"The parents," Stanley said. "Call me if you're approached."

"I owe you. I'll do what you say."

Later at the office, Stanley sought out his father.

"I have a dilemma," he stated flatly.

Hubert got up, and as he closed the door, he told Rose to hold his calls.

"How did it go in court?"

"Two hundred hours of guard duty at Brown's house that will rob Cooper Egan of playing on the Fresh Soph team this season, plus he has to drop honors math. Ten thousand punitive plus actual plus legal fees."

"Sounds like a big win."

"Oh it is, but Elias Finch said...oh, hell, Dad...he admitted he knew it wasn't a stunt, but now...what am I going to do about my leg?"

Hubert chuckled. "Which leg? The one you don't have any more or the one you used to stand up on when the judge entered."

"It's not funny. I could stand so I did." Stanley charged. "It wasn't a stunt!"

"Was the judge affected?"

"Who can tell with Jacobi?"

"She knows you lost your leg recently. I don't think it affected her judgment."

"I don't want to appear to be grandstanding."

"Why not? I think the fact that you stood on one leg was grand."

"Dad, you're playing with words and I'm serious."

"So am I. Sitting would have been grandstanding."

Stanley frowned as he considered what his father had said.

Finally, he shrugged.

"I can't win," he muttered.

Hubert smiled. "You won today."

"I mean people will criticize no matter what I do."

"You're just learning that?" Hubert asked and then added, "How's Aleta?"

"I think she knew I was there." Stanley said. "She seemed to like the massage."

"Don't read her involuntary movements as voluntary," his father advised.

"It helps for me to believe she's responding," Stanley said.

"I can't see a harm in that, actually." Hubert responded. "I keep forgetting that Aleta is not an ordinary person, after all. She could well be reacting positively to your touch."

"I am not sure I'm strong enough to stay the course," Stanley confided.

"My door's always open to you, Stanley. You can come in anytime and watch my fish."

Stanley looked over at what had been a blank aquarium.

"I didn't know your fish came."

"Like them?" his father asked, smiling.

"You have all Aleta's!" Stanley exclaimed.

Hubert laughed.

"I love fan-tailed gold fish. Robert ordered angel fish."

"Isn't anyone creative?" Stanley griped.

"We lawyers are not artists, Stanley," his father replied. "Speaking of artists, are you going to the opening of Paul's exhibit tonight?"

"If I go, I won't make it back in time for my scheduled visit with Aleta," Stanley responded. "I am going into the city tomorrow afternoon. I will visit the exhibit then."

"It won't be the same."

"I know, but Paul might appreciate a friendly face tomorrow."

"I think you should go tonight," Hubert said, a touch of urgency in his voice. "Even if you can't stay."

"I wouldn't have time to see the whole exhibit," Stanley explained. "That would be rude."

"I understand you're in for a surprise," Hubert said. "You need to see it first."

"I have seen all Paul's work."

"Not all," Hubert said. "He did an experimental piece."

"Who was the subject?"

"You."

"Me?"

"I haven't seen it, but I understand it's one of his best," Hubert said. "The gallery is opening its doors at seven for the critics. You could go then. The rest of us are planning to arrive at eight."

"You're pushing, Dad. Why?"

"Tomorrow the exhibition is open to the public," Hubert said. "Trust me. You need to see the painting tonight."

"If I don't like it, I will remove it," Stanley vowed.

"You signed a release. In fact, you signed multiple releases," Hubert said. "Paul says the painting is named in the release."

"That was my idea," Stanley remarked dourly. "But I don't remember posing."

"Don't overreact. Your mother saw the painting. She told Paul to include it in his exhibition."

"And how did she think I would feel?"

"Exposed."

Stanley's jaw dropped. "She used that word?"

"Yes."

"Why then did she approve?"

"She said the painting moved her deeply. She said it wasn't just good. It was great."

"Dad, you've just ruined my day," Stanley snapped. "I don't want to be the subject of a great painting. I don't want to be stared at by a multitude of people, especially exposed. I like the one where I was in a suit and Aleta's back was bare. She doesn't mind being slightly exposed. I do. I never posed nude. I will not go on display nude. I absolutely will not no matter how many releases I signed!"

"When you serve him with a restraining order," Hubert advised, "do it with restraint."

"Why?" Stanley grumped. "He was a guest in my home. He took advantage."

"His words exactly," Hubert said. "Your mother talked him into letting the critics see it. She showed it to Mrs. Cook and she bought it."

"I thought everything not commissioned was subject to a silent auction with a beginning bid suggested. How could it be sold?" Stanley asked, his voice petulant.

"Martha already told Paul she would add one hundred thousand to any bid."

"Suppose I want to buy it."

"Aleta said you would never want it in the house."

"She saw it?"

"Just a beginning sketch," Hubert said.

"Has every woman I know seen it?"

"Pretty much."

"Dad, he's never seen me nude." Stanley railed.

"Didn't he help you shower?"

"Oh my God!"

"Stanley, you're talking to someone who hasn't seen the painting, but I trust your mother's judgment," Hubert said calmly. "Trust her."

"You trust her," Stanley quipped. "I am going to get a court order."

He turned his wheelchair around.

"Chief Peets made an appointment with Alice."

"How do you know that?"

Brushing aside his son's query, Hubert glanced at his watch. "He should be arriving in a few minutes."

"You purposely kept me here after you told me so I wouldn't have time to get a restraining order."

"You have a staff."

"I can't involve the staff in this."

"You have this afternoon," Hubert said.

"You're right. I do," Stanley conceded. "Dad, I'm sorry I bit your head off."

Chief Peets was waiting for Stanley in his office. He was calmly sitting watching the Koi swim lazily up and down their long tank.

"Alice didn't buzz me," Stanley apologized as he entered.

"Your father's secretary said you weren't to be disturbed."

"I will tell Alice you are allowed to interrupt from now on," Stanley said. "What brings you here?"

"We need to talk. I need help if I am to get the Shacklefords on conspiracy."

"I told LaVerne to call me if anyone offered to settle out of court."

"He's been approached."

"How do you know?"

"Brown was down at Glascock's dealership looking at new trucks," Chief Peets revealed.

"LaVerne just received a sizeable award," Stanley pointed out. "But not enough for a new truck."

"Remember what you said about service people being invisible."

"Someone heard?"

"Seems Glascock apologized quite effectively for the actions of his son, Drew. He then offered LaVerne a new truck at half price."

"Which would cost Glascock only a couple thousand," Stanley interjected. "And LaVerne could afford that. And his truck is pretty old."

"LaVerne wants that truck," Peets said.

"Did he close the deal?" Stanley asked.

"He said he was late for a shoeing appointment, so he had to go. He promised to come back at noon."

"Bless LaVerne Brown's work ethic!" Stanley exclaimed. "We may be able to stop him."

"How?"

"He doesn't want to go back to court because it interferes with his shoeing schedule. I made a mistake by not taking his commitment to his work seriously."

"But he would get more money," Peets said.

"He doesn't want the money. It embarrassed him
when he got it. All he wants is an apology and for it not to
happen anymore."

"So the money didn't make him feel better."

"Having a guard on his house was the best part he
said."

"He doesn't dare start over," Peets said thoughtfully.
"His possessions have been destroyed too many times."

"We need to go to where he's working," Stanley
determined.

"He's at the stable next to Bessie Dobbin's place,"
Peets said.

"You're a fount of information."

"I keep track of what goes on in my town." Peets
returned without explanation.

Stanley rolled his wheelchair through the door.
"Alice, I am off to see a client. I have my cell on."

Huck Dirkson was surprised to see Stanley emerge
from Chief Peets' car.

"You aren't planning to return Minx, are you?" he
asked, worry lines crossing his forehead.

"Never!" Stanley exclaimed. "She's a jewel. I plan
to ride her. Robert built a hoist to help me get on her. Aleta
and Bertha think I should learn to ride bareback to strengthen
my upper legs. I trust Minx not to throw me."

"You aren't being fitted for an artificial leg?"

"Eventually."

"So why are you here?"

"To talk to Mr. Brown."

"The farrier? Is he in trouble?" Huck asked.

"No, not at all."

"He said he was in court this morning."

"He was," Stanley said. "He won."

"He seemed troubled for someone who won."

"That's why we're here," Stanley said. "We'd like to
talk with him privately."

"He's alone behind the barn, but I'd better go with you. I'm not sure the horse he's shoeing won't spook at a man rolling up to him in a wheelchair. I don't know if she's ever seen one."

"Maybe he should come out," Peets suggested.

"No!" Stanley declared. "I will walk if I have to." Both men stared at him.

"Okay, okay. I will need help."

"Why don't you have crutches?" Huck inquired.

"My doctor doesn't want me to put weight on my right hand."

It turned out the mare wasn't bothered by the wheelchair. In fact, she ambled forward a couple steps and nuzzled Stanley.

"Poppy's a rescue," Huck said slyly.

"I have a barn full of horses," Stanley protested.

"Robert doesn't have a horse. He's been practicing on her and others. He likes Poppy best."

"LaVerne, what do you think?" Stanley asked.

"She's a good one. Been mistreated, but she's pretty sound."

"Okay," Stanley said. "How much?"

"Your usual donation would be appreciated."

"I am never coming here again. Next thing I know I will have to buy Jack a horse."

"Jack? Hubb's helper?" Dirkson asked.

"Don't even think about it!" Stanley declared.

"I keep a lookout for one that can carry the boy."

"I said, don't think about it."

"It might take a while. Mostly the horses we get are underweight and he's a hefty lad."

"You're thinking about it," Stanley declared, exasperated.

"You're a rich man. You have a full-time groomsman and a helper. You have pasture land. And you like animals."

"Where'd you get that idea?"

"Poppy told me. The only other person she nuzzles is Robert.

Stanley pulled out his checkbook and signed a check and handed it to Huck Dirkson. "Fill in the rest."

"You trust me."

"Yes," Stanley said. "Deliver Poppy today if you can. Robert and Bertha ride Saturday mornings."

"I thought you were full up."

"Robert's a carpenter. He can build Poppy a stall. There's room for one next to Jezebel."

"Until then?"

"Hubbs will take care of her."

Huck Dirkson went up to the horse and stroked her on the neck. "Well, Poppy, old girl, you got the home you wanted. Mr. Brown, I will be taking a quick trip when you're done. I will need help getting Poppy into the trailer."

"Sure," LaVerne said.

Dirkson walked back through the barn to the house. Stanley knew he'd take care of the check right away.

"LaVerne, you really don't want to go to court again, do you?" Stanley asked.

"Don't like it none."

"Chief Peets and I have been talking it over. If you don't want to, you don't need to go to court again."

"Not even to tell what they did?" LaVerne asked.

"We have pictures," Stanley said.

"Not even to say I didn't do nothing to those boys?"

"No," Stanley affirmed. "Is that what you're afraid will happen? You think the defense attorney will make it your fault?"

"Something like that."

"Thanks for telling me," Stanley said. "Now for sure, I don't want you in the courtroom from now on."

"But you'll be there."

"Oh, yes, I will be there."

"You ain't mad?"

"Not at all."

"Mr. Glascock offered me a truck at half price," LaVerne said. "Weren't much of an offer. I was gonna go back at noon and bargain a bit, but I suppose I shouldn't, huh?"

"No, Chief Peets needs to be the bargainer. He wants to nail the adults behind these attacks."

"Does he know who they are?"

"Yes," Stanley said. "And he knows why. Now, what he needs is for you to stand firm so he can get the boys to cooperate."

"He's got more than one?"

"Drew Glascock and Anthony Gambetta," Peets disclosed.

"If we can get them both to cooperate and testify," Stanley explained, "We can prosecute everyone involved over the past four years."

"Four years?" Chief Peets asked, surprised. "Isn't there a statute of limitation on vandalism?"

"Yes, but not on conspiracy. And that's current," Stanley said. "We have an ongoing chain of influence with information continually passed down. It will be tough to link them all into an unbroken chain, but, Alan, if you can do it, Aleta will run with it."

"So I have two months, right?"

"Cooper Egan has ten weeks of guard duty. We don't need the next one to start his stint until Cooper's done," Stanley commented positively.

LaVerne smiled.

"I might just get me a real comfortable couch."

"Can you hold off on that truck?" Stanley asked.

"I don't want a fancy new truck. My customers will think I charge too much if I drive up in one." LaVerne said. "But I need one that don't give me trouble when it's cold."

Twenty minutes later, Stanley rolled into his father-in-law's office and despite the fact that Robert was on the phone, announced, "I bought you a horse. She's being delivered this afternoon."

Hastily Robert told the person on the phone he'd call him back.

"Did you say you bought me a horse?" Robert asked. "Why would you so that?"

"I am about to be very angry with your brother and I don't have Aleta around. I feel as if I have been gut-punched and Dirkson talked me into it."

"You get talked into nothing," Robert stated flatly.

"Is that why Paul is going to put a painting of me in his show without showing it to me for my approval?"

"Paul is my brother," Robert declared. "Paul is not me. What painting?"

"Some painting my mother says exposes me."

"Paul wouldn't paint you nude."

"If he did, he didn't have me pose."

"He's never even seen you naked."

"He helped me shower a couple times when I first got home."

"I assume he didn't have a sketch pad in his hand. He never paints anything he hasn't sketched first."

"Well, he did this time!"

"So you bought me a horse because you plan to yell at my brother. Don't you think that's strange?"

"Dirkson says you like her," Stanley stated.

"Poppy? You bought me Poppy?"

"She nuzzled me."

"Huck says she doesn't do that much."

"Just you and me," Stanley remarked.

"Do you suppose he said that because he knew we'd be suckers for that line," Robert suggested.

"Does it matter?"

"No. I really like her, only the barn is full."

"I figured you can build her a stall next to Jezebel."

"Over my lunch hour?" Robert quipped.

"Use hay bales temporarily. Put Poppy in Jezebel's stall and put Jezebel in the makeshift stall. She's too old to do anything but try to eat her way out."

"I'm not sure Hubbs will want her doing that," Robert said.

"Won't she stop when she's full?" Stanley asked.

"I know even less about horses than you do."

"That's not possible. You have two daughters that ride."

"Bertha and Hubbs will figure it out." Robert concluded. "Let's get back to why you're so upset."

"Paul didn't ask. He showed the painting to half the women I know but to none of the men. I feel like I've been cast as some type of porn star."

"Do you want me to drive you down to the gallery so you can reclaim the painting."

"Dad says I signed a release."

"Has he seen the painting?"

"No, but my mother approved; Aleta approved the sketch or the outline or whatever, and I think your wife approved and Martha Cook bought it. I am so upset I can barely function. I can't take time off because I have things to do. Besides being idle would be worse. But I'm testy. I almost bit Peets' head off. I almost insulted a client. I rudely interrupted you. I bought a horse for you without consulting you at all!"

"Maybe you will like the painting. Maybe Paul didn't show it to you because you've been through hell this past week. Maybe that's why he elicited the opinion of the women you respect. They all know and love you. It's not porn."

"I don't want it to be Michelangelo's David either."

"Paul doesn't sculpt."

"I don't want to be stared at, even if it's not actually me."

"You can get a court order to prevent its display, but you will need to have a reason."

"I need to see it, don't I?" Stanley said.

"You can't say something's offensive if you can't say how," Robert said. "But Paul's a reasonable man. Let me drive you down to the city after lunch. I have to tell Bertha and Hubbs about the horse coming."

"Will Paul be at the gallery?"

"There are always last minute adjustments. Arranging art is like rearranging the living room furniture. It's a never-ending process."

"I need to squeeze in a meeting before we go," Stanley said. "But I do need to go down before the critics come, before anyone."

"I'll be ready when you are," Robert promised. "But what about your police guards?"

"They can't come," Stanley said. "I will tell Lyle."

Chapter 30

In the end it was Lyle himself who drove Stanley to the gallery in Chicago. Two Arborville police officers followed him in a separate marked car. They were met by a Chicago patrol car that escorted them the rest of the way.

"You did it by the book this time, didn't you? How was I introduced to the Chicago Police Department?"

"As an officer injured in the line of duty that was still in danger."

"Who is going to an art gallery?" Stanley queried skeptically.

"To his uncle's art exhibition for a private showing," Lyle said. "Made sense to everyone."

"Are you prepared to cart the painting home?"

"I won't have to. Paul said if you didn't want it displayed, he'd store it in back."

"Of course I won't want it displayed!" Stanley said. "Have you seen it?"

"No. But Mrs. Cook says it's one of the most moving works of art she's ever seen."

"Moving?" Stanley pondered. "Mother told my dad I was exposed."

"I asked Mrs. Cook if you'd object to it," Lyle said.

"And what did she say?"

"Yes."

"Aleta said she'd never hang it in our house," Stanley remarked.

"Soon the mystery will be solved," Lyle said.

"I don't know if I want you to see it," Stanley said hesitantly.

"Paul said it's hanging in an alcove. I can stand outside," Lyle said.

"I would appreciate that."

"Then that's what I will do," Lyle declared.

A short time later, Stanley's wheelchair was unloaded and Lyle wheeled Stanley into the gallery.

Paul took over the pushing of the chair and Stanley let him position the wheelchair inside the alcove off to the left near the back.

The alcove was dark. Stanley could just make out the gilded frame and some slashes of white.

Paul slowly turned up the lights. First Stanley saw the tremendous sorrow etched in every line of his face. His eyes followed the gaze of the man in the portrait as the diffuse light let him see the fingers clenching his thigh just above the knee below which was the white bandaged stub of his left leg.

He remembered the moment vividly. Paul had memorized and memorialized it. He felt tears running down his cheeks as he empathized with the man in the painting, the man that was himself, the man that was every man who had ever sustained such a loss. It was a private display of deep sorrow. He was exposed, but not in the way he had imagined.

"Call Lyle in," he said in a voice choked with emotion.

He heard movement behind him and then silence. A hand fell softly on his shoulder.

"I didn't know," Lyle whispered. "I never even guessed at how deeply you felt the loss."

"It happened when I was waiting for Paul to come help me shower," Stanley explained softly. "I looked down and realized what I had lost. My leg was gone. I would never..."

Stanley paused.

"Paul captured that well," Lyle murmured.

"You're an artist, Lyle," Stanley said. "I don't want it to be criticized. It would hurt too much."

"You're asking two questions," Lyle said. "First, this is great art. A moment of truth revealed by one man and captured on canvas by another. The execution is worthy of the subject matter. Second, the critics don't matter. If Paul's portrayal is honest, nothing else matters."

Stanley wiped his eyes and said, "Paul, it stays. Thank you. Now show me the rest of your exhibit."

Later that night, Stanley told Aleta about the exhibit. Then he told her about his day and how worried he'd been.

Suddenly, he broke down and cried.

His words when they came exited haltingly. "I am not strong enough for this. It is too much. I felt the sorrow all over again. I thought it was gone. It rushed over me like a tidal wave.

"I need you, Aleta. I am not ashamed to admit that. I know you're sleeping, but please wake up. Please."

His words trailed off and he put his head down on the bed next to his wife's hand and fell asleep. He lay like that for half an hour.

Her voice woke him.

He started and raised his head.

"You spoke!" he exclaimed. "Please tell me what you said."

But Aleta was silent.

"All I heard was 'no leg.' What does that mean?"

He glanced at his watch.

"I've wasted half an hour sleeping," he muttered.
'Where's my energy?" Why can't I seem to move?"

Despite berating himself, Stanley continued to sit motionless, his emotions spent.

"Love me," she breathed softly.

Her words cut through the stillness and pierced through the cloak of despondency that had wrapped itself around him, restricting his thinking to his own emotional distress and thus binding him to the wheelchair which masked his physical inability to move freely.

"Love me," she repeated.

He rose on his one leg and muttered, "I need two legs to do this right."

"One leg," she murmured.

"You don't want me to be fitted with an artificial leg until you're well? You want me to hobble around on one leg until you wake up?"

His questions shot out of his mouth with a bitterness born in the despair that his feeling of helplessness had given rise to. He put his hands on the bed and leaned on them and stared at his wife. He couldn't walk. He couldn't care for himself. He couldn't care for her.

Death seemed like a release. He wanted the pain to end. He didn't want to grieve anymore. He could no longer tell what he was grieving for--the loss of his leg or the loss of his wife's presence. Or was it for the loss of his feeling of control, the feeling that he was the master of his fate. He had been followed around all day by police guards. After the first hour, he realized how easy it would be for someone to kill him. Every second after that he lived with his vulnerability.

"Blessed are they that mourn for they shall be comforted," he recalled aloud. "I am not being comforted."

"Love me," Aleta whispered again.

He stared at her thoughtfully. He had been wishing she would communicate with him. Three times she had made a request. The first time the words could have been a random uttering. The second time he had been so absorbed in his own emotional turmoil that he had dismissed her words. This, however, was her third request.

What kind of effort did she have to expend to utter those few words? Three times took the utterance out of the random realm, especially as her first words had been about his leg. He had automatically argued with her. He hadn't completely ignored the fact that she had communicated with him as if it didn't matter. But he had been so tuned in to his own disheartened state, he had not even seen the gift he had been given.

He took the ring off his finger and placed it on Aleta's. He held her hand between both of his and gazed at her lovingly.

"With this ring I thee wed," he murmured. "I promise to love, honor and cherish you forever."

Then with a slight smile he added, "And tonight as well."

Twenty minutes later, he kissed his wife and bid her good night.

"Twice," she murmured.

He smiled. Leave it to Aleta to remember that covenant, not that they had adhered to it faithfully.

"I will be here first thing tomorrow morning," he promised.

When he left, he had a smile on his face. He could still do something. He could stay connected to the woman he loved deeply. She needed him. He had thought the nightly massages were trivial. Evidently, they were important to her.

That night Stanley fell into bed a happy man. Aleta had spoken to him. She had given him an order. He was to wait for her to wake up before being fitted for a prosthesis. That was the Aleta he knew. She was still alive.

And the one thing he was certain about was that she would not have given that order if she didn't believe she were going to wake up.

The one thing that puzzled him was her earlier explanation for the coma.

God didn't demand penance. Jesus had already paid the price for the sins man committed.

On top of that, Aleta didn't heal him. God did that. And asking God to heal him was not a sin.

Two recollections flashed into his mind almost simultaneously.

Chief Milani had urged Lyle to call upon Stanley right away because he had the most analytical mind of them all.

It hadn't occurred to Stanley to analyze what had happened to Aleta until the second remembrance of what she had said to him crowded into his mind at the same time.

Why hadn't he analyzed what had happened to his wife? Why had he put blinders on?

He didn't like her explanation, but he didn't question it. He just accepted her weak-kneed excuse that she didn't quite understand, but God had asked her for her complete obedience.

Why would she need to obey if she were comatose?"

His mind wrestled with that question for an hour before it settled on the answer.

The baby was in danger. Aleta's pregnancy was more precarious than anyone imagined. She had to be in a coma-like state for the baby to survive.

The obedience part was that Aleta was to accept the state and not fight to emerge from it.

God hadn't revealed the reason to Aleta, so she had come up with her own explanation.

"Every man has his own proper burden to bear," Stanley recalled. He and LaVerne Brown had joked about that. Neither of them wanted the burden of the other.

Now Stanley realized that his sole responsibility was to support his wife.

The explanation had been God-given. He knew it was confidential. God would reveal it in His own time.

Stanley felt singularly blessed as he closed his eyes in sleep. God had revealed a tiny bit of His plan to him. It was enough.

The Prophet Series

The Reluctant Prophet

The Apprehensive Prophet

The Bewildered Prophet

The Overwhelmed Prophet

The Beleaguered Prophet

The Dreaming Prophet

The Recuperating Prophet

The Silent Prophet

THE STILL SILENT PROPHET